WITCH OF SHADOWS

A.N. SAGE

OLIVERHEBERBOOKS

CONTENTS

Prologue   1
Chapter One   7
Chapter Two   19
Chapter Three   27
Chapter Four   35
Chapter Five   43
Chapter Six   49
Chapter Seven   57
Chapter Eight   69
Chapter Nine   77
Chapter Ten   83
Chapter Eleven   93
Chapter Twelve   101
Chapter Thirteen   111
Chapter Fourteen   119
Chapter Fifteen   129
Chapter Sixteen   139
Chapter Seventeen   147
Chapter Eighteen   157
Chapter Nineteen   163
Chapter Twenty   169
Chapter Twenty-one   177
Chapter Twenty-two   189
Chapter Twenty-three   197
Chapter Twenty-four   205
Chapter Twenty-five   213
Chapter Twenty-six   221
Chapter Twenty-seven   231
Chapter Twenty-eight   239
Chapter Twenty-nine   247

Chapter Thirty   255
Chapter Thirty-one   265
Chapter Thirty-two   273
Chapter Thirty-three   283
Chapter Thirty-four   293
Chapter Thirty-five   301
Chapter Thirty-six   309
Chapter Thirty-seven   319
Chapter Thirty-eight   325
Chapter Thirty-nine   331
Chapter Forty   341
Chapter Forty-one   349

Acknowledgments   361
About the Author   363

Prologue

It was a dark and dreadful afternoon, even by Shadowhurst standards. I walked the wide corridor of the academy with a scowl on my face and my clammy fingers wrapped around the cool silver handle of the dagger. The magic of the etched runes on the handle slammed into me with their power. By some luck, I remembered to pull out the dagger from the hidden compartment of my boot this time. Looking around the lengthy line of lockers on both my sides and the shadows that crept along them, I somehow had a feeling that dagger or not, I was in it deep this time.

The tattered strap of my backpack dug into my shoulder and I couldn't help but hiss and curse under my breath with each slow step. Why did I find it necessary to pack my grimoire for school today out of all days? I couldn't very well chase the creature I followed here with two pounds of book strapped to my back. On the bright side, if I was right and a shadower was lurking on school grounds, I could always chuck the grimoire its way and hope to hit bone. *Get it together, Billie!* If I survived this, I would need to get my hands on the High Coven's cloaking spell so I can leave the damn thing home next time.

Home. Such a strange word to process after so much time spent on my own. Somehow, Shadowhurst had almost seemed like one and if I was being honest, I didn't totally hate that fact. I might have liked it a little, which was saying a lot for me. I didn't even like myself on most days.

With a grunt, I rearranged the backpack's straps and wiped the unyielding sweat off my palms before continuing to make my way down the corridor. It was so empty and cold that I couldn't believe this was the same place filled to the brim with students just a few hours ago. By now, those students were off the premises, leaving only me to roam the academy's halls like I had a death wish. *Why did I chase that shadower again?* I mean, I could have just as easily packed my stuff and left with the rest of them. But no, I needed to be a hero as always. If only there was a spell to wipe someone's conscience away because you know I'd use that in a heartbeat.

As if on cue, a low growl rose from down the corridor, just beyond my sightline, and I froze in my place. My heart jumped so high in my throat, I was sure I could bite right down on it. I took a deep breath and tried to wet my dry lips with whatever saliva was still left in my mouth without success. Around me, the air shifted, turning from a steady cool to an eye-reddening burn and confirming my suspicions. There was only one type of shadower that could radiate this much heat and luckily, I had my fair share of encounters with shapeshifters to know what to do.

My fingers regained their grip on the hilt of the dagger, and I used my free hand to pull an amber crystal from the side pocket of my backpack. Nothing got rid of a shifter faster than silver and fire, and I knew well enough to carry both with me at all times.

Another growl filled the air, closer this time, followed by the sound of scurrying feet. The steps quickened, and I sped up to match their pace. *This sucker is quick!*

As I ran, my messy braid bounced from side to side, catching on the studs in my leather jacket and making me curse through gritted teeth each time. I rounded the corner, throwing my hands up to ready for an attack.

The corridor was empty.

DAMN IT! I picked up speed and ran toward the end where the door to the library was still wide open. There was only one place for this bastard to hide now and I was not letting it get away. My legs pumped, and I tried to think of the last time I went on an actual run, though judging by how my pathetic lungs were pulling air, I'd have to say it's been a while. The dagger felt heavy in my hand, and I used its weight to pick up momentum as I sliced my arms through the air. When I reached the library door, I skidded to a stop.

The scent of iron filled my nostrils, but that wasn't what gave me pause. There was something else at work here— something magical. I don't know how I knew, but I just couldn't shake the feeling that things were very wrong beyond that door and that magic had something to do with it. *Better safe than sorry,* I thought and reached for the power of the amber in my left hand. The crystal warmed against my skin before sparking to life. *Shit! That's hot!* I yelped and nearly dropped the ball of fire to the ground.

This definitely wasn't the best way to start this, but it would have to do. Not like anyone else was here to kill this monster.

Frustrated, I peeked around the large, wooden door-frame to scan the room. The library was quiet, which wasn't unusual, most students avoided this place like the plague even during school hours. My breath hitched and I forced myself to move. *Nothing you haven't done before, just keep going. Don't be a wuss.*

Step by shaky step, I walked into the library, the ball of fire glowing in my palm as I held it up to light my way. As my nerves settled, the flow of the flames spread wider, brightening the dark stacks of books that spread around me like curtains. Tomes upon tomes of information that was almost redundant in a modern school such as is. Why bother keeping so many books around if no one even bothered to read them?

My eye caught a glimpse of movement and I spun on my heels to face a row of shelves on the back wall. Without breaking my pace, I lunged for them, flipping the dagger in my hand as I ran.

"I know you're in here!" I yelled out, pausing at the edge of the shelves. "I could smell your stank breath from the hallway!"

I looped around only to find a whole lot more of nothing in front of me. Whatever this damn shadower wanted, it sure enjoyed playing games. Guess it didn't account for the fact that unlike most students, I didn't have much of a social life, so I'd be open to chase its sad, little tail around all night if I had to. I hated to admit it, but I enjoyed this a little too much. The chase, the fight, the magic—it was like having an infinitesimal part of my life back from before the High Coven cast me away to this dreadful, dead-end of a town without so much as a good bye. But being here, in this library, about to vanquish a shadower, brought me back to myself. This was who I was and, for the first time in a long while, I didn't have to hide it. This filthy creature did not understand that it was about to be handed the ass whooping of its lifetime.

I swallowed hard and crept to the end of the shelf. My back pressed against the books until I could all but make out the etched words on their spines like brail against my shoulder blades. The smell of iron intensified, and I squeezed around the shelf, ready for whatever lay on the other side.

My eyes widened as I emerged into the adjoining aisle. The thoughts rushing through my brain scrambled, and I fought against the bile that rose in my throat. There, in between two large bookcases lay a frail and lifeless body. From where I stood, I could tell it was a girl. Smaller than me and with a much fresher face. She was on her back, her thin arms spread to the side like she mimicked a cross. There was so much blood, I couldn't even recognize her, and I didn't need to move in closer to know there was nothing I could do for her. The girl was dead.

"NO, NO, NO!" I shouted and ran to her against my better judgment.

I dropped the dagger at her feet and blew out the fireball before gripping her shoulders. My index and middle fingers found her neck, confirming I was right—there was not a pulse to be found. I jumped back from her, staggering to my feet and taking a few steps back. My hands—covered in her blood—were shaking like crazy and I had to ball them into fists just to gain some form of composure. My eyes widened in horror as I took in the familiar signs of ritual around the girl's body. Salt, amethyst dust and burnt peach wood remains; your standard, very illegal, energy-draining spell. "For the love of..." I growled.

This was all wrong. Magical ritual like this was strictly forbidden, the High Coven would never allow for any witch to take the life of a human. Not this publicly. This was heresy at its finest and I was smack-dab in the middle of it.

A guttural hiss sounded behind me, and I turned just in time to see the shapeshifter lunge for my throat. It was smaller than I thought it would be—somewhere between a wolf and a coyote if I had to guess—but that wasn't enough to stop it from knocking me on my ass. The shifter's taloned teeth snapped as it fought to get a grip of my neck and I kicked my legs from under me trying to block its attacks. To make matters worse, my hair had come undone and was now fully soaked in the puddle of blood I landed in.

I stretched my arm, straining to reach the dagger that lay a few feet away from me. The fingers of my right hand inched toward it while I used my left arm to push the shifter off me. Its body slammed against mine over and over, teeth getting dangerously close to my windpipe. I tried to call for my magic, but without the crystal in my hand, it was pointless. I was strong, but not that strong. As I lay there, scrambling to kill the damn beast that refused to back off no matter how many times I kicked its sides, all I could think of was how much had changed in the last few weeks. It was only three weeks ago that I was still in Stamwick, doing the High Coven's bidding and smoking these suckers like it was nothing. But a lot can change in three weeks. Turns out, it was just enough time for someone to derail their life.

The shadower lunged for my throat again and I closed my eyes.

Screw you, Shadowhurst!

Chapter One

The drive into Shadowhurst was about as eventful as watching an ant burrow through sand. So far, the only exciting thing we passed was the gargantuan iron gate on the way in. It was almost as tall as some of the surrounding trees with the town's name inscribed in gothic font below a row of spikes. They looked so much like cemetery gates that I got whiplash looking from window to window to see if graves were lining the entrance into town. I rolled my eyes as we passed through. Shadowhurst may not have been a graveyard, but it sure felt like I was being driven to my deathbed. Each twist and turn of the intertwining streets shook the SUV and sent me sliding across the cold leather backseat from the momentum. I tightened the seatbelt around my waist and squinted my eyes to peer through the tinted windows. My eyes took in the small-town shops as we zoomed by them. Cafe, yoga studio, another cafe. This place was no doubt going to be boring as hell!

My fingers played with the moonstone ring on my left middle finger, twisting it around in lazy circles. I pressed a button on the door panel and listened for the whirring of the window as it rolled down. The cool air hit my face with an obnoxious slap and sent my long blonde hair whirling around my face. I spat out a loose lock, rolled up the window, and plopped back in the seat with a huff. Why couldn't the High Coven send me somewhere a little warmer? I mean, I wasn't expecting some beach paradise, but this sad town was the last place I'd expect to be banished to. "It has a small-town charm!" Luna chimed when they first told me what my punishment would be for accidentally using magic in the presence of a human. Leave it to her to put a positive spin on basically the worst situation ever. I should have known this town would be a dud, something about the way the high priestess let the lie roll off her tongue when she described it so giddily. No one in their right mind would think this place had any kind of charm at all.

We rolled past a large clearing with a statue of an uppity old man in the center. Benches surrounded the statue in a semicircle and a few people were filling them despite it being the middle of the afternoon. *Great, town folk.*

I groaned and crossed my arms, pressing the moonstone ring close to my chest. It was one of the few belongings they allowed me to bring, and I was grateful to have at least one piece of home for the journey. The only other thing I was permitted to pack was my grimoire—since no witch could be without one—and the rune-blessed dagger I tucked into my boot. Okay, so that last one was not exactly prescribed by the High Coven but what the high priestesses didn't know couldn't hurt them. Besides, they couldn't expect me to live in this weird little place without protection. Especially when I was strictly prohibited from using my magic. I was relieved when they let me keep the ring, probably because I begged them like an idiot and cried for days about it. I'm still unsure why they caved but it likely had something to do with the fact that the moonstone crystal was the most useless element conductor out there. Sure, it was good to direct balance and was handy to have during rituals and spell-work but other than that, it was just a pretty rock. Still, it was *my* pretty rock, and I was happy to have it, since I couldn't have anything else I loved. One minor mistake and I'm suddenly the black sheep of the entire family. Go figure!

Fine, it wasn't a minor mistake, but still... They could have at least given me a second chance. The shadower I fought was vanquished, and the coven wiped the human girl's memories, so what was really the harm here? The witches have been killing off the dirty creatures that threatened humans in the nighttime for ages, but I vanquish one pathetic soul sucker and get sent off? What reason did they have to tear into me this hard?

Of course, I knew what the reason was. If I was anybody else, they likely would have looked the other way, slapped me on the wrist, and sent me back to patrol the night streets of Stamwick. But I wasn't anybody else. I was the daughter of Beatrix Stonewall, the biggest damn criminal witch the High Coven faced. Unlike my mother though, I wouldn't dare be so arrogant as to fight against the high priestesses for violating the number one rule of the coven—no magic around humans. *For the love of the Goddess, Beatrix, couldn't you just do as you're told for once?* She couldn't, so it served her right to be locked away in the High Coven's magical prison for the rest of her days.

I haven't seen my mother in over ten years, not since she got caught in her wild dealings and dragged away by the high priestesses. Which was fine by me. Good riddance. Not like she was ever around before that. In my sixteen years on this earth, I could not remember one day where I felt like a kid, where I felt like *her* kid.

We stopped at a stop sign and the cheerful sound of children laughing jarred me back to the car ride. If this is what I had to put up with to make sure I never cross the High Coven as my mother had then so be it. There was no way I would end up like her.

I unzipped my jacket to let the sweat-soaked band tee underneath dry out in the air-conditioned air. "How much longer, Damien?"

"Almost there, Miss Stonewall," the driver responded in his thick, Eastern European accent. "Three more blocks and we're there."

"Outstanding," I said and rolled my eyes. "And Billie is fine."

As I snuck another glance outside, I realized that we were no longer in the shop-ridden streets we drove through before. The alternative views left much to be desired; nothing but spanning, lush grass, and prim homes with pristinely arranged flower beds lining the porches. The entire town looked like it was trying to put on an act. A collection of houses tailored to give the feeling of humbleness built by people who didn't understand the word. Shadowhurst was nothing like Stamwick. It was small and proper and not at all what I was used to. I was a street kid, through and through. My boots were still covered from the dirt they collected walking the filthy alleys of the city and yet here I was, in some posh town I would never fit into.

The SUV rolled to a stop, jerking my body forward hard enough to knock the breath out of me. The driver door slammed shut and Damien rounded the car to grab my bag from the trunk, giving me a chance to inspect my new home. As I scanned the yard, my jaw slacked. The driveway curved around a massive, stone fountain, leaving us parked in front of what I could only describe as a very over-the-top entranceway. The yellow Victorian-style house had all the details of a small-town home but amplified. Every white window frame had one pane too many hiding behind white shutters, and the doors were so large that they looked like they belonged in a mansion. There was a wraparound porch housing a few chairs and hanging planters that seemed to be freshly watered. To the right of the almost-mansion was another smaller house, just as yellow and just as obnoxious. Though this second structure did not have the mass of the first, it had the same eye-burning etchings of florals and vines that decorated the door frame.

This was going to be actual Hell.

I stretched my neck, rolling out my muscles from being cooped in a car for hours and opened the door. Damien was already standing guard, one hand in his pocket and one clutching my beaten down bag. His gaze met mine and he smiled before ushering me to the front door. My eyes danced as we walked, trying to peer through the upper windows and guessing which one would be my prison for the next Goddess knows how long. I was still spying when the door opened before us and a thin man in his late sixties stepped on to the porch to greet us. His face was blank and the gray suit he wore did not have a single wrinkle. His eyes narrowed on my slender frame behind the gold framed glasses that perched on the edge of his nose.

"You must be Billie," he said, so slowly I nearly fell asleep. "Please, come in."

"'Kay..." I stretched out an arm his way and he jumped back in surprise. "Good to meet you!"

The man scrunched his nose before awkwardly shaking my outstretched hand. "You as well, my dear. My name is Silas."

He looked to me like I was supposed to know some unspoken secret that hung in the air, and I immediately regretted not reading more of the notes the High Coven gave me to prepare for my stay here. All I knew was that the coven arranged for a false identity, staging me as a troubled teen that required a place to stay after escaping charges at her last school. It wasn't too far from the truth, though the only school I've ever attended was that of the High Coven's. I vaguely remembered reading about the couple that took me in. A well-to-do husband and wife who crowned themselves the token do-gooders of Shadowhurst. If I was being honest, I couldn't even place their names or pick them out of a lineup. In my defense, I wasn't planning on staying long. I doubted these people had any intention of adopting the trouble maker student they were housing for the remainder of the semester. I scoured my memory to find some reference to Silas and drew a blank. *Damn it, Billie! You really should have brushed up on this crap.* If I didn't get my act together, I would blow my cover before I even stepped foot in the door.

"I am the Head Butler of the Chandler household," Silas said with a grin. "Welcome to your new home."

A maitre d'? Are they kidding me? This place had a freaking butler!

My eyes darted to Damien, who only shrugged in return and handed me my bag. He nodded to me, bid Silas good bye, and turned on his heels to leave. And just like that, I was alone.

Hesitantly, I stepped past the threshold and into the house. My fingers twirled around the loose strands of my hair and as I followed Silas through the main hallway, I couldn't help but feel a sense of loss the further we got from the entrance. It was almost like this house and my alternative life was swallowing me whole.

Silas walked slowly and I wasn't sure if it was because of his age or if this was his way of letting me explore as we wandered. The interior of the home was less intrusive than what we first drove up to and the thought put me at ease. Looking around the open layout living room and dining area, I felt almost comfortable in this place. Sure, every little detail of the house screamed luxury and was a direct contrast to my black, ripped jeans and faded t-shirt but at least it wasn't an actual mansion. Hard as I tried, I could not find one tacky thing in the house. It even smelled good! Like cinnamon and baked goods. It was modern and clean and had all the features of a well-designed home. Everything from the marble countertops I spied on the large kitchen island to the plush leather sofas looked like someone had plucked this house straight out of a magazine. Each room had an obtrusive chandelier and the crystals glimmered in the light that fell from the enormous windows. There was very little in the way of décor, but everything was chosen with exquisite detail and I instinctively compared this home to Sebyl's. Unlike the home I've grown used to over the years, the Chandler residence was airy and did not have a knick-knack or detail out of place. *Fewer things to dust, I guess...*

We stopped in front of a wide staircase that pointed to the second floor and I turned to see Silas hover next to it.

"Is my room upstairs?" I asked, eager to put my heavy bag down.

Silas pointed past the staircase to a doorway down the hall from us. "Oh, no, no." He smiled. "The Chandlers felt you'd be more comfortable having your own apartment. They arranged for you to stay in the guesthouse."

"They..." I swallowed. "Gave me an apartment?"

"Correct," he said with another warm smile. "You'll find it has everything you need ready for your stay. I've arranged for fresh linens and towels, so you can get cleaned up before dinner."

He pointed to the door again and I took it as my cue to keep moving. To my dismay, my fake parents remained a mystery as there was not one photo hanging on any of the walls. It was almost as if a personal touch would have set the place on fire. I made a mental note to take extra caution to keep my messy ways under control while I was here and kept moving.

Silas led me through the doorway and into the backyard, which, no surprise, was the approximate size of a football field. There was an endless array of flowers that spread around the sizeable space, but I only focused my eyes on one thing—the long, very welcoming, pool in the center. *Maybe this won't be so bad, like a vacation or something.* I grimaced and turned back to follow Silas to the smaller house I saw when we first turned in. *Holy mother of...*

"I'm staying here?" I asked, gawking at the miniature version of the main house.

"Yes." Silas nodded and though he said nothing else, I had a feeling he was laughing at me.

"Silas?" I turned to face him.

"Yes, miss?"

"Where exactly *are* the Chandlers?"

"Oh, my," he whispered. "They must have forgotten to

send you a warning. The Chandlers are away on a business trip until later this week. They are very sorry they couldn't be here to meet you, but I am certain you will have plenty of time to get to know each other upon their return."

"Oooookay..."

"Will that be all, miss?"

I choked on a laugh. "You can call me Billie. Miss sounds, well, pretty weird."

"Very well." Silas paused. "Billie."

I smiled, gripped the handle of my bag tighter, and started up the slight steps of the guesthouse.

"Oh, Billie?" Silas chased after me. "Dinner is served at seven PM sharp. I have taken measures to stock your closet with a few things, but perhaps you'd like to go into town to pick out a few other items before tomorrow."

"Why? What's tomorrow?"

"Your first day at Shadowhurst Academy. I'm sure you're eager to start."

I scowled and dropped my gaze to my feet. New house, new butler, new school. This is turning out to be the worst week ever. Magic slithered beneath the surface of my skin, and I took a few deep breaths to push it away. My back slouched as I struggled to lug my bag up the steps. Even through the thick leather of the bag, I could feel my grimoire call to me. One pleasurable thing about being away from the main house and prying eyes is I could study my spells in private. The High Coven said no magic use, but no one said anything about reading and from what little I knew about high schools full of rich kids, it's that keeping your head in a book was the best way to stay out of the spotlight.

"No worries!" I yelled out over my shoulder as I rushed inside. "I'm sure whatever you picked out is fine!"

I closed the door without waiting for Silas to respond, which, in hindsight, was rude, but I couldn't wait to get out of my sweaty clothes and into a shower. The guesthouse was small and just the way I like it. It was set up in the same open concept the main house and had similar finishes that all looked to be too expensive for my current attire. As soon as I walked in, I was greeted with a compact galley kitchen with a fridge I hoped was filled with iced coffees and snacks. To my right sat a cozy nook with a couch, a loveseat, and a TV longer than my body. My jaw unhinged as I looked around and my lips curled into a grin.

I found my bedroom with ease and stepped in, tossing my bag on the wood framed canopied bed with a sigh. My fingers trailed along the silky fabrics of the bed coverings, and I had to toss myself on the plush mattress next to my dirty bag. Gaze drifting over the bedroom, I tried to memorize every inch in case someone decided this was all a huge mistake and they sent me to the wrong house. My unused bed was sandwiched between two glass side tables that had been exquisitely arranged with a few books, the most recent fashion magazines, and a faux flower arrangement that matched the lilacs stitched into the duvet. To the right, a gigantic window opened up to the backyard and I could smell the scent of cut grass drift through it each time the wind picked up outside. There was an inky wood dresser in the corner with a vanity table next to it and though I hadn't inspected it, I knew it was filled with the most luxurious makeup money could buy. Maybe now that I was here, I'd start wearing more than just lip gloss. Next to the vanity were two sliding doors with mirrors covering them from top to bottom. One of the doors was left open and I gasped when I saw the walk-in closet that hid behind it. There were more clothes in that closet than in some boutiques in Stamwick and I couldn't believe they were all mine. From here, I could see so many colors, it made my eyes bleed. Someone hadn't been alerted to my standard style of all black and gray...

At the far edge of the bedroom was another door that led to the bathroom, and I didn't need to look to know it would take my breath away much as everything else had so far.

The silk cradled my face in heart shattering perfection, and I smiled at the relaxation this little oasis offered. My muscled ached from the trip and being able to stretch out on the most comfortable bed I've ever laid on was nothing short of Heaven. My eyes focused and unfocused on the crystal chandelier—that was bigger than my freaking bedroom back at Sebyl's—above the bed and all the nerves that plagued my bones dissipated. Even the hum of magic that normally ran through me slowed and I stretched my arms out to the side. It's delicious warmth spread through my body and I giggled. There was no explaining what it felt like to have this locked away inside. Magic was a part of me, like a second heart. *Just a vacation,* I thought with a smile and set a timer on my phone for six. The last thing I wanted was to miss the seven PM sharp dinner on my first night here.

Chapter Two

Silas was not kidding when he said I should have everything I need in my closet. Getting ready for my first day of school was like shopping in some fancy department store and by the time I was done, I felt even more out of place than before. I opted for a simple black blouse and black leggings, choosing to don my leather jacket and boots to keep at least a slight part of myself intact. With my hair brushed and the smallest coat of mascara on, my blue eyes twinkled in the sunlight as I rode the brand new bike the Chandlers left for me down the streets of Shadowhurst.

Winding the small streets and leaning into the curves helped uplift my spirits and it relieved me to have convinced Silas not to drive me to school. Something about showing up in a private car seemed way too pretentious, and I wanted as little attention drawn to me as possible.

As I rounded the corner, I realized that biking to Shadowhurst Academy was the worst decision I could have made.

This place was nothing like the schools I was used to seeing in the city.

The academy's campus was monstrous and covered in such perfect grass that it looked like a country club and not a school. There were four colonial buildings that surrounded a massive quad in their center with trees lining its perimeter. Each building had dozens of windows facing the quad and I felt unease thinking of all the classrooms hiding behind the plates of glass. Knowing me, I'd get lost just looking for a bathroom. Students had already trickled in, and my heart pounded with worry that I was, once again, late to something important.

In a hurry, I found the bicycle racks tucked in the corner of a parking lot that had more expensive cars in it than a dealership. It took me a few tries to fumble with the lock to secure my ride but after a few loud sighs and cursing, I crammed it into a slot. Aside from my own wheels, there was only one other bike in the station, and I scanned the area to see if I could spot who it might belong to. I searched over the prim and proper faces of the students around me and realized that none of them would dare ride a bike to save their lives.

The students of Shadowhurst Academy looked more like movie stars than average teenagers. Their clothes were carefully put together, their nails manicured and every girl I passed had a full face of makeup on. *Well, this is different.*

I stumbled over a rock on my way up the tiny hill that led to the main quad and nearly lost my backpack to gravity in the process. Thank the Goddess for the training the High Coven provided, I recovered with only a few people noticing my clumsiness. Their eyes scanned my plain attire before looking away and continuing to chatter about whatever topic

held their interest that morning. Making friends was definitely out of the question in this place.

After brushing a loose strand of hair off my face, I started
my way to a sign post covered in directions. Because, of
course, this place needed a map to navigate. My eyes landed
on an arrow pointing to reception and I walked the
perimeter of the quad to the tallest building of the four.

Jaw slacked, I took in the size of the main hall. It was
almost as large as some buildings in Stamwick and had a
triumphant bell tower perched above its roof that added
unnecessary grandeur to an already humongous design.
Above the steps, lay an overhang held up by six, two-story
columns and beyond them, ornate wooden doors flung open.
Students filed in the doors and disappeared into the darkness
beyond, making me feel even more alone than I already was.
I rearranged the straps of my backpack and followed them in.
As soon as I entered the hall, I regretted the jacket choice I
made this morning. While the weather of Shadowhurst
seemed to be in a constant state of fall, it was hot as Hell
inside the main hall. Sweat beaded down my neck and I had
to pause to pull my hair into a loose bun at the nape of my
neck. The school's sterile scent of bleached floors jammed
into my nostrils, and I had to rub my eyes from the film it left
on them.

Inside the hall looked like I expected, brown and boring
with a touch of rich kid detailing thrown in just for kicks.
The principal area opened to a wide entryway with corridors
spanning in each direction. One glance around told me I
would hate it here. Tan colored lockers lined the corridors on
either end, breaking only to make room for large mahogany
framed doors with frosted windows in the center. Above me,
a three-tiered chandelier caught the light streaming in from

the overhead windows. This town and its chandeliers—I seriously did not get it. My eyes traveled over the crystals and to the panes of glass that were surprisingly sparkly clean. Through them, I could see the gold of the bell I noticed outside as clear as daylight. Its sheer mass was impressive, but what attracted my attention was the etched writing that ran along its perimeter. I couldn't make out any of the words but somehow, they drew me in. *Interesting.*

With a groan, I made my way to another sign on the wall opposite me and tried to locate the school's reception area to sign in for the day. *Science, drama, tools...* I read off the titles in my head until my eyes spotted what I was looking for. Without pause, I turned on my heels and ran for the office.

As always, my feet were quicker than my head and my already rising nerves made me oblivious to my surroundings. As I turned the corner, my shoulder bumped something, and I turned around, startled to see a tall girl rubbing her shoulder from the impact of my clumsiness. Her hair fell over her bronze skin in perfect ringlets as she brushed off invisible lint from her way-too-short romper.

"Ouch!" she yelped, narrowing her hazel eyes at me. "Watch where you're going!"

My hand clasped my mouth as the horror of almost running down a stranger set in. As I looked over the girl in front of me, I could feel my pulse race. She was stunning. Her auburn hair fell in perfect, tight ringlets down to her shoulders and she brushed it off her high cheekbones as she stared me down. How did someone even get cheekbones like that? Mine were pretty much nonexistent and I sometimes wondered how my face stayed in place. This girl, however, was all bone structure and flawless bronze skin. She looked like a freaking super model.

"I'm so sorry! I wasn't paying attention, I'm new—"

"I don't need your life story," she snapped. "Just stay out of my way!"

"You okay, Savannah?" another girl yelled out a few feet away from us. Her fiery red waves bounced as she jogged to meet her rude friend.

"Yeah, I'm fine. Whoever *this* is decided to try to kill me, apparently," Savannah bit out.

Her eyes zeroed in on me and I could sense her stare burrow into my bones. My magic screamed beneath my skin, and I tightened my lips into a thin line to keep myself from lashing out at her. *So much for staying unnoticed.*

"I'm really sorry," I said through clenched teeth. "It's my first day and I'm just trying to find reception."

"You should try finding your balance first," Savannah growled.

Was this asshole for real right now? It was an honest mistake, and she was way extra with her responses. Though judging by her appearance, I doubted anyone at this pathetic school dared do anything to anger this chick. I've seen enough movies about human high schools to know a mean girl when I saw one and Savannah was as wicked as they came. Snarl and all.

The redhead next to her snickered and turned away, hiking up the straps of her floral tank top to reveal a sliver of midriff. "Abigail! You coming?"

From behind them, another girl appeared, trailed by three boys that all looked like they just finished auditioning for some beach babe movie. The girl, Abigail, had her fingers entwined in the hand of one of them and she walked over to us, dragging him behind.

"Calm your shit, Morgan. We still have ten minutes to

class." She rolled her eyes and turned to plant a kiss on the boy's cheek. "See you at lunch, babe."

The four of them turned to look at me and I froze in my tracks. It felt like I was being pulled into something I would definitely regret later. I needed to get away from these jerks and fast. Squaring my shoulders, I made a beeline to the left to give them a wide birth. I was already past them when a deep voice called out behind me, causing me to pause.

"Reception is around the corner from the music room!" a boy from their group yelled out. "Just make a right at the next turn."

My face blushed as I turned to face him. I mean, sure, I've seen my fair share of hot boys in the city, but this guy was out of this world gorgeous. My gaze drifted over his messy brown hair that sat just past his ears and landed on his dazzling green eyes. He was tall, not much taller than Savannah but well built for his height. He had on a pair of ripped jeans—designer, no doubt—and a fitted golf shirt that hugged his chest muscles in all the right places. And that jawline... wars have started for less, I was sure of it.

I shook my head. "Thanks," I said, my voice catching in my throat. "First day."

"No problem." He took a step toward me, and I backed up. "Welcome to Shadowhurst, I'm River."

River outstretched a hand and I hesitated before taking it. Fire lit in my belly as soon as our skin touched, and I cursed the Goddess for putting this fine piece of man in my way. I seriously needed no more distractions today. River studied me with calculating eyes, like he wasn't sure what to make of me.

"This is Tyler." He pointed to the round-cheeked boy

Abigail kissed. "And his girlfriend Abigail. The spit fire is Morgan and that over there is Jayden."

River pointed to the boy next to him and Jayden bowed in a theatrical bow to me. His Shadowhurst Academy varsity jacket rode up so high when he lowered his head that it seemed like he had no neck at all. Though to be fair, jacket or not, the muscle in this boy's shoulders likely trumped his neck, regardless. "Pleasure to meet you, m'lady," he joked, running his hand through thick, black hair.

"And you've already met Savannah. She takes some getting used to." River smiled and I nearly fainted. "So, where are you from?"

"Um," I stumbled, trying to remember if I was allowed to tell these people anything. "Stamwick."

"Ooooh!" Jayden crooned. "Big city girl! To what do we owe the pleasure?"

I sighed and gave my moonstone ring a few flips. "Long story."

"We'll be late for class," Savannah said with venom in her voice. Her long legs strode toward River, and she wrapped her red tipped nails around his bicep to pull him away. "Let her figure out her own way. We're not hall monitors."

She turned and pulled him behind her with a huff while the rest followed. As they stomped away from me, River turned back smiling and a single dimple deepened in his left cheek, melting my already overheated body into oblivion. Blood cells hummed and expanded in my veins, and I could feel a familiar tingle of nerves at the edges of my skin. All around me, the air became solid until I could almost hold it in the palms of my hands. My vision blurred and as I tried to blink, sparkling white lights frayed in my peripheral. My magic was going into overdrive, and I wasn't sure if it was because of his hotness or the fact that I wanted to rip Savannah's throat out but whatever it was, I had to keep it together. I blew out a lengthy breath and turned in the direction he instructed. As I walked past the scurrying heap of students, I had the distinct impression that I was being watched. It felt like there were eyes on me with every step I took, but each time I turned around, there was no one that drew my attention. Either I was losing it or whoever was stalking me was even more invisible than me.

I saw the sign for reception and sprinted in its direction, eager to get out of the hallway. *So much for a good first impression, Billie.* I scoffed and turned the knob to walk in.

Chapter Three

School dragged on for hours like a bad movie set on repeat. Every class was the same and I found myself daydreaming more often than necessary. Luckily, Savannah and her team of hyenas was only in two of my classes that day and I sat far enough in the back to avoid their judging gazes. Every once in a while, my eyes locked on River, and I had to shake myself to concentrate on the lessons. Is this what normal kids dealt with every day? This constant fear that someone will notice them combined with pointless infatuation? I hated every second of it.

The classrooms in Shadowhurst Academy left much to be desired. Unlike the grandeur of the buildings on campus, they were small with rows of tables lined up at the center. It was pretty much a regular classroom, chalkboard and all, and I wasn't sure why expected anything else. Oh, right! Maybe the freaking gold bell and crystal chandelier in the Main Hall threw me off kilter. All around me, students whispered whenever our first period teacher, Mr. Blair, turned his back to scribble something on the board. I couldn't believe the nerve of them. Back in the coven, a head witch would singe the hairs off your arms if you talked during a lesson. I guess money really doesn't buy class, or obedience.

The lessons were simple enough to keep up with and I found I had no trouble staying on track despite this being my first day. The hardest part was keeping my backpack out of sight when I took out my binders in class for fear of the grimoire making an appearance. I was too afraid to leave it in the guest house, so the leather-bound, hefty book of spells travelled with me to school and stayed hidden at the bottom of my pack.

When it was time to break for lunch, I stuffed my books in the surprisingly large locker assigned to me and made my way to the bustling courtyard behind the main hall.

The academy was so much bigger than I expected, and it took me almost ten minutes to find a spot to sit on the freshly cut grass. I picked the one furthest from the pond as it seemed to be a hub of activity, Savannah included, but made sure to give myself a clear view of River in the process. Might as well have a good show while I ate.

River, Tyler, and Jayden tossed a football while the girls cackled about something Savannah said and I found myself rolling my eyes on more than one occasion. Their laughter echoed through the courtyard and drew in crowds like they were celebrities. Girls swooned over Savannah and her friends, while boys tried to cozy up next to them. It was truly a disgusting act to watch.

I bit down on my veggie sandwich and tried to remember the last time I was surrounded by this many people. The answer was never. The High Coven consisted of a substantial group of witches, but we never gathered in big crowds so as to not attract attention. Aside from Sebyl's home, which we used as a meeting point, the witches kept to themselves unless ritual called for it or there was a big hunt taking place. I always loved spending time with the other witches, especially the high priestesses. Sebyl, Theodora, Luna, and Rhiamon practically raised me after my useless mom was arrested and I spent every free moment trailing behind them like a love-sick puppy. As far as I was concerned, they were what magic was all about.

There were a total of eighty-seven witches in our coven back in Stamwick, though I knew there had to be more spread out across the world. If there were though, I never got to meet them. The High Coven's main initiative was to control the infestation of the beasts that threatened human life in the shadows, or shadowers as we called them. Once, when I was still too young to know better, I asked the high priestesses why we had to vanquish them in the first place. It seemed odd to me back then that we couldn't just let the shadowers be and go on with our lives. I don't think I've ever seen Sebyl that angry with me before. She even had to leave the room, like she couldn't bother to look at me. See, what I didn't know then was that our magic was the reason shadowers existed in the first place. The more we used our magic, the more it grew and intensified, seeping out a little more each time we wielded it. The elements have a balance of sorts that needs to remain constant and if it's overused, anomalies begin to form as a result and the magic can go bonkers somehow and attach itself to human cells and restructure them. By the time the witches realized what was happening, it was too late and plain old humans were turning into shadowers right, left, and center. I guess since we were responsible for the creation of these creatures, it was our job to clean up the mess. Of the three types, I feared the soul suckers the most since they could literally kill you with just a touch. Unlike the rest of the evil beasts that went bump in the night, the soul suckers were the hardest to lure out and deadly once they got there. Mind reapers were my next least favorite in the haunted house that was my life. On the outside, they seemed to be peaceful and kind, but that was just a front to get close to the humans. One touch and these pathetic, two-faced bastards could get a lock on your brain so tight, you'd be crying for your mommy in no time. Unlike the other shadowers, these guys took their time killing you and they didn't stop until you were nothing but a void of forgotten memories and confused thoughts. If I had to pick my opponent, I'd no doubt go for a shapeshifter. They were nothing but dumb beasts with a pack mentality and easy enough to trap. Shapeshifters were less damaging and fairly easy to vanquish; though with the right spell and a few weapons, anything could be killed. Anything except the fae, but we haven't seen any around for decades. So, as far as I was concerned, they were as good as dead already.

I took another bite of my lunch and ran my fingers through the grass. It was weird but something about the ground here felt steeped in magic, which would explain why I had so much trouble keeping my own under control this entire time. A witch's power stemmed from her surroundings and the stronger your connection was to the earth, the harder it was to keep your magic contained. Since I entered Shadowhurst, mine was on a whirlwind. It was like I could tap into it even without crystals or herbs, which was an absolutely ridiculous thought. No witch could wield magic without external sources.

"This seat taken?" A light voice sounded next to me, turning my attention outward.

I turned to see a petite girl glare at me from above. Her narrow eyes took me in, and she flipped her straight bob cut to the side to reveal streaks of red that peeked through her black locks. Unlike Savannah and her friends, this girl was dressed head to toe in black. Everything from her biker vest to her ripped shorts was studded with metal and I found myself staring at her in shock. Much like me, this kid was way out of her depth.

"Uhm, no. It's a field, so all the seats are open." I smiled and patted the grass beside me.

She plopped down with a sigh and tossed her navy, jean backpack to the side. Her tiny nose pointed up as she surveyed me. "Thanks! Name's Peyton. Peyton Ling."

She stretched out a hand and I ogled the ring tattoos on her fingers before shaking it. "Billie Stonewall. Nice to meet you."

"First day?" Peyton asked, digging though her bag to pull out a Tupperware container. When she opened it, the scent of Dim Sum filled my nostrils and my mouth salivated uncontrollably. I looked to my half-eaten sandwich in dismay before forcing myself to take another bite.

"Yep." I nodded between chews.

"Saw you this morning, you looked lost. Glad you found reception okay."

So that's who was watching me, I thought and looked down. *Great, first day and I already have a stalker.*

"Oh, yeah. This place is a maze."

"You'll get used to it," Peyton said. "Aside from the trust funders, it's not so bad."

"Trust funders?"

Peyton pointed to Savannah and her friends. "The annoying rich kids."

"Ah..." I pursed my lips. "I've had the pleasure already. Unfortunately."

"Don't let them get to you. They're pricks but totally harmless. Savannah would never do anything her parents might deem as unsavory. And the Queen Bee does whatever they tell her, so you're safe."

"So, what's the deal with them?" I asked, genuinely curious.

"The usual. Money and power." Peyton smirked. Her phone vibrated and she fumbled with lock before frowning. "Crap! It's my dad. I gotta take this!"

She jumped to her feet and tossed her half-eaten food back in her backpack. Peyton already had her phone to her ear when she turned back to me.

"Let's hang out later, 'kay?" she yelled out without waiting for me to answer before she rushed off.

As I watched her run down the slope, I let out a deep breath, shrugged my shoulders, and continued eating. This day had already exhausted me, and we were only halfway through. I turned my ring around mindlessly while I ate, each turn leveling out my spiking body temperature. The cool breeze of Shadowhurst spun around and I closed my eyes. I could not wait to be back in the guesthouse and away from this place.

The rest of the day flew by surprisingly fast. I had two more classes after lunch and was relieved that gym wasn't one of them since I completely blanked and forgot the gym bag Silas left for me in the main house. I tried to find Peyton after school, but there was no sign of her and I had no intention of running through the halls in search of someone who I wasn't even sure truly wanted to hang out with me. Maybe she was just being nice to the new girl.

After my last class, I was instructed by the teacher to proceed back to reception to fill out paperwork, which was just as boring as it sounded. By the time I was done, the sun had already started to set, and the school was all but abandoned. As I unbuckled my bike from the rack, I could hear a few hollers from the football field and my mind immediately went to River. Was he out there right now with the rest of his jock friends?

Why do you even care, Billie?

I pulled the chain off the rack and secured it back in place before wheeling the bike out of the stand. My head was pounding and all I wanted was to be back in the guest house. My eyes looked at the clock on my phone and I hissed. It was already half past five and I still had to bike back and get changed before dinner! From what I gathered of Silas so far, he was not a man that appreciated tardiness and I didn't want him telling the Chandlers about what a poor house guest I was on my first week here.

Securing my backpack to the small seat at the back, I started to mount the bike when a low scuffle caught my attention. My head jerked to the bushes behind the bike rack, and I was hit in the face with thick, warm air that made me gag.

"Crap!" I yelped, dropping my bike with a loud bang and reaching for the hidden dagger in my boot.

Before I had a chance to grab it, the bushes split open, and a large tiger pounced at my throat. My breath hitched and I jumped back, avoiding the creature before it could make contact. The tiger slid through the lot, its large paws kicking my bike out of the way and sending it flying across the cement.

What in the actual hell?

While the tiger rebounded, I ducked down and grabbed the dagger, holding it in front of me defensively. Beneath my skin, my magic piled to the surface, pushing its way through my blood stream. The hairs on my arms stood on edge and I shivered from the feel of the power inside me multiplying. My irises narrowed and my face flushed as I surrendered to its call. As the air thickened, I blinked to focus my vision and refused to look at the thousands of twinkling lights around me. The magic danced in circles, beckoning me to close my eyes and surrender. I patted my pockets, searching for anything I could use—a crystal, an herb, a damn stick even—but there was nothing in my reach.

The tiger's golden eyes landed on me, and I swear I could almost see it smile. It lunged again and I swerved out of the way. My backside collided with the bike rack, and I tripped on my loose shoelaces, falling to my knees.

"Damn it!" I screamed and scrambled to get up.

The dagger glistened in the setting sun, and I held it fiercely, hoping to scare off the beast. I had nothing with me to use in a vanquishing spell and if I tried to fight a shifter with just the dagger, there was good chance I'd lose. Sure, silver hurt these bastards but if I wanted to get rid of it for good, I'd need to vanquish it. *This is a bloody mess!*

My fingers clammed and I shakily rose to my feet, pointing the tip of the dagger at the tiger's glaring stare. It growled and the sound sent shivers down my legs and spine. I took a step back and ground my feet into the cement just as the beast shook its brown fur before barreling toward me.

Chapter Four

The tiger's body slammed into me. The force knocked out my breath and I gasped as I flew back across the parking lot. Its massive paws framed my hair, and I could smell the foul stench of its breath on my face like molasses. A rush of nausea hit me as I thought of the poor sucker the shadower ate before this. My fingers wrapped around the hilt of the dagger in my hand, and I swung it upward, kicking the tiger's chest and making it yelp out.

Blood coated the silver blade, and I didn't need to look at the beast to know the fury that must have been coating its face.

"Take that, you asshole!" I yelled and swung my blade again.

This time, the tiger was faster, and it swerved out of the way to avoid my attack, leaving me just enough room to wiggle out from under it. I crawled back, my ass scraping the cement and ruining a good pair of leggings. Silas would not be impressed with my state when I got home. If I got home, that is.

I jumped to my feet, trying to will my magic to the surface. I could feel it just under my fingertips, eager to play, but no matter what I tried, it refused to comply. My cheeks reddened as my blood surged to the surface and I took in a shaky breath. Feet planted, I trained a sharp gaze on my opponent and tried to recall what Rhiamon instructed me to do in these situations. She was the fiercest fighter the High Coven had, and it was no wonder she was one of the four high priestesses. Unfortunately, I was no Rhiamon and my mind drew a complete blank. I widened my stance, spreading my arms wide. On my finger, the moonstone ring caught the light of the still setting sun and the sparkle flashed across the tiger's face. It twitched in its spot. Its heavy body froze, following my ring as my hand wavered in the air. *What in the Goddess does it want?*

I took a step forward, flipping the blade in my palm to point it at the beast. Its golden eyes narrowed on my frame, and it shook its thick fur and hissed. I took another step— there was no way I was backing down now.

To my surprise, the tiger growled, turned on its heels, and leapt away from me and back into the bushes it emerged from. Without a second thought, I gave chase. My legs pumped and I could feel the muscles tense as I ran after the beast. I sliced through the foliage, twigs catching the skin of my neck as I fought to get to the other side.

When I reappeared on the other side, the field before me was empty and the tiger was gone.

My eyes jerked from side to side, but it was no use. Shadowers were quick when they needed to be and with the sun already this low, there was no chance of me catching up while it hid in whatever hole it crept from. This was an absolute disaster. One day in and I was already in trouble. I thought the High Coven sent me here to prevent me from using magic but how what I supposed to do that with shadowers sprouting from nowhere? And on school grounds! I would never go against the coven's wishes, I wasn't my mother, but this would be an impossible task.

I let out an annoyed sigh and fought my way back through the bush to the parking lot.

"You had to pee or something? 'Cause they have bathrooms inside." Peyton smirked, shocking me with her presence.

Her arms were crossed at her chest, and she tapped her foot like she was waiting for me the entire time. As fast as I could manage, I tucked the dagger in the waistband of my leggings and stepped onto the cement. "What? No. I..." I paused. "I dropped my ring, but I found it." I held up my moonstone ring to prove my lying point.

"Cool." Peyton smiled. "Looks like your bike's out of commission."

I followed her gaze to my limp ride and rolled my eyes. *Damn shifter!* "Shit. I must have knocked it over when I went looking for the ring. Well, that's just great."

"No worries," Peyton said and nudged her head to a yellow Jeep Wrangler a few spots over. "I'll drop you off."

"Thanks, but honestly, it's fine. I can walk it."

"You're kidding?" She smirked. "It will take forever with that sad excuse for wheels. Hop in!"

I looked back to my useless bike on the ground and nodded. The faster I got back home, the better. With a grunt, I hoisted the bike into the rack on the back of her car and Peyton helped me secure it in place. My nerves were still jagged from the fight, but I tried to look as relaxed as possible as we drove away, which was an arduous task at best with

Peyton at the wheel. The girl was a maniac! She took turns without slowing down, sped up when lights changed, and had a complete disregard for pedestrians. And it was brilliant! I latched onto the seatbelt more times than I blinked but every time we hit a bump and I went flying upward, I couldn't help but laugh. This was the most fun I've had in days!

"Soooo…" I peeled my eyes from the blurring road ahead to peer at her. "You always drive like you're in a race?"

Peyton's bubbly laugh filled the car. "Pretty much. My dad is way overprotective, so this like the only chance I have to rebel."

"One way of putting it." I laughed.

"How was your first day?"

I thought about her question before shifting my weight in the seat. The point of the dagger had dug into my skin, and I tried to rearrange it before I ended up shredding my leggings in her car. "Different," I whispered.

"Savannah give you any more trouble?"

"No. But I made sure to stay away."

"Don't take her too seriously. She's not worth it."

"Ooooookay…"

Peyton pumped the brakes at a stop sign and sent us flying forward.

"Whoa!"

"Sorry!" she yelped. "That came out of nowhere."

My heart was racing but I forced a smile her way. "So, what do people do for fun in this place?"

"Fun in Shadowhurst? Unheard of."

"Awesome."

"But seriously, what's your poison? I'm sure we can find something to do."

I tried to figure out what my poison would be, but all I could think of was spell ingredients for an actual poison and I had a feeling that's not what Peyton had in mind. "I don't know. I like movies, I guess. Mysteries mostly."

"Me too!" Peyton exclaimed. "You like magic?"

A knot formed in my throat, and I choked on my spit. "Excuse me?"

"Magic. You know, abracadabra and whatever. This town is full of stuff like that! People love the occult around here, it's like their little obsession. You should have seen this place when that vampire movie came out. They pretty much had a parade in its honor."

"...Oh," I said, relaxing my shoulders. "Yeah, I guess. Kind of an occult wiz, sort of."

Peyton turned to look me over, her lips curling into a grin. "We should totally hit up the Crystal Cauldron later."

"The what?" I asked, baffled.

"The Crystal Cauldron. It's one of those new-age witchy shops, first one in town. I love it! It has all this weird crap and the owner, Ms. Broussard, is a complete weirdo. You'll love her!"

My face paled and I looked out the window at the rest of the shops that lined the street. As far as I could tell, everything seemed so normal, but somehow, I landed myself in a town obsessed with witches and magic. Just my luck. Hiding who I am was starting to look like a harder task than I originally imagined, and I wondered if the High Coven knew about this before they sent me here. Doubtful, they weren't that stupid. My eyes widened as a thought popped into my head.

"This cauldron place, do they have crystals and herbs and stuff?"

"Oh, hell yeah! The place is full of that stuff. Most people fall for that crap and spend a fortune in there."

Suddenly, my dampened mood brightened. If I could get my hands on some supplies, I'd be better prepared in case another shadower attacked me. I knew the high priestesses said no magic, but what did they expect me to do? Die here?

"Perfect! I'd love to check this place out!" I said giddily.

"We'll go this weekend, it'll be fun." Peyton nodded. She rounded the corner and I slid in my seat, my head bouncing off the window.

"Hey," I asked, "what's the deal with that River guy?"

"Mr. Abs?" Peyton wiggled her eyebrows playfully. "He's alright, for a trust funder. Despite being friends with Savannah. Why? You have the hots for him?"

Blood rushed to my cheeks. "No! He was just nice to me, so I was wondering. Back when Savannah and her hyenas tore into me this morning."

"Hyenas! I love it!" Peyton laughed. "But like I said, don't worry about them. Everyone's been on edge lately."

"Really? Why?" I arched one eyebrow and turned to face her.

"Wait, you haven't heard?" Peyton asked. "Is it a left or a right here?"

I looked up, confused by her question, and noticed we stopped at a fork in the road. My mind raced trying to remember the way to the Chandler residence and I had to lean out the window to see if I could spot it in the distance. Sure enough, there it was—my favorite eyesore—just down the street. "Right," I said and leaned back. "What I haven't I heard though?"

"About that kid? You know, the one that died last week? Lacey or something. I never knew her."

"A kid died?"

"Yep," Peyton said and put the car in park across the street from the front gates of my house. "Not just died, killed. It was all over the news. Super creepy too."

"Creepy how?"

"I don't know all the details, Dad wouldn't let me read the news that week. Like I said, overprotective. But from what I heard around school, it wasn't pretty."

"What do you mean?"

Peyton's eyebrows kissed and she trained her eyes on me, her thick eyeliner making her look like a demon from an old horror movie. "They said when the cops found her, she looked like she was mummified or something."

"Wait, what?" I gasped.

"I know! I told you, creepy!" She shook her black hair and unlocked the side door. "Anyway, you need help getting the bike off, or are you good?"

The goosebumps on my body spread from my toes all the way to my ears, but I tried to shake the feeling of dread that threatened to eat me alive. I climbed out of the Jeep and turned to shoot a fake smile Peyton's way before unbuckling my bike and dragging it to the gates.

"See you tomorrow?" Peyton yelled out behind me.

"You sure will," I answered and waited for her to peel out.

Tiger shapeshifters and a mummified kid—the High Coven sure knew how to pick a good spot for my so-called vacation.

Chapter Five

My head was reeling as I walked up the steps to the main house. *A mummified kid? Were they kidding me?* Thinking of what this could mean was making it hard for me to catch my breath and I had to pause before I gathered the courage to turn the knob. Here I was thinking the shadower was my biggest problem when there was something else—much more gruesome—lurking in Shadowhurst. Sure, it could have been a plain old coincidence and a perfectly plausible explanation was out there for why a student from the academy was found dead in a strange, very magic-related manner. But knowing my luck, this was something to worry about. Besides, my witchy senses were going haywire ever since Peyton brought up the dead kid and that had to mean something. I had to get some more information on the murder as soon as I got back to the guesthouse.

With renewed excitement, I turned the doorknob and burst into the house. My feet skidded to a stop in the entrance as I took in the two people standing in front of me.

"Welcome home," the woman sang, her arms

outstretched like she was about to hug me. "We're so excited to finally meet you!"

Goddess-freaking-damn-it! I cursed while inspecting the couple before me. *They must be the Chandlers!*

For two people who had been traveling for a week, they looked fresher than a newborn lotus bud. Mr. Chandler was dressed in a pristine, white linen suit that struck me as an odd choice for Shadowhurst weather. His gray hair was brushed to the side and adorned with so much gel, it looked to be plastic. To me, he resembled what I could only imagine as a well-aged Ken doll. If a Ken doll could grow a beard that thick, that is. I tried to recall his name from what I briefly read about the two, but my thoughts were mush. Mark, Michael... I seriously drew a blank here.

As much as I wanted to keep playing the guessing game, my eyes could not stop traveling to Mrs. Chandler. Imala, from what I recalled—a beautiful name for an even more beautiful woman. Unlike her stocky husband, Imala was tall and slender with a figure that wouldn't quit. She looked much younger than him, we're talking at least fifteen years here, and I couldn't help but wonder how the two met. Imala's deep bronze skin glistened in the chandelier's light that hung in the hallway and from where I stood, she looked just like an oil painting. Her long ebony hair hung effort-lessly over her shoulders and even I knew that the pink suit she donned must have cost a fortune.

"Mr. Chandler! Mrs. Chandler!" I yelped in false excite-ment. "I'm so glad you're back. It's wonderful to meet you!"

I walked over to them, shaking their respective hands and trying to keep my shaking arms under control.

"Please, my dear," Mr. Chandler said with a smile. "Thomas and Imala will do."

Thomas? Wow, I wasn't even close.

"Thank you for letting me stay here." I nodded.

Imala reached out to wrap an arm around my shoulder and it took everything out of me not to brush her off. Physical contact was not something I had grown accustomed to. The high priestesses were not a touchy-feely bunch and even when Beatrix was around, she was more interested in teaching me to wield magic than hugs and cuddles. My skin recoiled from Imala's touch, but I tried to not let her see it, having a troubled teen in your house was bad enough, there was no need to let them in on the mess I was on top of it.

"How was your first day at the academy?" Thomas asked, his blue eyes inspecting my appearance. "It's quite the school, is it not?"

I stifled a cough. "Yes, quite."

"Have you made new friends? I hope you met Savannah and her friends! They're lovely ladies!" Imala cooed and I all but barfed in my mouth.

"I haven't had a chance to talk to many people," I sighed. "I met a girl named Peyton. She seems nice."

"Peyton Ling?" Thomas asked, one eyebrow arched.

"Yep."

"Oh."

What the hell did that mean? Did these people not like Peyton?

His wife brushed past him and pulled us into the living room, her eyes narrowed on her husband in disapproval. "Don't mind Thomas," she whispered when were past his earshot. "Him and Mr. Ling had some disagreements over a business deal and he's still a little stuffy about it."

Of course. I rolled my eyes. *Rich people problems.*

"No worries," I said. "I understand."

I did not understand at all.

"Will you be joining us for dinner tonight?" Imala asked. "We'd love to hear more about you."

"You mean other than what my file said?" I scowled.

"Darling." Imala flashed her teeth. "Files are for the average. We'd like your side of the story."

Mrs. Chandler patted me on the back and turned me toward the backyard door like I was a puppet she was commandeering. For someone that slim, the woman sure had some strength in her bones. I forced another smile her way before pulling out of her hold and making my way to the exit. "Oh, Imala?" I turned back. "I kind of had trouble with the bike. It might be a little broken."

Imala's black eyes sparkled, and she spread her red painted lips into a wolf's grin. "Not to worry about, we'll have Silas secure another one for you tomorrow."

The heat of the jacuzzi jets warmed my aching bones as I lay in the large, marble tub inspecting the wounds from my fight with the shadower. I had a few scrapes down my shins and an already darkening bruise on my left thigh but other than that, I saw nothing worth worrying over. I'd have to make sure to spread some lavender oil on my legs before bed in case I had to wear shorts for gym class tomorrow. If I was careful about it, I could use a tiny bit of magic, and no one would be the wiser.

My fingers flipped through the cream colored pages of my grimoire and a sense of emptiness bubbled in my gut with each turn. Dragon's Blood, chamomile, eyebright—I read off the ingredients listed before me. It was a simple scrying mirror spell and one I perfected before I was eight but it seemed as far away as anything could be. I missed spell casting and I missed the coven—my only family in this wretched world. I even missed Luna and her batshit crazy, mystical nonsense. Out of all four high priestesses, she was the one I could never connect to. Likely because all she talked about was prophesy and the moon cycles. I never understood that part of our practice, why bother with guess-work when you can use spells to do your bidding? But the witch's code was strict for spell work and the High Coven was unbudging when it came to rules. Everything had a point, and everything had a result. Disobeying coven rules could get you into more trouble than you bargained for, just ask my mom.

I flipped another page and my eyes trained on the messy hand writing. *I really needed to work on my lettering, this thing was a disgusting mess!* I trailed the words with the tip of my finger, making sure not to smear the ink. It was a basic water-binding spell to calm one's mind. I read the instructions and dropped the grimoire at the side of the tub. What harm could one little spell do?

Slowly, I flipped my palms to hover over the water and took a deep breath, inhaling the warm scent of eucalyptus bath salts in the air. With careful calculation, I lowered my palms closer to the water's edge and closed my eyes. As soon as the water reached my skin, my magic exploded. I could feel it flow from my heart to my fingers, craving the energy the element provided. It wasn't as strong a connection as I could form next to a natural body of water, but desperate times called for desperate measures. I pulled on the power that rushed through my veins, calling for the water to reach me. Those damn blinking lights crowded the space under my lids, and I had to blink several times to stay focused. From here, I could smell the coolness of the water as clear as if it had submerged me. I had it in my control. At my command, the tub bubbled and beads of water rose to the surface. I continued to breathe through the spell, welcoming the beads into myself. One by one, droplets of water rose from the surface and hovered in the surrounding air until I was covered by them. In a flash, I snapped my eyes open and plummeted my hands into the full tub. The droplets exploded, raining down on my face and neck in a mixture of hot and cold.

A light laugh burst from my lips, and I looked around to make sure I was still alone in the room. When I was satisfied that no one had witnessed me perform a spell, I sunk back into the tub and closed my eyes.

The peace I felt lasted only a brief moment before my mind was full of gruesome images of the murdered student. I could see the girl as clear as day. Her ashen, dry skin, and sunken cheekbones that were once full of life but were no more. She was no more.

My eyes burst open, and I gulped a breath of air, realizing for the first time that I've been holding my breath. This was it, this was why I came here. The High Coven shunned me for my mistake and hid me away but maybe there was a way to get back into their good graces? I splashed water over the edge of the tub as a renewed sense of hope engulfed me. I had to find out what happened to that student and, if my hunch was correct and this *was* an act of a witch, I would be the one to find her and bring her to the coven. It was the only way for me to get back home.

Chapter Six

Our calculus classroom was colder than an ice tray and despite having my leather jacket zipped to the top, my teeth chattered while I tried to take notes to keep up with the lesson. Math has never been my strong suit and I hated every droning second of this class. My eyes continued to shift to the clock over the door as I counted the minutes to lunch. *Five more to go, you can do it, Billie.*

Mr. Abbot, our teacher, spoke in a monotone voice with little pause between sentences, which made it even more difficult for me to stay focused. To my left, Peyton sketched in her notebook, winking at me to let me know she was just as bored. The other students seemed oblivious to the lesson except for Savannah, who raised her hand to answer questions so many times, I wondered if she'd pull a muscle by the end of class. Today, she opted for a skin-tight miniskirt and a geometric print top, which was no doubt chosen strictly for the point of showing off her upper assets. I looked down at my ripped boyfriend jeans and frowned. Someone should tell this girl school isn't a fashion show.

A few seats ahead of me, Abigail giggled and tossed a wad of paper at Tyler, who swatted it effortlessly out of the way. Their affection and ongoing flirtations drew me to River. With his back to me, I had nothing else to stare at than the wide set build of his shoulders and heat rushed to my neck each time he rearranged his weight in his seat. I was staring so much, I had to wipe drool off my chin.

I was still ogling his semi-sheer white tee when the bell rang, and I jumped from the sound. River's head swung in my direction, and I sank back into my seat, pretending to rearrange my books. Not that I was shy around guys, quite the opposite, but something about River made me think he was way out of my league. Though that could have been the nerves talking since the last guy I hooked up with was in college and forgot I existed as soon as a better piece of ass caught his attention. Let's just say my ego was more than a little bruised at this point and River had trouble written all over his hotter than hell body.

"Having fun?" he purred, flashing his pearly whites my way.

"Oh, yeah," I said. "Time of my life."

He laughed and got up to stand, tossing his bag over his shoulder. As he opened his mouth to say something, Savannah pounced on his desk to draw his attention to her. She flipped her curls over her shoulder and though I couldn't be sure, I was convinced her arms pressed closer together to amplify her already way too exposed cleavage. "Finally!" she exclaimed. "Lunch time!"

Dragging him by the arm, she led River out the door with the rest of the hyenas without giving me so much as a nod. The hairs on my arms rose and I fisted my hands as I watched them walk away. *Are they a thing? Is that why she hates me? Because her boyfriend was nice to me?* The idea of Savannah and River dating made my stomach turn. What a surprise, the one hot guy I found in this stupid school that was actually nice to me was already taken by the worst person I've ever met. Just my luck.

"Yo, B!" Peyton knocked my shoulder to snap me back to the room. "You alive?"

I cleared my throat. "Yeah, sorry. This class put me to sleep."

"Every class puts me to sleep." She laughed. "Come on, let's go!"

I followed her out of the room to the courtyard, eyes scanning the halls for River as we walked. We weren't even past the lockers when I spotted him leaning against the exit doors with one foot hiked up on the frame. *Man, whatever they're feeding this kid, it's working!* His eyes met mine and he waved me over to join him. I was so taken aback that I had to look around to make sure he didn't mean someone else, but it was just me and Peyton in the hall now, so unless he was talking to his invisible friend, he was definitely waving at me. Peyton tugged at my sleeve to pull me back, but I flashed her a reassuring smile and ushered us forward. My smile widened as we approached and my breath quickened. River's single dimple glared back at me as he widened his smile and my neck flushed in return. This guy had some effect on me I couldn't explain and I liked it. *It's because he was nice,* I told myself. *Nothing else.*

"Hey," I said when we reached him.

"Wanna join us for lunch?" River asked with a grin, "We're going down to Main Street to hit up a coffee shop. This place is in a serious need of better lattes."

"Oh, um..." I looked to Peyton, who shrugged. "Sure, I guess."

"Oooh!" Peyton said. "We could pop into Crystal Cauldron while we're there so you can have a look around!"

Loud heel sounds tattered behind us, and I swung around to find Savannah standing with her hands on her hips, her eyes shooting daggers my way. Next to her, Jayden shuffled from foot to foot, oblivious to her fury.

"You have got to be kidding me!" she snapped. "We don't hang out with the weirdos, River!"

"Cool your jets," River blurted. "It's just coffee."

Savannah stomped my way, looking me up and down before turning her back to me. "You can't be serious. Peyton Ling and this thing? No thanks!"

"You're acting like a bitch." River sighed. "Give it a rest."

My cheeks puffed and I held all my breath for fear of lashing out at her. *Who the hell did this chick think she is?* My fingers tingled and the anger made my magic rile like a hungry snake. I could sense the silver of my moonstone ring cool the heated skin of my palms and tried to will myself to calm down. What I wouldn't give to find out Savannah is shadower so I could smoke her right here in the middle of the hall; nothing would give me more pleasure.

Beside me, Peyton crossed her arms and looked away as though she had grown bored with the conversation. I had to give it to her, unlike me, Peyton sure knew how not to hold a grudge. I could only imagine what Savannah and the hyenas have put her through all these years for being different. I had no words, well, that's not true, I had many words, but none that would justify this behavior. Savannah wasn't just a bully, she was evil through and through and I've had enough of it.

I turned to Peyton and nodded to the door, stepping around Savannah close enough that I bumped her shoulder and shoved her forward. Her head spun my way, and she blew out a breath so low, it sounded like a hiss. "Excuse you!" she wailed, regaining her balance.

"Sorry." I smirked as I passed her. "Didn't see you there. Guess my mind is on more important things right now."

With that, I pushed past her and walked out, not bothering to look back at River. If this was the type of girl he wanted to be around, I did not need this guy in my life.

My steps quickened and when the cool chill of the outside air hit my face, I could all but feel my tense muscles relax. Peyton ran to catch up with me and we made our way to our regular spot under the trees. With a grunt, I tossed my backpack on the grass and kicked it for good measure.

"She is unbearable!" I screamed. "I mean, seriously, who talks to people like that?"

"She's just jelly. Don't worry about it." Peyton smiled and sat down.

"Of what? She clearly thinks she's the best, so what's to be jealous of?"

Peyton arched an eyebrow. "You're joking, right?"

"Huh?"

"Um, girl, River? He obvi likes you."

"He is just being nice!" I yelled, quickly realizing how loud I was being in front of at least two dozen other students. "She could learn a thing or two from him about not being mean to the new kid."

"Shit, I keep forgetting that you're new here." Peyton sighed. "One thing you have to know about Savannah is that she's had a crush on River since like third grade."

I loosened the zipper on my jacket and sat down next to

Peyton, pulling my pack to my chest. From here, I could feel the edges of my grimoire press into my ribcage and their familiarity slowed my racing heartbeat by a few notches. "So, what does that have to do with me?"

"'Cause you're like the first girl River paid attention to," she said. "Savannah has to hate that. If she can't have him, no one will, or whatever."

"Well, she can have him!" I wailed. "'Cause I don't want him!"

"Yeah." Peyton winked. "Right..."

I shot my friend the dirtiest look I could manage, but it was hard to stay mad with Peyton around. Something about her personality exuded positive vibes and I couldn't help but smile when she was nearby. I wished more people were like that in this school, but the more I thought about it, the more I realized that I would never belong here. Not in the Chandlers' posh home, not in this academy, not even with Peyton maybe. These were regular kids with regular problems, and I was something else entirely. I had zero urge to worry about petty things like mean girls and hot guys, no matter how hot they were. I had a mission and I'd be damned if I strayed from it.

Shadowhurst was not my home.

My home was back with the High Coven. It was with the witches and the dangerous nights of Stamwick's alleys. My thoughts landed on the dead student again, but I pushed them away. Nothing would make me mess up again. Looking into the murder would only put me in a position I didn't want to be in, and I couldn't afford that right now. I had to keep my head down and stay out of trouble so I could be out of this place and back with my family. So I could be back home where everything made sense.

My mind was decided.

I reached into my bag to pull out my lunch, but my hand jerked back when Peyton's fingers dug into my arm. I turned to her, eyes widening as I followed her finger scroll the phone, face paling with each word she read.

"Peyton?" I asked, "What's wrong?"

She tossed the phone in my lap. "You gotta read this!"

As I skimmed through the text on the screen, my stomach dropped. I felt the blood rush from my head and my legs get heavy under their own weight, pulling me into the grass below.

This couldn't be happening...

Chapter Seven

'Shadowhurst Academy student found dead in Gentry Park early this morning.'

I read the article, again and again, hoping each time that the words would rearrange themselves to spell out something more cheerful, but there was no use fighting what I knew was true. Another student was dead, and I was having trouble accepting it. The article didn't disclose the student's name but all around us, people whispered and guessed, taking inventory of who was in school to figure out who's missing. Since I only knew a handful of people, I didn't bother joining in. Instead, I pressed my backpack closer to my chest in some hopeless attempt to tap into a calming spell in my grimoire through the thick fabric. Forget the no magic rule the High Coven forced down my throat, I had to get my hands on some supplies before I lost my mind in this town.

"Who do you think it is?" Peyton asked.

Heat swam through me, and I turned to my friend, eyebrows kissing. "I literally only know you and the hyenas, so you tell me," I retorted.

"Clay wasn't in biology today," she said, "but I think his dad took him camping for the week. I don't know, maybe Chloe?"

"Who's Chloe?"

"Some girl I used to chill with." Peyton sighed and I got the sense there was a story here I'd like to hear more about later.

"We'll probably find out more later," I said. I've had my fair share of hunting down the news in Stamwick when I was hunting shadowers to know that information is always withheld in the initial stages. "It just happened, so I doubt they'll write anything about it in the papers for a while."

Peyton's shoulders rose and she froze. "You think it's a serial killer?"

There was a loud screech downhill from us, and I looked over to see a few students arguing. A boy that looked to be in one of the younger grades ripped a football from another boy's hands and ran off with it before tossing it back. *Were these people seriously more worried about a game right now? A kid was dead! Someone they knew!* Anger rose in me, and I tried to keep it under control. I didn't know these people, for all I knew, a student dying was standard operations in this weird town.

"Is this out of the ordinary here?" I asked bluntly.

"A murder? Heck, yeah!" Peyton chirped. "I don't think Shadowhurst had this many murders since, you know, the witches."

Her words hit me like a loose air-conditioner falling from a second-story window. Whatever saliva I had in my mouth evaporated and I found it difficult to catch a breath. I crossed my legs, dropping my backpack in my lap. "What witches?"

"Girl, serious?"

I nodded, my eyes straining to refocus.

"You know the history of this town, right?"

"I really don't," I said, my jaw tighter than a vice.

Peyton rearranged herself to sit more comfortably in the grass and turned to face me. "Shadowhurst is like one of those witch-burning towns, from way back when. Like Salem, or whatever."

Well, that explained all the references to magic and the town's love of the occult. *Why the hell did the High Coven not warn me about this?* It was like they wanted me to fail.

"They burnt witches here?"

Peyton's smile dropped and she pointed a purple lacquered finger to the bell tower above the Main Hall. "Yep, right up there actually. They built this whole school on the same spot they used to do it on. It's pretty gross if you think about it. We are literally going to school on top of some big old murder fest." She crossed her arms. "I have an idea!"

With a quick hop, Peyton jumped to her feet and pulled me up with her. Her red streaked hair blew in the wind, and I barely had time to snatch my backpack before she had us running downhill toward the parking lot.

"Peyton, wait!" I shouted. "Where are we going?"

"We're getting out of here," she said, tugging harder on my arm. "You and I will find out who this kid was and what happened to them."

Twenty minutes later, we were whipping through Main Street in Peyton's Jeep with my hands white-knuckling the seatbelt. As we drove, Peyton's mouth worked faster than a motor while she spewed every bit of history on Shadowhurst she could remember. To my surprise, my friend was quite the history buff when it came to Shadowhurst and I sat in silence, taking in every bit of information I could that the High Coven didn't disclose to me.

Turns out, Shadowhurst's past was dark and gruesome when it came to witches. Outsiders, a group of European descent had originally formed Shadowhurst, or at least that's what the town's archives stated. No one knows what became of them, but from what Peyton had gathered, they disappeared as quickly as they came, leaving only a handful of the founding families to run the place. Everything was fine and dandy until rumors of witchcraft spread, and fear trampled the small streets of Shadowhurst, spreading like a disease. At first, the town's members attempted to live together with the so-called witches but after a while, they drove them out, which was how Carriage Hill was formed. From what I could recall of the map I studied on my drive in, Carriage Hill was still up and running just a short distance from Shadowhurst to this day.

My memories flashed back to when I first drove into town. "That explains the creepy gate on the way in," I mumbled.

"Yep!" Peyton said. "Carriage Hill has one just like it, but those tools are always flexing like they're better than us."

"So, all the witches ran off to Carriage Hill?" I asked when Peyton took a breather from talking.

"Uh-huh." She nodded. "At least at first."

"At first?"

She turned the wheel, whipping the car to the left and I held on for dear life while the wheels smoked and screeched as she leveled us off. "I think they were all still scared over here, so they started forming some creepy little groups that would go into Carriage Hill and bring witches back here. To burn them. Isn't that cool?"

Peyton's eyes danced and I found myself fighting the urge to vomit on the dashboard. Our ideas of cool were very, very different. "I guess," I whispered and swallowed hard. "They burnt them in the bell tower?"

"Yep."

"And no one ever found out what happened to the Euros that created the place?"

"Nope. They disappeared into thin air. Like magic."

Like magic? Right.

"People don't just disappear, Peyton," I said and lowered my eyes to the ring on my finger. Well, some people do. Like dads—dads definitely disappeared sometimes.

Peyton's eyes widened and she turned to stare at me, oblivious to the road. "That's what *I* said!" she yelled. I had to nudge my friend's attention back to the windshield. When she finally looked away and I could breathe again, she tapped her index finger on the wheel and smiled. "Wanna know what Ms. Broussard told me?"

I nodded, my excitement rising. Peyton's attitude was definitely infectious.

"She said that they never really left. She thinks whoever these mystery strangers were, they're still here. Or at least a part of them."

"Like their kids or something?"

"Great, great-grandkids more like it! But yeah!" she exclaimed. "Isn't that cool?"

"I guess..."

The car accelerated and we sped by a group of students gathered outside a cafe. My eyes scanned the crowd, hoping to spot River in the midst, which was stupid since I wanted nothing to do with him and his friends. Then why was I even bothering to check?

"What you thinking?" Peyton asked and I realized I'd been staring out the window for longer than necessary.

"Just that it makes sense now, how much this town likes all this paranormal stuff."

"Told you!" Peyton grinned. "But wait 'til you see where we're going. You're gonna freak!"

"Where exactly are we going?"

Peyton swerved the car again and pumped the gas. "Crystal Cauldron, of course. It's time you saw this place and its glory!"

The Crystal Cauldron was located smack dab in the center of Main Street, and I felt way too exposed following Peyton down the busy street. Shoppers filled every inch of the side-walk, picking out knick-knacks from display tables and laughing with their friends. It was so busy that it almost made Shadowhurst feel like a big city. Almost. The tiny shops with cheerful window displays and intricately hand drawn signs on the windows were nothing like the cold, modern storefronts back home but I had to admit, I loved how they looked lining the streets. We passed at least three different coffee shops as we walked that all smelled delicious and a cute restaurant terrace with the name "Handsome Devil" running across the small iron fence that surrounded it. Peyton guaranteed that this place had the best steak in town, so I vowed to come back later for dinner, if this Handsome Devil was serving up good meat, I was in!

The sun was high in the sky, and it was a surprisingly hot

day by Shadowhurst standards. The town that was in perpetual fall was starting to feel like a sauna today and I was ready to call it quits when Peyton paused in front of a dusty, glass door. She turned back to me and wiggled her eyebrows. "This is it!"

My gaze flew from her to the small sign hanging off metal chains above the doorway and my heart skipped a beat. The font was the same handwritten style as the rest of the shops but what caught my eye was the cute drawing of a bubbling cauldron with a witch's hat in its center. I couldn't help but laugh at the ridiculous way paranormal shops portrayed my kind. I mean, no one actually used a cauldron or wore stupid pointy hats like that. It was impractical.

The bell rang as we walked in, and I was struck with an overwhelming scent of peach wood and patchouli. Looking around, I was glad Peyton had forced us to skip school to come here. The Crystal Cauldron, though still very much a small-town shop, was the closest to home I've felt since I arrived at Shadowhurst. It was tiny, about the size of my bedroom in the guest house, and filled to the brim with everything one might expect from an occult shop. Shelves lined the walls on either side, full of crystals and tarot decks and dried herbs. Passing by them, I could feel my magic pull in all directions as though it was trying to decide which element to latch onto first. The Crystal Cauldron had the distinct scent of myrrh and chamomile, and I couldn't help but smile as I walked through, inspecting every item on the shelves. It smelled like home.

I spotted a small, glass counter at the far end of the shop with a few display cases of crystal jewelry atop it. More dried herbs hung from the ceiling over the counter in an array of bushels ready to be picked. My eyes slid to a small door behind the counter adorned with leaves carved into the wood.

"Why are we here again?" I whispered, eyes never leaving the door.

Peyton smiled and pulled me forward. "Because if anyone knows what happened to that kid, it's Ms. Broussard. She knows all the good gossip!"

She jogged to the counter while I walked awkwardly behind her, careful not to knock anything over with my backpack. As soon as Peyton reached the counter's edge, the door behind it swung open and a gust of dust burst into the air. I shielded my mouth with my sleeve, coughing into it to clear my throat. When I thought I'd be able to breathe without choking, I looked up to survey the small woman that perched in the doorway. She looked to be almost in her seventies, which you'd never know by looking at her smooth, caramel skin. The only thing that gave her age away was the white hair that was messily wound into a bun atop her head. She meandered in the manner of someone not used to keeping up with time and I noticed rows of beaded bracelets adorning her frail arm just under the long, loose blouse she wore. Her gray eyes, full of time and wisdom, lit up when she noticed Peyton.

"Miss Ling!" the woman exclaimed. "Welcome back!"

"Hi, Ms. Broussard." Peyton nodded and stepped to the side to reveal me. "This is my friend, Billie. She's new here."

Ms. Broussard's eyes landed on me, and she tipped her thin nose upward to motion me forward. Hesitantly, I took a few steps to stand next to Peyton, relieved for the distance the glass counter put between me and the woman. Ms. Broussard reached over the counter and tucked a loose strand of hair behind my ear before I could jump back. "Welcome to the Crystal Cauldron, Billie," she whispered.

The tone of her gruff voice gave me pause and I felt like I had met this woman before, though I knew well that it was just my nerves talking. Something about being surrounded with all the knick-knacks in the shop and my magic on overdrive made me uneasy. It was like I was torn between running and staying.

"Thank you," I said after a lengthy pause. "It's quite the shop you have here."

"Do you like it?" Peyton asked.

"I really do. We have a lot of these in Stamwick, so it's nice to be somewhere familiar for a change."

Ms. Broussard's eyes widened when I mentioned my hometown and she turned to the jewelry counter, running her slender fingers over the dangling necklaces. The crystals bounced off each other, drawing my attention to them immediately. "I see you've found what you're looking for," the shop owner said and snatched an amethyst pendant off the display. She pushed the necklace my way and I shook my head.

"Oh, no," I blurted. "We're just browsing. Though I wouldn't mind picking up a few things for fun later."

"On the house." Ms. Broussard winked. "Think of it as a welcome gift."

I wanted to refuse her kind gesture but something about the way she kept waving the pendant told me the shop owner would not take no for an answer. Despite my mind telling me to walk away, I stretched out my hand and took the necklace from her. My fingers curled around the crystal, and I felt my magic calm. The energy of the amethyst flowed through me, digging its roots into my core. My mind stopped racing and my shoulders relaxed as my knees got weak beneath the weight of my body. *Goddess, how I missed this.* I unlatched the clasp of the pendant and fastened it around my neck, turning to Peyton for approval.

"You wear it well." Ms. Broussard winked again before returning her attention to Peyton. "And how can I help *you*, Miss Ling?"

Peyton's cheeks blushed and she rubbed one of her finger tattoos so hard, I thought she was trying to scrub it off. "We, um…" She paused. "Wanted to know if you heard the latest news?"

"You're referring to the murder plastered all over the papers, I assume?" the shop owner asked.

Peyton nodded and I followed suit. "Peyton said you can help us figure out who it was."

"Child," Ms. Broussard said and widened her smile to reveal a row of broken, blackened teeth. "I've lived in this town for almost seventy years, there is little I do not know."

"So, you know who it was?"

"Why does that matter to you?" the shop owner asked, her leer sharpened.

"Just wondering," Peyton said without missing a beat. "Juicy gossip is what I live for!"

The shop owner laughed, and I swore I could hear the shelves rattle from the sound. Her brow furrowed and she tore her eyes from me to look out past us and into the busy street outside. "Such a shame," she said. "Such a young life to lose."

"So, you *do* know?" I gulped. "Who it was?"

"Well, of course, I do," Ms. Broussard snapped.

"Told you…" Peyton whispered my way. "Who was it?"

The tension in the shop dissipated as Ms. Broussard

lowered her eyes and rested her hands on the counter. Her fingers tapped on the glass, sending shivers down my spine but the cool touch of the amethyst on my chest relaxed me. "Grady Sanderson," she said. "His poor family."

"Holy crap!" Peyton yelped, "Grady? Really?"

"Who's Grady?"

"One of the juniors. I think River and Tyler knew him pretty well, actually. That sucks."

"Is there anything else you can tell us?" I asked.

Before I could stop her, the woman reached over and patted my chest where the crystal pendant lay against my skin. "Only that whoever is responsible for the untimely end of these students' lives is not someone you want to cross. You girls should be careful out there, evil is afoot in Shadowhurst."

Chapter Eight

Despite Peyton's insistence to drive me home, I decided to walk. She fought me, but in the end, left the matter alone and promised to pick me up for school tomorrow since I left my bike behind when we rushed off.

Shadowhurst evenings were much cooler than those back home and I found myself speed walking down the darkening suburban streets as I made my way back to the Chandler residence. At some point, I'd need to think of something else to call that place that wasn't such a mouthful. I turned on one of the streets, facing an uphill climb I wasn't ready to take and took a deep breath before moving on. The yards of the neighboring homes were lit by garden lamps, and it was so quiet that I could hear the trickle of water from some of the surrounding fountains. *These people sure loved their fountains!* I sucked in a breath and willed my legs to move faster, eager to be back in the guest house.

Around me, twilight coated the street in luminous shades of red and purple and I couldn't help but inhale its beauty. At this hour, Shadowhurst was almost picturesque, like they staged it for a showing. The homes sat far from the road and as I passed by them, they felt like feral eyes watching my every step.

My thoughts drifted in circles, always landing on Ms. Broussard's last words to us at the Crystal Cauldron. *Evil is afoot.* She didn't know the half of it! A second murder only confirmed my suspicions and I have never been more sure that a witch was responsible for the deaths of those students. I didn't even need to read the news to know what they'd say —that the student was left in a mummified state, their energy sucked dry. There was only one spell I knew that could steal someone's energy and no one in the coven dared go anywhere near it. It was dangerous and dark, something most witches avoided unless they wanted the High Coven to rain hell upon them. This was definitely the doing of a rogue witch. But why now when I was in town? It was like the entire thing was planned just for my arrival and I couldn't help but worry over what that might mean.

As far as I knew, I was supposed to be the only witch in Shadowhurst, but these murders said something else. The worst part wasn't that students were being murdered, though that should have been enough to send me running for the hills, it was how they were being killed. With magic, and dark magic at that. And this town's history with witches didn't help matters one bit. Who's to say that they wouldn't burn *me* at the stake if rumors got out that magic was involved in the murders?

It was a foolish thought, deep down I knew that. People didn't go around burning each other anymore, not in the civilized world we lived in now, but something about Shadowhurst felt different. Like they wouldn't think twice to strap me up in the bell tower and light a match. There was no way in fresh hell I could stay out of the murders now. My fate was decided as soon as Grady got killed. I had to protect myself before fingers started pointing my way. I mean, who better to blame than the new, weird kid with the so-called troubled past? Besides, if the High Coven found out that this was happening and I did nothing to stop it, I'd never hear the end of it. Worse, I might end up sharing a cell with Beatrix in the magical prison and I had no intention of ever seeing that woman again.

I was so wrapped up in thought that I barely noticed how far I'd walked. I spun around, trying to find the homes I was just next to, but all I could see were trees and bushes blocking my view. Somehow, I ended up on a hiking trail without even realizing it. I backtracked my steps, trying to orient myself back to the major road that led to the Chandlers. Just ahead of me, I could see the streetlights twinkle in the dark. I hoisted my backpack higher and took off in a sprint.

Jogging down the trail, I could feel the air thicken as night took hold of the town and ran faster. A whimper sounded to my left, and I froze, skidding to a stop and digging my boots into the gravel beneath. My irises widened as I scanned the area for something unusual. That was when I saw him.

A few feet from me, perched on a park bench, sat a young boy no older than five. His legs were curled close to his chest and his head shook as he gasped for breaths. Not thinking, I rushed toward him, wanting to cradle him into my chest to stop him from crying.

"Are you okay?" I asked when I reached the bench. "Where are your parents?"

The boy didn't answer. His back rose and fell as he continued to cry uncontrollably.

My hand stretched out to touch his head. "I'll help you get home, okay?"

When my fingers contacted his hair, my breath hitched. Something was wrong here, undeniably, creepily wrong. What was a tiny boy doing by himself at night with no parents in sight? I tried to back away, but my legs refused to cooperate. No matter how much I willed myself to run, I stood still.

The boy looked up, his tear-stained eyes locked on mine. My heart leaped in horror as the little boy's lips curled into a vicious grimace and he strained his back, hopping from the bench to stand in front of me. His small hand grasped mine and my brain exploded. Heat rushed from his palm to mine, boiling my blood from the touch. I wanted to scream. I wanted to push him back and get the heck out of there, but I couldn't do anything. My muscles ached and my head felt like someone was crushing it from either side.

Goddess help me, I cried. *He's a mind reaper.*

Tears flooded my vision, and the boy took another step toward me, his hand still latching onto mine. His smile was maddening, like a creature from a fairy tale, which wasn't surprising because a creature was exactly what he was. A tiny finger stroked my skin and my temples pounded with the echoing sound of laughter. I felt him inside my brain, digging and digging until he got what he came for.

Few could survive a mind reaper once they had a hold of you and those that did were barely alive enough to tell the tale. When I was young, Beatrix took me to the hospital to visit a mind reaper victim to teach me some lesson about staying safe in the field, though it had quite the opposite effect. After seeing the young woman strapped to tubes and unable to even speak, the last thing I wanted was to be a witch. For weeks, all I could think of was what that girl must have gone through and what she must have felt when the mind reaper destroyed her from the inside. Standing here now, with this creature's hold on me, I could definitively say that this was so much worse than I ever imagined.

The creature smiled again, and I could feel myself grow faint. *I swear, if I get out of this, I'm knocking your baby teeth right out, you little bastard!*

A car zoomed by in the distance and the boy swung his head toward the sound in alarm. Before he could regain his hold on me, I took my chance. I yanked my hand from his and stumbled back, my mind still swimming from his power overtaking me. I threw my hand into my shirt, ripping off the pendant from my neck and tightening a fist around the amethyst. The crystal cooled my heated palms and I screamed from its power.

The boy flashed his eyes my way and leaped but he was too slow, too small, and much too inexperienced. I swerved out of the way, sending him falling to all fours on the gravel. He swung around, his eyes feral and wild as he readied to lunge for me again.

He was so tiny that I almost felt bad for him. Almost. *This isn't a kid, Billie,* I told myself as I pulled on the crystal's powers. *YOU CAN DO THIS.*

But I couldn't.

Vanquishing a full-grown shadower was one thing, but destroying a small child, creature or not, was something else and I wasn't sure I'd be able to go through with it. Correction, I knew I couldn't.

My mind raced to think of a solution, some spell that

would free me of the creature without killing it. There was no time to consult my grimoire. It's not like I could ask the kid to hang tight while I found a way to defeat him.

Suddenly, an idea sparked just as the boy threw himself at me. I jumped back, leaping in the air to land on the bench in a crouch. My fingers pressed into the amethyst, and I willed its magic into existence. Mind reapers fed on thoughts and memories, so all I had to do was take enough back to render him useless.

"Let's see how you like it!" I roared and flipped my palm at the boy.

The crystal hummed in my grasp, and I closed my eyes, forcing its energy outward. A flash of purple spread from my palm, creeping toward the boy. He fell back, crawling away from me but I pressed my palm further as the crystal's energy enveloped him in its grasp. The purple light surrounded him, twisting and turning in a beautiful blaze of power.

The boy screamed and I pulled back, yanking on the crystal and pulling the boy's memories out with it. His small body shook on the ground as I pulled, further and further until I could taste his energy in the air. He yelped and I yanked on the crystal harder, sending the purple ring of light back into the pendant in my hand.

I stayed in a crouch while I inspected the boy's body that lay on the gravel below. His chest rose up and down, taking in air.

"It worked!" I hollered, hopping off the bench to stand above him. The toe of my boot kicked his side to make sure I knocked him out before I turned and took off in a dead sprint. In my hand, the amethyst pendant vibrated with the energy of the mind reaper's memories, and I nearly dropped it several times before I reached the main road. I'd have to cleanse the crystal when I got in to rid it of the dark magic it held, but that wasn't my priority at the moment. My legs pumped as I ran down the road, heart still racing from what just happened. Two shadower encounters in just as many days were nothing to laugh at. The residents of Shadowhurst were in deep trouble and it seemed I was their best chance. Just what I needed, to be stuck saving a town that used to burn people like me without a second thought.

Chapter Nine

"I couldn't sleep at all last night!" Peyton complained while I crammed books from my locker into my backpack. "You?"

She didn't know the half of it. I don't think I got so much as a nap in after I got back from the trail. My head was a mess even this morning and I knew it would be hours before my thoughts cleared up. That little asshole sure did a number on me last night. I still couldn't believe that I got attacked by another shadower, a mind reaper none the less. Things were looking bleaker by the second and I couldn't imagine what else Shadowhurst had in store for me. *What's next? I find out Silas is a soul sucker?* I laughed internally. Silas being a shadower was as likely as me running into fae on the way to first period.

"Not really," I admitted and zipped up my pack.

"I was thinking." Peyton smiled. "Since you're new here, we should totally catch you up on all the weirdness of this town. Sooner rather than later."

I laughed. "And why's that?"

"Um, hello? Because we're like a team of detectives or whatever. You and I are going to figure out what happened to those kids. It's gonna be fun!"

Fun was exactly what it was not going to be, but I didn't have the heart to tell her that. The less Peyton knew about what was going on in Shadowhurst, the better. I couldn't protect everyone, but I could at least protect her, my only friend in this stupid town. I tossed my bag over my shoulder and looked down the corridor. "Hey," I asked and nudged my head toward a large, wood door at the end. "Think the library might have something we can use?"

Peyton's eyes twinkled and she flashed her pearly whites my way. "Genius, B! Let's go!"

We ran down the hallway, zigging and zagging to avoid students in our way. When we arrived at the doors, I looked at my friend and winked before turning the handle. The doors opened with a creak and the scent of musty old books overtook my nostrils. The library at Shadowhurst Academy was a sight for sore eyes. It was deserted and quiet. A graveyard of knowledge long abandoned.

We walked past a row of shelves full of books with tattered spines that looked to be older than the school itself. As we marched, I ran my fingers down the length of the shelves, letting the ancient leather bound edges of the books roughen my calloused skin. When we passed the first row, the library opened up to an enormous hall with empty wooden tables lining its center. Each table was adorned with a reading lamp that had more dust on it than some crypts I visited back home on History tours. A few of the tables had stacks of books piled on top and I wondered if they were there to encourage students to read. Aside from Peyton and me, it seemed no one had any use for the library. At least not when they had all the information they needed on their phones and tablets.

"Where's the librarian?" I whispered, careful not to raise my voice. From what I remembered of libraries, they weren't exactly places where yelling was encouraged.

"The what?" Peyton asked.

"You know," I said, "whoever keeps this place under control."

Peyton looked around and waved her arm around the space, snickering. "Oh, yeah! This place needs someone to keep all these people in line!"

She twirled in a circle and pulled my sleeve.

"Come on! The Shadowhurst stuff is over there!"

I followed my friend past the rows of tables to three large bookcases on the back wall. The floorboards creaked under my weight, and I couldn't help but look around occasionally to make sure we were, in fact, alone in the library. Peyton seemed oblivious to any of the noise from our clumsy steps, her eyes trained on the books ahead. When we reached the cases, she started to pull out tomes and volumes, flipping some open to scan their indexes before piling them into my outstretched arms. By the time she was done, we each had half a dozen books in our hold, and I was almost toppling over from their weight. Peyton gestured to a small side table in between the bookcases, and we dumped our findings with relief.

I opened the first book in front of me and read the title out loud. "'The Grim History of Shadowhurst'."

"Oooooh!" Peyton exclaimed, hopping from foot to foot. "That's a good one! Turn to page forty-seven. You'll die!"

I followed her instructions and flipped the pages, my eyes landing on a stamped sketch of the school's main hall.

The other buildings on the campus weren't illustrated and when I looked down the date etched at the bottom, I realized that this sketch was likely done well before the academy existed. Above the main hall, stoic and proud stood the bell tower, though, in this image, there was no bell in its center and no roof overhead. Instead of the large iron bell that hung in the tower today, the image portrayed a wooden pole that sat secured to the floor.

"What's this?" I asked, my finger tracing the poll up and down.

"That's where they did it."

I jerked my hand back, disgust coursing through my veins. This was it, the place where they strung up my kind before setting them alight. My vision blurred and I had to back away from the book from fear I would pass out. I wanted to rip off the page and burn it with my magic, tear it apart in the same way my people were torn apart for nothing more than existing. Grim History was right, Shadowhurst was nothing but a monstrosity created by close-minded humans that let their fears rule their judgment. My eyes found Peyton's and she smiled sheepishly my way.

"I told you," she said. "This town is creepy."

Reluctantly, I squared my shoulders and turned back to the bookcase, hopeful to find a volume that could give me some clues to the town's history that didn't make me want to burn the library to the ground. As I scanned the shelf, my eyes snatched on the spine of a book that felt out-of-place amid the others. There was no writing etched on its side and the leather was not as worn as the rest. I reached to pick up it, but the book wouldn't budge. It was as though it was glued in place. My determination was limitless, and I tugged on the spine again, pressing the sole of my boot into the shelf for leverage. Slowly, I could feel it give way before surrendering to my incessant pulling. The book ripped off the shelf and sent me flying back to land on my butt. Next to me, Peyton's jaw slacked just as a loud, creaking screech rose over us. I watched in astonishment as the bookcase slid on a hidden rail to reveal a secret doorway.

"What in the..." Peyton yelped, running to the door.

"Peyton, wait!" I shouted, but my friend was already turning the doorknob before I had a chance to reach her.

The wood of the door scratched against the floorboards and Peyton pushed her way inside and into the darkness before us. I jumped to stand and took off after her.

"What is this place?" I whispered, my arms stretching to find the walls.

"One sec!" Peyton yelled out somewhere not too far from me.

I could hear her cursing and stumbling about in the dark. She hit something and yelped, and I swung my head left and right, squinting to see her. There was a sharp click and the room illuminated in dim yellow light. I turned to see Peyton in the center, her fingers wrapped around a hanging light switch.

"Sweet!" she croaked and looked around.

The room, though small, was larger than I expected. It looked like it belonged in the basement of a haunted house and not in a prominent academy's library, but that wasn't what caught my attention. What drew me in were the piles of books stacked around the perimeter of the walls. There had to be hundreds of them in here, perched in the darkness and hidden from watchful eyes. "Where are we?"

"Don't know. Some secret room."

"No kidding, Sherlock," I growled and crouched next to a book pile.

As soon as my fingers reached the books, my heartbeat sped up. My sweatshirt felt suddenly constricting and the walls seemed to have inched closer. The energy in the room shifted and I could feel the moonstone of my ring pulse against my skin. Even the amethyst pendant on my neck burned and I had to pull it through my tee to keep it from touching my chest. With unease, I pulled out one book from the stacks and carried it to the center of the room and closer to the light. My hands shook and my palms clammed against the binding as I opened the book to the first page.

"Holy actual crap!" Peyton yelled out but her words were lost to me.

I glued my eyes to the worn-out, cursive font that spelled the title of the wretched book in my hands. "'A Witch Hunters Guide to Entrapment'," I read aloud.

"Oh my God!" Peyton screeched. "You know what this means?"

I had no idea how to respond. I knew exactly what it meant. Shadowhurst Academy was not what it seemed on the outside. This place would be the end of me.

Chapter Ten

The rest of the school day passed in a blur. I got at least ten messages from Peyton between the time we left the library to the time I rode up the driveway to the Chandler residence. My white tee was soaked with sweat and my hair was a mess, and I couldn't wait to get into the guesthouse and reset my energy. Finding the hidden room in the library was like stepping into a minefield. I felt like every step I took in Shadowhurst only led to more questions, more secrets, and so much more danger. How long had that room been in the library? Years? Decades? Worse, was it still in use today? And if it was, who used it?

Questions raced through my mind as I walked the bike around the side of the house to park in the garage. Was the academy just a front for witch hunters? If it was, I was done for.

I climbed the steps to the front door and brushed my hair back behind my ears before entering. All I could hope for was that the Chandlers weren't home, and I could hide in my room and process what I just discovered. Unfortunately, hoping had never done me any good and as soon as I walked in, I heard hushed tones rise from the living room. I tiptoed down the hall, trying not to attract attention to myself to avoid interrupting whatever company the Chandlers were hosting.

"Billie, darling?" Thomas' voice echoed behind me just as I reached the main stairs. "Come in here, we have guests."

I rolled my eyes, plastered on a fake smile, and marched into the living room. When I entered, my lips pursed and my mouth dried. There, in the middle of the Chandlers pristine living room, sat the four high priestesses. My arms felt too heavy for my body, and I let them drop at my sides as my eyes moved from one priestess to the other. The room smelled like a potent mixture of a dozen different herbs, and I could hear the jingle of crystals as the high priestesses shifted in their seats to see me walk in. My magic reached for theirs, clinging to the stones and herbs tucked into every orifice of their attires. There was so much magic in the room, I couldn't stand it.

Rhiamon and Luna sat on one of the sofas, their hands entwined as they often had been. Luna's small, rune-covered hand was almost obliterated from view by Rhiamon's muscled grasp but somehow, it didn't feel out of place. Those two had been best friends since as long as I can remember, so much so, that I often wondered if their relationship was more than platonic. If it was, no one spoke of it, and I kept my mouth shut for fear I might entice Sebyl's anger. Rhiamon grinned, flipping her long braids to one side to reveal her signature black leather choker encrusted with crystals. Beside her, Luna's compact frame fidgeted and the sound of the bells adorning her long, lace gown filled the room.

To their right, Theodora perched at the edge of a

loveseat, her bright blue hair teased higher than a skyscraper above her head. As always, she donned an over the top outfit made of feathers and silk, all in the same shade as her hair. After Rhiamon, Theodora was a favorite of mine from all the high priestesses. Mostly because she reminded me more of an actress from an old Hollywood film than a witch. Her eccentric personality carried the room and I remember watching her in awe as witches huffed and puffed around her while she chattered away before some of our rituals.

But today, it was Sebyl's eyes that I could not shake. The high priestess commanded the room, as she had often done. It was no wonder the witches followed her lead without question. Sebyl's cat-lined eyes burrowed into me as she reached a black-gloved finger to brush a loose strand of her blunt black bob into place. The edges of her lips curled into a smile, and I could almost hear the unspoken words flow through her false smile. *Keep your mouth shut and behave.*

"Oh," I choked out, "hello."

"Billie!" Imala clasped her hands in excitement. "Isn't it wonderful to get a visit from your caseworkers?"

"Splendid," I hissed and walked over to sit across from Sebyl, my gaze still focused on the deep red lipstick of her forced smile.

The white leather of the couch swallowed me whole and I wished I picked a different spot to sit in. With the fabric wrapped around me like a cocoon, I felt more like a restless child than the witch I was.

"Wilhemina, dear," Theodora cooed, "you seem to be settling in well. The Chandlers have told us such wonderful things about you."

I cringed at the use of my full name, it made me feel like a kid in trouble.

"They have?" I asked and arched an eyebrow to Imala.

"Of course, darling!" she said. "We love having you around!"

My eyes snapped back to the high priestesses. The tension in the room was palpable and I knew that whatever they had to say would not be something I wanted to hear. Maybe I was wrong. They might simply be here to check up on me to make sure I was doing okay. *Doubtful.*

"Thomas, Imala," I mumbled. "Would you mind giving me a moment with my... *caseworkers* in private?"

The Chandlers exchanged glances. There was a long pause before they got up from their seats in unison and exited the room, leaving me alone with the priestesses. Out of the corner of my eyes, I could see Luna twirl a raw amethyst in her fingers, her wolf's grin spreading as their backs disappeared.

"Luna!" I snapped. "Don't use magic on them!"

The high priestess turned her lavender eyes my way and tucked the crystal into a pouch that hung from her wrist. "Careful, Wilhemina. You don't get to make demands, not after what you did to land yourself here."

I ground my teeth to oblivion and bit on the inside of my cheek to keep from screaming. I wasn't a child, and I didn't need them here checking in on me. I knew what I was doing and somehow, I got through this total mess even with the lack of support they've shown me. This was ridiculous!

"So," I said after forcing myself to calm down, "was anyone going to tell me that this place used to burn us to the ground, or was that just a fun little mystery you wanted me to solve by myself?"

Sebyl and Theodora looked to Luna and Rhiamon, their faces blank.

"That's what I thought." I scowled, crossing my legs to sit a little higher. "So, what now?"

"What do you mean?" Sebyl asked.

It was the first time she'd spoken to me since they shipped me off and the cool tone of her voice gutted me. Sebyl was always frank and straightforward, but she was never cold. She wanted to teach me, to turn me into the powerful witch I knew I could be. But now, her stare was rigid and full of... Well, I wasn't sure what but whatever it was, I didn't like it.

"I mean, I'm sure you don't expect me to stay here," I said.

Sebyl narrowed her eyes my way and smiled, though the gesture barely reached her eyes. "Why would we not expect that?"

"Um, let's see, because I'm a witch in a town that hates witches."

"Wilhemina, please," Theodora interrupted, "don't be so dramatic. It's a quaint insignificant town with a sordid history, the world is full of them."

"Not my world," I hissed under my breath.

Slowly, Sebyl rose to stand, taking a few steps until she towered over me. Her tall frame obscured the light falling in from the windows and I could see the lines of her aged face grow deeper as she frowned. She placed her hand on my shoulder and squeezed. "We simply wanted to make sure you are getting along fine here and staying out of trouble. As we had instructed."

"Kind of hard to do when you tossed me into a witch-hunting school," I blurted, immediately regretting my decision to speak.

Sebyl staggered back and Luna reached for Rhiamon's other hand.

"A what?" Theodora asked, baffled.

"I found a room," I explained, "in the library. A room no one wanted to be found, I think. It's full of books on witchhunting. Instructions on the worst things. Goddess, they even have an entire section on weapons to use against us and how to spot a witch in a crowd."

The high priestesses exhaled in unison, their eyes finding mine in an instant. To my surprise, Sebyl stepped in and lowered to sit next to me. Her long fingers found my shoulder again though this time, she pulled me into a hug. My body relaxed into her. My hands cupped in my lap, and I looked at my dirty boots before looking up at her with tears in my eyes.

"There's more," I whispered. "I've been attacked by two shadowers. The mind reaper almost killed me. I can't stay here, Sebyl. It isn't safe."

Sebyl looked from me to Theodora then back to me again. "This is very interesting indeed."

"Interesting?" I pushed back from her. "That's what you have to say about this?"

"Wilhemina, why is it you think we've placed you here?"

"Because I was bad, and I messed up and I had to be punished?"

She nodded. "Partially, yes. But also, because we believe in you. We know the good you can accomplish in this world, and we need you to know that too."

Tears flooded my vision and I swatted them away with the back of my hand. Sebyl had never said such words to me. Her only act of encouragement was to push me further. Her saying that she believed in me meant everything. It meant that I wasn't like Beatrix. It meant I was good.

"What do you need me to do?" I choked between tears.

"Well, that is quite obvious, is it not?" Sebyl grimaced. "We need you to stay and find out if any hunters are operating in Shadowhurst."

"So, there *are* hunters out there? I thought you told me there haven't been one in years? Like the fae."

"There are some left, here and there. We didn't want to worry you or the other witches," Sebyl answered. "We have to be careful and gauge the situation as it unfolds."

"And if I find them," I said fearfully, "what should I do?"

Sebyl squeezed my shoulder, pulling me into the black leather of her suit until I was almost suffocating on her musky scent. "You play the part, child. You infiltrate their group and report back. Can you do that for us?"

I nodded. I would do anything they wanted as long as they took me back.

Evening air filled the guest house as I toweled off my hair before falling back to lie on the soft covers of my bed. Thanks to Luna's magic work, the Chandlers had no clue what hit them. As far as they were concerned, the visit with my so-called caseworkers went over smoothly and everyone parted on acceptable terms. I, however, knew better. There was even more at stake now that the high priestess barreled into town with instructions. There were witch hunters in the world! Real-life hunters that wanted my kind dead and no one bothered to tell me! I wondered what else they've been hiding in their placid attempt to keep me safe. But what could I do? I had to follow their directions. They were my high priestesses for Goddess' sake. Their word was law.

My body ached and I idly played with the pendant Ms. Broussard gifted me when my phone vibrated. I caught it just in time before it plummeted from the edge of the bed and tapped a key to unlock the screen. The light from the screen filled my unlit room and I had to blink a few times to focus on the message that popped up.

It was from Peyton.

Meet me tomorrow after school in the parking lot.

I tapped the keys to respond. *Why?*

Three dots flashed on the screen before Peyton's answer came through.

I have an idea on how we can find out more about this hunter business.

I rolled my eyes so hard, they almost got stuck in the back of my head. This girl was way too into solving mysteries but luckily, this was one mystery I needed her help to solve. *I'm in,* I typed. *What's the plan?*

Those incessant dots filled the screen again then disappeared. A few moments later, Peyton's message showed up.

We need the trust funders.

My fingers entered the keys angrily. *What? Why?*

There was another pause before her text appeared. *They know everyone in the school. We can use them to dig up info on the students to find out who might have a special interest in a certain secret library room.*

"Ugh, great." I sighed and started typing. *What makes you think they'll tell us anything? Savannah isn't exactly a fan of mine...*

They will if they think we're their friends, her message

read, followed by a second text bubble. *Ready to go undercover?*

I groaned and rolled over on the bed. Why did everyone in my life think I'm some kind of secret spy? Is this what James Bond felt like all the time? It annoyed me, to say the least, but mostly, it left me tired. My head was clouded from the day, and I couldn't wait to get a good night's sleep. I was already under the covers when my phone vibrated again with another message from Peyton.

Just a heads up, it spelled, *River's coming too. Nite!*

Chapter Eleven

I hightailed it to school first thing in the morning and sped down the hills of the residential streets of Shadowhurst like a maniac. My loose braid wove behind me in the breeze, and I was sure that when I reached the campus, I'd look like a disheveled mess. *You don't care;* I convinced myself. *So what if the hot guy will be there?*

The wind hit my face, flushing my cheeks with its icy fingers, and by the time I parked my bike in the lot, I was out of breath and full of energy.

Scanning the parking lot, I found Peyton leaning against her newly washed Jeep, her hands tucked into the pockets of a brand new denim jumper I haven't seen her wear before. Her hair was shiny and shampooed and I swear I could see lip liner from where I was standing. Next to her, River leaned with his elbow on the side window and whispered something I couldn't hear. Peyton threw her head back and laughed so loud, I thought my eardrums would burst.

Wow, she's taking the whole make friends with your enemies thing to heart...

They hadn't noticed me roll in, so I took the chance to straighten out my braid and reapply a thin coat of lip balm to my wind-chapped lips before marching toward them. My breath hitched when I approached at the sight of River in yet another hotter than the sun ensemble of white jeans and a red v-neck tee that did all the right things for his body. My eyes rolled over his pecs and down, down, down.

"Hey!" He waved when he saw me, and I shot my eyes up before he could see me drool over the dangerously low cut of his waistband.

"Morning." I brought my hand up to my forehead in a salute.

Did you seriously just salute him? What is he? Your army general? Idiot.

I chuckled nervously before turning to Peyton. "So, what's going on?"

"Well," my friend said in a sultry tone I wasn't used to, "I was just telling River, here, about the weird little chamber in the library."

My eyes snapped to Peyton's and I gave her the death glare of a lifetime. What was she thinking of telling him about the witch-hunting room? Was she crazy? I was beginning to think Peyton was not as good a detective as I thought she might be. She's going to spill all our secrets before we even fool the hyenas into being friends with us!

Peyton nudged her head toward my hand where my knuckles turned white around my phone case. I looked down, noticing a new message alert on my screen. As I flipped my phone over to check, she turned her body to block River's view of me. "So, what were you saying about the quarry this weekend?"

"We're having a party there Saturday," he answered. "You guys should definitely come."

His eyes peered over Peyton's shoulder and burnt into me. Blood rushed to my face, and I licked my lips, wondering what that perfect mouth of his would taste like. Before I could make a fool of myself and blurt out something stupid again, Peyton shifted her weight, hiding me from River's attention once more. "Tell me more," she purred.

I shook my head, focusing my mind back to my phone and the text message my friend wanted me to read.

I'm telling him only what he needs to know to pique his interest.

Okay, maybe I was wrong, and Peyton was a better detective than I thought. She clearly had some plan concocted in that odd brain of hers and I had to admit, I didn't even see her type the message. The girl was slicker than tanning oil.

And great, now I'm thinking about River tanning.

I rolled my eyes and stepped around Peyton's aggressive stance to fit myself into their conversation. My gaze locked on River and when he looked back at me, I choked on the spit I hadn't realized collected in my mouth.

"Peyton told me you're kind of a witchcraft expert," River noted, his eyes never leaving mine. "Didn't take you for an occult junkie."

"Uh, yeah. Got it from my mom, I guess."

"Your mom?" he asked, arching one perfect eyebrow my way. "I thought you were, you know..."

"An orphan?" I laughed. "No. Well, sort of I suppose. I haven't seen her in a long time."

"How come?"

I blushed and looked down at my boots. *How come?*

Because she's in a magical jail for the rest of her life. Cool story. "I'd rather not get into it," I said bluntly. "So, you like witchy things too, I take it?"

"Not really." He shrugged. "But can't get away from it in this town."

"Yeah, I'm starting to realize that."

At my side, Peyton coughed then giggled like a schoolgirl with a crush before nudging me with her elbow. I followed her gaze to River's chest, realizing that the V of his tee has rolled down far enough for me to make out every curve of his chest muscles. I nudged her back, shooting her a side glance. We were here for a reason for Goddess' sake.

"So, what did Peyton tell you about this room so far?" I asked, "And why are you even interested?"

River raised his arms. "Whoa, officer! She said it's for some history project you guys are working on. My family has been in Shadowhurst for generations, so when she asked for help, I figured there was no harm in it. I can leave if you'd prefer…"

"No!" I yelled out a little too eagerly. "I mean, thanks for helping. Anything you can tell us about the town's history would be great."

River took a step toward me, his green eyes brightening in the rising sun of the early morning. He licked his lower lip and my stomach turned. He was so close, I could smell the woodsy scent of his cologne and it sent shivers down my thighs. Beneath the surface of my skin, magic stood at attention as I caught it at a crossroads. The heat off River's tanned skin rushed toward me and my mouth dried up when he took another step in. For a second, I forgot Peyton was even there. It was as if everything around me dispersed, leaving only me and him in the empty school parking lot.

"Wanna show me this room?" he whispered, his lips just inches from my ear.

My body froze and I turned my moonstone ring around my finger so many times that it ripped into my skin. I nodded, swallowing hard. "Sure..."

"Great!"

I exhaled the breath I've been holding and cast a side glance at Peyton, whose eyes were so wide, I thought they might pop out of their sockets. She snickered and turned to reach for her backpack in the passenger seat, her jumper riding up as she bent over. My eyes turned to River's and it surprised me to see him looking at me despite my friend's ass almost hanging out a foot away from us. What kind of guy didn't drool over a girl's exposed behind when he had a chance?

"Ready!" Peyton yelled out, pushing past us to run up the path leading to the school. "You guys coming or are you just gonna stare at each other all day?"

River shrugged and we turned to follow her, my legs shaking with each step we took. As we strolled, I noticed that River hung back to keep pace with me, his arm brushing against mine every so often and sending my inappropriate thoughts into overdrive. He didn't seem so bad, for a trust funder, that is. His hand swayed and knocked into mine and my eyes widened. Whatever I felt when this guy was next to me wasn't normal, it was different somehow, dark.

"What about Savannah and the rest of your friends?" I asked when we turned into the quad.

"What about them?"

I glanced his way, choosing my next words carefully so as not to sound too desperate. "Are they from a long line of Shadowhurst families too?"

"Savannah and Abigail are. But Tyler, Jayden, and Morgan are fairly new here. Jayden is actually from Stamwick too. Maybe you guys knew each other."

"I doubt it. It's a pretty big city."

"Yeah." He blushed. "That was stupid. I guess growing up here where everyone knows each other you just assume it's like that everywhere else. It must have been fun living in the city."

An image of me slicing off the head of a snake shifter in a dark alley flashed before my eyes. "That's one way of looking at it," I replied with a grimace.

"What's another way?"

"I don't know," I whispered. "...Lonely."

River slowed down and turned to look at me. "I won't ask about why you're here," he said, "but do you at least like living with the Chandlers?"

"They're cool and thanks for not butting in."

He brought his hand to his forehead and saluted me in the same, awkward way I had done earlier. "Anytime, soldier!"

A laugh burst from me, and I punched him on the shoulder before rolling my eyes.

"So, tell me more about this room," River said.

"I don't know," I answered in the best nonchalant voice I could manage. "It's a room of books, but Peyton seems excited about it. Has a bunch of weird tomes about witch-hunting, so that's cool."

"Huh," River whispered.

"What?"

He shook his head. "Oh, nothing. Just a secret room in a library that no one knew about. Sounds like something out of a movie."

"I wouldn't get too excited. It's literally just books."

"Whatever you say, soldier." He winked and pulled me forward. "Come on! Let's go check it out!"

When we caught up with Peyton, she already had a million questions for River. Knowing her, she likely stayed up all night memorizing them so she could suck as much information out of this poor, clueless boy as she could. I couldn't help but laugh every time she fired another one but to my surprise, River was more than eager to play along. We marched through the quiet hallways of the academy in unison, laughing and joking like we were old friends that knew each other for a lifetime, and with every minute, I could feel the tension in my body ease away. Even if we couldn't get what we needed from River and his friends, I was glad he was here. It was nice to have another normal friend in this town.

For a second, I even forgot about why we were there. It wasn't until Peyton burst through the library doors that reality crashed down on me like a heavy wave of agony. As soon as we walked into the library, every sense of comfort I felt before disappeared and I was back to my old self and the girl I knew I had to be no matter how much I wished for something different. *You're not normal*, I had to tell myself. And I wasn't, not really.

I was a witch. A witch with a mission and a town to protect. A witch that had a murder to solve before anyone else got hurt.

Chapter Twelve

Peyton and River bent over one of the library's tables, their fingers flipping through book pages, while I took notes on the opposite side. We only had a half-hour left before first period and so far, could not find anything in the books of interest. At least not anything that could help me figure out who the hunters in the town might be. My friends shouted off new bits of information as they came upon it, and I tried my best not to let the bile in my throat make an appearance. Each time we turned a page, we came across detailed accounts of witch killings from the last hundred years and it made me want to scream. How could anyone be so close-minded and brutal? Witches weren't the problem and whoever put these books together had no actual clue what was going on in the world.

From everything we've read, there was no mention of the shadowers, which wasn't all that surprising to me. The High Coven was adamant about covering our tracks and, as much as we wanted to keep the existence of witches out of the public eye, we were just as concerned with the shadowers.

Humans had enough to be afraid of without worrying about soulless creatures hunting them in the night. Back home, if a shadower attack got out of hand and a human got hurt or killed, there was always a witch nearby to erase all evidence pointing to anything supernatural. I had to admit, the coven has gotten so good at covering our tracks that sometimes I wondered if even I existed. Keeping secrets had become such an enormous part of me, it was easier to lie than tell the truth. Though I was sure I'd inherited a lot of that trait from Beatrix, who couldn't tell the truth to save her life.

I was growing frustrated by the second as we scoured the pages of the books. Everything we've read was nothing but propaganda against my kind. It was such a joke! As far as the hunters—if they even still existed in Shadowhurst—were concerned, witches were evil and deserved the worst kind of death. The kind of death that apparently required a lot of sharp weapons and a good burning. My stomach twisted into knots and my lungs felt like lumps of coal in my chest. These books were leading us nowhere.

"There's nothing in this one." I sighed and tossed the volume I was going over to the side. "I don't think we'll get anything here, you guys."

"What are you two looking for?" River asked, still confused about our fake project. His eyes scanned over the book in front of him and a smile flashed over his face. He looked up, noticing me staring and crashed his lips into a thin line before jerking his gaze away from me. Was I imagining this, or did I just make Mr. Varsity League nervous? *Interesting.*

Peyton smiled. "Pretty much anything on this town's obsession with the occult. We want to put together a timeline to see where it all started," she lied without missing a beat.

I, of course, knew better. We didn't need a timeline at all. Any fool could see it all started with the witch burnings in the bell tower that perched not too far above our heads. What we needed was to find some connection between the two murdered students, but that was looking like a lost cause. Aside from the obvious misinformation about what witchcraft was, the books had no information on the town's background. As far as I could tell, Lacey and Grady had nothing in common.

This was a dead end.

River shut the heavy tome in front of him. "Have you checked the town's archives?"

"I've basically lived in the archives," Peyton noted. "Nothing there."

"You sure?"

"...Why?" I asked, my eyes locking on his.

"Just that if you're looking to see how it all started, it would make sense to check the genealogy of the founding members. At least, that would have been my first guess."

Peyton and I exchanged glances and I could see the wheels turn in my friend's head. She pushed the book she was holding to the side and narrowed her eyes on River. "Isn't your family one of them?" she asked as though she didn't already know the answer.

"Yep. Savannah's too."

"So, what can *you* tell us?"

Footsteps pounded in the hallway outside as students trickled in for the day and I was suddenly very aware of the fact that we were not alone in the academy. I checked the doors to make sure they were still shut before turning back to my friends. "Was Grady's family one?"

In front of me, River's face grew ashen, and he bit his lower lip. He ran his fingers through his tousled hair and sunk deeper into the chair. "Um, yeah. I think."

"And Lacey's?" I asked before I could stop myself.

His eyes snapped to mine and I jumped back in my seat. The green in them burnt like fire as his gaze burrowed into me, and I couldn't help but smile his way. Why couldn't I stop acting like a fool around this guy?

"I think her family has been around for a while, but I don't know how long. So maybe," he finally answered. His fingers tapped on the edge of the desk, and I got the sense that he didn't want to talk about this with us. Peyton's comment back in the Crystal Cauldron drew me in, connecting the dots. River knew Grady, they might have even been friends. It can't be easy for him to have to talk about it and us quizzing him about Grady's death was a terrible idea. The last thing I wanted was to upset him, but I had to know more. If both Lacey and Grady were from one of the founding families, this could be the connection we were looking for.

Could the witch killing these students be out for revenge?

"Do you think that—"

"Probably just a coincidence," Peyton interrupted me, forcing the words back in my mouth. "And has nothing to do with our project."

She fluttered her thick lashes my way and I shifted my weight in the chair, dropping my eyes to the table. Whatever Peyton had in mind, it was something she'd tell me about later and I trusted her to lead this.

"But good call on the archives," she added. "We'll check there next."

The bell rang, jolting my nerves with its sharp tone. We had fifteen minutes left before we had to leave for class. My mind raced with possibilities of who the witch might be and what her business was in Shadowhurst. I wished I could call on the High Coven to help, but that would not be the smartest move. I needed to have more to bring to them and Peyton's hunches would not do the trick. As soon as school was done, I'd have to get Peyton to take me to the archives so I can confirm my suspicions. Somehow, I knew that I was right. The witch was killing students from the founding families. But why?

And who was next?

Agony twisted and turned under my skin as I looked up at River. He was one of those family lines, could he be next? Savannah too, but I was a lot less concerned about her. Not that I wanted her dead, but if I was being honest, I could see why someone would. My breath quickened just thinking about River being in danger. I had to warn him somehow, I had to keep him safe.

"This quarry party," I said, "who else is going?"

River leaned in on the table and smiled. "All of us and if you're worried about Savannah, don't be. I'll make sure she plays nice. And I want you to come."

His eyes met mine again and I turned as red as blood and looked down at my hands. Having River around was distracting me from what I was here to do, and I hated it. Not the staring part, that I had no problem with. It was the fact that my stomach turned every time he was near me that had me all twisted up inside. I couldn't remember the last time I felt this nervous around a guy and it was taking me for a loop. *He's just being nice, Billie. As if he could like a little weirdo like you.* I grimaced and forced myself to think about the party River invited us to, willing my nerves back to a comfortable level.

The quarry party would give me a chance to get closer to the possible targets without looking like a complete creep. *Right. That's what this is. You're not just excited to spend more time with him,* I recited in my head over and over. I wasn't looking forward to partying with Savannah, but I had to stay near the two of them. If I was right and the witch was targeting the Shadowhurst founding families, they were in more danger than they realized. Maybe if I could stay by their side, I could be there if she tried anything. Then again, maybe I was dead wrong and someone else would get hurt while I was playing bodyguard to a bunch of trust funders. Either way, it was my only lead so far and I had to follow through.

"Cool," I breathed out. "We'll be there."

"We will?" Peyton gasped.

"Yep." I nodded and forced myself to look away from River. "It'll be fun."

The guest house was so hot that I had to chuck the covers to the floor as I tossed and turned, unable to sleep. My eyes focused on the clock above my dresser, and I groaned. It was two-forty in the morning, and I was still wide awake. Under normal circumstances, I dropped like a log as soon as my head hit the pillow but that was back in Stamwick where I could use my magic freely and would wipe myself out every night. Here in Shadowhurst, where magic use was prohibited to me, I was nothing more than an agitated teenager stuck in a loop of thoughts. *Ew. Is this what kids had to deal with all the time? No wonder they had attitude problems!*

I let out another loud sigh and got out of bed.

Tightening the belt around my plush robe, I put on a pair of furry slippers and tiptoed through the backyard to the main house. Since I've already cleared out all the snacks Imala stocked in my small kitchen, I was fresh out of food and my insomniac stomach was growling louder than a shifter.

I twisted the handle and made my way through the downstairs hallway to the kitchen. Mostly, I tried to stay out of the main house for fear of being an imposition on the Chandlers, but right now, my need for snacks took priority.

As I rounded the corner, I noticed the kitchen light on and stopped dead in my tracks. The wood creaked under me, and I cringed at the sound. Just ahead, Thomas snapped his gaze to me and smiled.

Crap. Too late to turn back now. I returned his smile with my own and scooted into one of the chairs, my elbows banging on the tabletop.

"Can't sleep, kiddo?" Thomas asked.

"Yeah," I said, "long day."

He dunked a knife into the Costco-sized peanut butter jar in front of me and spread the delicious goodness over toasted bread. "This should do the trick," he said and slid the toast over.

The bread crunched in my mouth, and I swallowed so fast, I almost forgot to chew. Beside me, Thomas laughed and made himself an identical sandwich. He took one bite and sighed in relief before turning to face me. "If you ever find yourself not sleeping, chances are, I'm over here stuffing my face. You're welcome to join at any time."

I smiled, blushing. "Thank you. I didn't want to bother anyone, but I was starving."

"You're not a bother, Billie. We love having you around."

"Really?"

I was genuinely shocked. No one had ever said they loved being around me and his words knocked me back. Thomas was probably just being polite, but the tone of his voice made me think he might have meant it. *Super weird.*

He laughed again. "Yes, really. Imala especially, I think you remind her of herself when she was your age."

"So, how did you two meet?" I asked. *Was that crossing the line? Whatever, I want to know.*

"HA!" Thomas exclaimed. "It's a tale as old as time..."

"Seriously?"

His grin widened and he plowed another mouthful of peanut butter toast. "Not at all," he said between chews, "we met in a lounge. Imala was there for her friend's bachelorette party, and I was out with some boys from the office. But as soon as I saw her, I knew I wanted to marry that woman."

"No kidding. She's gorgeous."

"And smart. Way smarter than me, that's for certain."

I took a few more bites, swallowing loudly after each chew. "I'm really glad you guys let me stay here."

"Kiddo, you can stay here as long as you need. Like I said, we love having you around."

As we sat there in the kitchen in the middle of the night, scarfing down peanut butter sandwiches and talking about pointless things like school and movies we like, I felt my muscles relax. Whatever agitation I had about seeing River and the rest of the students at the quarry tomorrow evaporated and soon, I found myself yawning uncontrollably. Thomas' own mouth couldn't stay closed and after a while, we agreed it was time to call it a night, but not before I promised to have breakfast with him and Imala. He seemed so happy that I agreed and surprisingly, I was happy myself. Being around them felt normal somehow. There was no magic talk and no pressure. If this is what it was like to have a family, I was all in.

Chapter Thirteen

The sun was high in the sky by the time we pulled the Jeep into the parking lot next to the trail that led to the quarry, and I was glad I listened to Peyton and left my token biker jacket at home. Wind clipped at the sliver of flesh of my exposed waist where my loose tee barely reached my cut-offs. Beside me, Peyton awkwardly tucked and re-tucked her tank top into her jeans.

"This will definitely *not* be fun," she announced as we looked down the trail to the small beach below.

"Hey, you're the one that wanted to be buddies with them!" I said and nudged my elbow into her ribs. "So, let's go."

She rolled her eyes and followed me down the trail, huffing, and puffing the entire way.

The quarry River told us to meet them in was beautiful and I couldn't help but giggle with each step we took toward it. The water was the brightest shade of aquamarine I've ever seen and reminded me of the photos I used to scroll through online while planning out a dream vacation. We stomped down the stone-covered trail, my boots catching on loose rocks every so often. I should have worn sandals but the idea of being even more exposed than I already was made me queasy. Besides, if we had to hightail it out of here, I'd rather have my boots on than some fashion-friendly lace-ups.

When we reached the bottom, my jaw slacked. Around us, encasing the quarry from all sides, stood a large ravine. The rock looked like it was carved out, framing the water in its hold. I could feel the energy of this place tug at me, and, without surprise, my magic could too. The air, the water, and the lush trees pulled me in. Even the sand under my feet had power, it seemed, and I could already feel myself getting stronger just by standing in it. The stupid and debilitating lights that showed up each time like a warning bell blurred my vision and I closed my eyes, praying I don't fall over.

Peyton rustled beside me, her eyes scanning the crowd of teenagers on the beach.

"Ready?" she asked.

I nodded and pulled her toward them.

There were at least twenty people there, most of them split off into smaller groups. I noticed a group of girls in revealing bikinis tanning on beach towels at the far end and scowled. Why didn't I wear a bathing suit again?

I hiked up my top to sit higher on my waist and let the warmth of the sun spread through me. Stamwick was always cold and rainy, and I had almost forgotten how amazing it felt to be out in the sun like this. Beads of sweat ran down my neck and I had to toss my hair into a messy bun above my head to keep it off my shoulders.

There was a loud thud to our left and both Peyton and I turned to a group of teens tossing a frisbee around. My eyes spotted Jayden on the ground, the frisbee locked in his teeth.

"Told you I'd get it!" he yelled before jumping to his feet. His eyes landed on me and Peyton, and he waved us over. "New kid! Welcome to the party!"

As soon as Jayden yelled, all eyes were on us. I could see the confusion roll off everyone in the quarry as they tried to understand why the two of us were there. *This was a mistake,* I thought, and turned to leave when a powerful hand grasped my shoulder.

I swung around, ready to clock whoever it was that thought they could lay a hand on me without getting a fistful of my knuckles in their teeth. When I turned, my body vibrated and a low moan crept up in my throat.

"You made it!" River exclaimed, his hand still resting on my shoulder.

My eyes flowed over him, and it took everything I had not to say what I was thinking. Which was difficult at best because all I could think of was *Goddess help me,* over and over.

River's bare chest glistened in the sunlight, drawing my attention from his pecs down to the sculpted V at his waist. My eyes lowered, following its direction, and landed on the palm trees that decorated his swimming shorts. This guy was set on killing me with his hotness. I shook my head and met his stare, taking a wider stance in case I passed out from the view.

"Yep," I choked out, "we said we would."

"Awesome! Come meet everyone."

In my peripheral, I could see Peyton whisper something under her breath and I knew that it was directed at River's muscled body. My friend's face lit up and she followed him to the edge of the water where a large towel spread out over the sand. On it was a cooler full of ice with beer cans crammed in and an epic array of snacks. My mouth salivated at the overflowing bowl of chips, and I bent down to pick up a handful, eager to stuff my face. Better a mouth full of chips than a wagging tongue.

River chuckled beside me before grabbing a few for himself and sitting down cross-legged on the towel. "Glad you two came," he said, gesturing for me to sit next to him.

Hesitantly, I lowered down, pulling Peyton with me.

"This place is beautiful," I said and swallowed the last of the chips. "We don't have this back home."

"Shadowhurst has its upsides."

"When people aren't getting killed!" Peyton blurted out and smiled sheepishly.

"Right..."

His gaze darkened and I scooted on the towel until I was face to face with him. River's scent threw me for a loop, but I kept my eyes on his despite the constant tugging at the back of my mind telling me to look away. "I'm sorry about your friend. Peyton said you knew Grady?"

"Uh-huh." River's eyes brightened a bit, but I could still the hurt on his face clear as day. "Since we were kids. He was a great guy. One of those people you could always count on to do the right thing, you know?"

I really, really did. After Beatrix, my limit for bullshit was quite low and if anyone I met even seemed like they were up to no good, I usually hit the road before I got too close to someone else that thought rules didn't apply to them. Except for that college guy but in my defense, I was too busy checking out his other assets to pay attention to the pea-sized brain he sported under all that hair gel.

"I can't imagine what that was like for you," I whispered. Next to me, Peyton busied herself with watching a few kids play volleyball not far from us so I knew she wouldn't be blurting out any more nonsense that hurt River's feelings. "I'm sorry for your loss."

River rubbed the back of his neck and forced a smile. "Thanks. I try not to think about it, but you know how it goes. The things you try not to think about are usually the ones that bite you in the ass so hard, you get whiplash."

"Yeah, no kidding."

"So, how's Shadowhurst treating you so far?"

"It's not bad," I said with less enthusiasm than I was hoping to convey. "It's weird to be somewhere everyone knows each other. In Stamwick, people are so obsessed with their own lives that getting to know your neighbors is out of the question."

"Ha!" River laughed. "It's definitely a trip here. Just don't do anything stupid or you know the whole town will know about it before lunch."

"Noted." I reached for another fistful of chips and was about to bite down on one when sand splashed over my hand.

"You have got to be kidding me!" Savannah screeched as she towered over me and Peyton. "You brought the Riffraff?!?"

Her high-cut blue bikini was encrusted with gemstones and burnt into my peripheral as she cocked her hips to the side. If looks could kill, I'd be dead already.

"It's a public beach," I scoffed.

"It's *our* beach!" she yelled out, kicking more sand into my hand.

In seconds, I was on my feet. My face leveled with her icy glare and my hands at my waist. I took a deep breath in to keep myself from punching her lights out though a large part of me wanted to do nothing else but that. "You need to get over yourself," I hissed.

"River, are you for real?"

Before he could answer and before I could stop myself, I pulled on her shoulder and swung her back around to face me. "Didn't your mother teach you it's rude to turn your back on people?"

Savannah's lips curled into a sneer, and she pushed me back. Her eyes burnt into me, and she took a step forward until she was so close, I could feel her minty breath on my cheek.

"Go home, new kid," she hissed.

"Or what?"

"Or you'll regret it."

She was so quick that I had no time to register what happened. One second, Savannah was ruffling her feathers to get a rise out of me, and the next, her fingers were curled around the amethyst pendant on my neck. She snatched at the chain, ripping it off. The back of my neck burned from the friction, and I gasped, stumbling back from her.

"Give that back!" I yelled.

Savannah shot me a vicious smile. "Go and get it," she growled and tossed my pendant into the water.

"What in the actual hell, Savannah?" River roared and jumped to stand. He pushed past her and ran into the water for my pendant, and I followed him in, cursing under my breath.

Behind us, Savannah cackled and said something else obnoxious and rude, but her words never reached me. Tears burnt behind my lids, and they filled me with so much rage that I could see the hair on my arms stand on end. The water hit my calves, cool and heavy, as I waded through the water to where River was digging the surface. My boots were soaked, and I knew I would regret not taking them off before jumping in, but wet leather was the least of my worries right now. I knelt beside him, burrowing my hands into the wet sand below.

"Don't worry," he whispered, "we'll find it."

"It's okay."

It was one hundred percent not okay. Nothing about this was okay and I wanted to tell him that. I wanted to tell him I wanted nothing to do with him or his stupid friends and that Peyton and I were leaving. Then how come I didn't?

Instead, I waded further in the water until my cut-off shorts were drenched and helped him look for the pendant. Our hands patted the sand, picking up shells and tossing them out of the way before continuing the search. My fingers buried into the fine grain and raked through over and over until my skin burnt from the friction. I was pissed. No, I was more than pissed. I was absolutely, positively livid. We should have never come here, and I never should have agreed to Peyton's dumb plan to be friends with these morons. They would never accept me, even if it was all fake.

When River's back was turned to me, I dug both my palms into the sand and closed my eyes. As fast as I could manage, I unleashed the magic through my fingers and into the baby blue water around us. The energy hit my body like a tidal wave, and I toppled back from its impact. Despite myself, I held steady, searching for the hum of the amethyst hidden somewhere under the sand. My eyes snapped open as my magic connected to the crystal's wavelength and I pulled back, forcing it to rush toward me like a magnet. To my left, sand spread, and I saw the amethyst appear over its surface. My eyes brightened and I dove, snatching the pendant in my fist.

"Got it," I said, clenching my jaw, and raised the pendant for River to see.

"Good catch!" He took a few strained steps toward me, and the water spread out around him in slight waves. "Wanna go back?"

I looked from him to the beach where Peyton cowered on the towel. Savannah, Abigail, and Morgan circled around her like hungry sharks. Her eyes were so narrow that they were just slits across her face and I noticed her trying to get a word in while the hyenas threw insult after insult her way.

My head snapped to River, and I pushed him away from me, hard enough to knock him back. "No, thanks," I snapped. "Have fun with your friends. We're out of here."

Not bothering to look back at him, I rushed from the water and stomped Peyton's way. I was fuming. In fact, I was so angry that even the crystal that vibrated in my hand did nothing to calm my thoughts. With a grunt, I pushed Savannah to the side, grabbed Peyton's hand, and pulled her up. We ran up the trail, leaving the quarry and its pathetic occupants in our wake.

I was done with these assholes. Murders or not, nothing was worth this torture. If the witch wanted to kill them, I would not stand in her way. They could all burn in Hell for all I cared.

Chapter Fourteen

y feet have done all but tear holes in the fur rugs in my room while I paced its perimeter. I made Peyton stop at the Crystal Cauldron on the way back from the quarry so I could stock up on crystals and herbs, telling her I needed them to meditate to cool off. Relieved when my friend was more than eager to oblige and even ended up picking a few for herself.

Screw the High Coven and their rules, I needed magic to get through this.

I wrapped my fingers over the amber crystal in my hand and let magic do the rest. A small flame burst from my fingers, and I brought it down to the bowl of sulphur, sea salt, and bloodroot, setting it alight. The flames rose as the fire spread through the bowl leaving a trail of black in its midst. I dipped my finger into the soot and brought it to the paper I prepared on the floor.

Savannah Michaels.

I traced the name over the paper three times. My hands

shook with rage as I used my free hand to dab castor oil over the letter. The soot spread into twirling lines, flowing like rivers drawn on a map. When they stopped moving, I brought the paper to a lit candle at my side and watched it burn.

A sneer formed on my lips as the paper and Savannah's name disappeared into ash.

If I couldn't get rid of Savannah, I could at least banish her attention from me, and this spell should do the trick. I smiled, blowing out the leftover embers of the paper remnants before dipping it into the bowl of water next to my feet.

"That should do it."

I could feel the tension roll off as soon as the spell was complete and I spread myself out on my bed, reaching for my cell phone. Still no messages from Peyton but to my surprise, an unknown number flashed on the screen.

Come to the front. It's River.

My eyes doubled in size as I typed furiously on the keyboard. *How did you get my number? Stalker much?*

Peyton gave it to me. Come on, it's freezing out here.

I jumped up and looked at the silver clock hanging above my door. It read nine thirty-five, well past dinnertime. No wonder he was freezing his ass off, who shows up at someone's house this late and just chills outside like a serial killer? *What in the Goddess is he doing here?* I had to get this guy to leave me alone if I had any chance of staying sane. I ran to the vanity mirror in my room and wiped the streaks of mascara from under my eyes. Good thing I haven't bothered to shower or change, or I'd be greeting him in my PJs. I twisted my long hair into a low bun, zipped up my jacket, and sprinted for the door.

By the time I reached the front stoop, River was already perched on one chair. His leg kicked up on the glass coffee table that lived on the front porch, and I found it hard to look away from him. His usual tee was hidden under a knit pullover and despite the layers, he looked as fit as ever. *That sweater is wearing him just fine...*

"Hey." I nodded, closing the door behind me and walking over to him. "What are you doing here? It's kinda late."

He jumped at the sound of my voice, ripping his leg off the table and straightening in his seat. "I wanted to see if you're okay. You left in kind of a hurry."

"Gee, I wonder why..." I scoffed and sat at the chair opposite him.

"I'm sorry about Savannah. She can be—"

"A bitch?" I blurted out.

River laughed and the deepness of his voice riled up the magic in me. I shifted in my seat, my cheeks blushing. It was a cooler night than usual, but I was certain that wasn't the reason I was shivering in my chair. This guy got to me no matter how much I tried to deny it.

"Yeah, that's the word." He chuckled and leaned back. "I don't know what got into her, to be honest."

"Right, because I'm sure she's usually a ray of sunshine."

"Guess not. So, you okay?"

I peered up at him through my lashes and forced a smile. "I will be." *Especially after the spell I did kicked in.*

"She wasn't always like this, you know," he said even though I didn't ask, or care. "We've been friends since we were kids and believe or not, Savannah actually used to be nice. Like, really nice. She was the first friend I made in kindergarten and for the longest time, we had each other's backs. Still do, I guess, but it's different now."

"What happened?"

River sighed. "High school."

Having zero experience with high school teenagers until I landed at Shadowhurst Academy, I had no reference point for his comment. From what I gathered, high school wasn't the best place, mostly. I always wondered why parents bothered shoving their kids into the intrepid establishments if they knew most of them hated it. I guessed not everyone had the luxury of being raised by a coven like me.

"And you're just friends?" I asked against my better judgment. "I mean, because Peyton mentioned her having a crush on you and whatever. And you know, if you two are a thing, I would kind of understand why she hates my guts. I'm sure you being here this late is not something she wants her boyfriend doing."

River's smile widened into something sinister and wild, knocking me off my ass in the chair. "Are you asking if I'm single?"

"Kinda."

River's eyes sparkled and he leaned in until our noses hovered half an inch apart. His breath was warm despite the chill of the evening, and I could smell the peppermint of the gum he was chewing in the air. His dimpled cheek brushed against mine and I lost it. My body twitched and I swallowed hard, unable to move.

"You really need to ask that?" he whispered. "I thought it was pretty obvious by now."

"Kinda do."

River's hand found mine and his strong fingers tightened around my palm. My legs shook as he ran his thumb across my skin, stroking it so gently that I tried not to pass out in his lap. "She's not my type," he breathed out.

"...Who is?"

What the hell has gotten into me? I was never this bold around boys, but something about this guy made me want to spill all my secrets. Thoughts raced through my mind, and I choked on a shudder. I waited for him to respond but River was as quiet as the surrounding night. His hand pulled on mine, forcing me even closer to him. I licked my lower lip and inhaled his scent with the hungry need of a starved animal. That same darkness I felt from him before invaded my senses and a gasp lumped in the base of my throat. My vision blurred and I blinked my eyes to refocus my gaze on his smooth skin. His other hand found the back of my neck and he pulled me, crashing his lips to mine.

The porch exploded in a rainbow of colors. At least it did in my head. River's lips pressed to mine, and I felt his need for me fill the air. My lips parted and his tongue found the tip of mine, demolishing my heart into pieces.

After what seemed like a lifetime, River pulled back, a goofy grin on his face.

"That answer your question?"

I nodded like a complete idiot and blushed, pressing my face into my hands. A giggle escaped me and when I looked at him again, he was smiling from ear to ear. "Took you long enough," I purred and entwined my fingers in his.

Seriously, who are you?

River chuckled and pressed his forehead to mine before pulling away again; I missed his warmth immediately.

"You know, for a new kid, you're awfully brazen, soldier."

"You've got no idea." I smirked.

We sat in silence for a good ten minutes before River spoke again. His hand never let go of mine and I grew fond of how it felt. I had my fair share of encounters with boys, but none of them riled my magic as much as this one. It was almost like my energy fed on his. My thumb twirled the moonstone ring around obsessively to control my hands from ripping the damn sweater off him right there on the porch.

"So why are you really here?" he asked.

I hiccuped.

"I, uh," I coughed out, "wasn't the most obedient kid back home. Got into some trouble."

"Do I even want to know?"

You really don't.

"It's a long story. I'll tell you some other time, but let's just say the Chandlers have their hands full with me."

"HA! That's what my mom says about me."

I laughed. "I find that hard to believe."

"No, seriously. After my dad left, I was, let's just say, a bit of a basket case."

I ran my finger over his arm and collected the energy of the amethyst at my neck, pushing some of my magic into him. It wasn't enough to cause alarm but sufficient to soothe him, make him relax a little so he felt comfortable telling me about his life. I wanted to know everything about this beautiful boy that sat across from me. I wanted all his secrets and I wanted them all to myself.

"I'm sorry," I said, still rubbing his arm. "How old were you when he left?"

"Around ten, I think. I can't remember anymore. We don't have the best relationship."

"And your mom?"

River's lips curved at the edges. "She's exceptional. Don't know what I'd do without her. Well, her and my friends."

"Even Savannah?" I asked, finding that to be impossible.

"Yeah, even her. My friends and I, we're kind of..." He paused. "Close."

"All friends are close."

"Not like us."

Something tugged at my brain, latching its claws into my mind and pulling me back. Magic rolled off me in waves and I yanked my hand away from him before it manifested into something I couldn't control. With a quick swoop, I pulled the pendant from inside my jacket and put some distance between my skin and its energy. "What do you mean?"

River shifted in his seat, his eyes tracing my face like he was trying to choose between speaking and not.

"You can tell me," I whispered, desperate to hear about every part of his life. *Just say it,* I whispered into his mind.

"It's going to sound crazy."

"Trust me, I've heard it all," I laughed.

With ease, River scooped up my hand and placed it on his chest. His heartbeat plummeted against my palm, and I let my hand rise and fall with his heavy breaths. "You know those books in that room you found?"

My eyes narrowed in his direction. "Yeah?"

"They're mine. Well, they're ours. Me and the others."

"What do you mean yours? Like, you found them or something?"

"Something like that. They've been passed down to us by our parents, and their parents before that. To study so we're ready."

I pulled my hand away and stared in horror as he continued to speak.

"Turns out this town is into all that witch stuff for a reason. My family, Savannah's family, and the rest of them, we're kind of like protectors of this place. From witches."

My lids fluttered and tears formed behind them. They burnt my eyes with the intensity of stars exploding and I could hear the screaming of my heart pound at my eardrums. What was he saying right now? What was happening?

River leaned back in the chair, his brow furrowed. "I'm sorry, I don't know why I told you that. It just came out!"

An icy wind blew past us, and I crossed my arms over my chest to keep from screaming. I knew why he told me—because I made him tell me. Me and my stupid magic. Why did I do that? I wished I could take it back, so I never found this out. I cursed myself, shaking my head back and forth.

"I told you it would sound crazy," River said after I've been quiet for basically forever. "You still here?"

I didn't know what to say. Did he even understand what he was telling me right now? Those books, that room, it was for witch hunters. Not just any witch hunters. It was for him and his friends. The trust funders weren't just spoiled brats with too much money and time on their hands. They were hunters. And he was one of them. No wonder he was so nonchalant when we were reading the books. Anyone else would have been shocked or at least showing a modicum of emotion, but River was as cool as ice. That should have been my first clue but no, I was too busy oggling his freaking biceps to notice. *Idiot!*

The world spun around me. The air thickened and I couldn't keep my eyes open. I clenched my hands into fists and forced myself to stand up. My vision swam and my lungs felt like they were about to explode. River's face darkened and I could see the hurt of my reaction register across his features. How could this be happening? How can the one boy I let myself like in forever be a hunter? This couldn't be real. I blinked rapidly as though I could blink the truth away. *Maybe if I shut my eyes real tight?* I closed my lids and prayed to the Goddess, but when I opened them, River was still there and looking as confused as ever. I had to get out of here. I needed to get him out of here. Now.

"I should get inside," I said and backed away from him. "It's late. You should go."

"Billie..."

"Please, go," I whimpered.

"Can I just explain? It's not as crazy as it sounds. You and Peyton will get a kick out of it!"

I'm about to give you a kick you'll never forget, you witch killing son of a bitch!

"Go home, River," I growled and turned away.

Tears streamed down my face and my shoulders shook as his steps retracted. I waited until the porch was silent before turning around to see his car peel out of the driveway. It only took a few moments for me to fall apart.

My knees hit the cold wood of the porch and I crashed to the floor. Sobs threatened to choke me, and my magic fought to grab hold of the earth's elements in the yard. My heart ached—it literally hurt—like someone had punched me in the chest with a mallet. How could this innocent boy be everything I had to hate? How could he hate me and my kind?

Hands fisted, I forced myself to rise, and my knees buckled under the weight of my sorrow. Why did I make him tell me?

A low guttural sound escaped from behind the fountain in the driveway and I spun around, mascara dripping down my face like clown makeup. My body still shook from the pain of what I found out about River, but as my eyes focused on the thick, orange fur in the distance, I knew my night was about to get even worse.

Chapter Fifteen

At the base of the fountain, paws wet, stood the tiger shifter that attacked me on campus a few days ago. Its front paws gripped the edge of the marble, monstrous claws digging into the tile. Its mouth parted to reveal glistening fangs that oozed with frothy spit. I didn't even have time to think before the tiger pushed off the fountain and flew toward me.

The streaks of my mascara felt cool against my cheek as I pulled the dagger from my boot, pushed off the porch, and ran to meet it. My legs bounced off the stone on the driveway, silent and quick just like Rhiamon taught me. The tiger was not as dainty and each time his thick paws landed on the ground, a booming sound echoed over the lot. My heart beat triumphantly and I turned on my heels to make a beeline for the fountain. The tiger skidded to a stop before turning his clumsy, muscled body my way.

It growled and I plunged my hands into the fountain, reaching for the water element with my magic. This would get loud and unless I wanted the Chandlers to roll out of bed to find me battling a shapeshifter in their front yard, I had to mask the sounds. My eyes fluttered and rolled into the back of my head as I called on the power within me. The glittering lights were everywhere and for once, I welcomed their presence. They meant that I was close to release. Heat rose inside me, tossing my emotions like a rag doll. My eyes cracked open, and my head tilted back. In seconds, I slammed my hands to the sky above, raising the water from the fountain behind me. The watery wall rushed upward, higher, and higher until it collided with the distant night clouds. My lips tightened when the first raindrop hit my face and the tiger shook its head, the orange fur darkening from the rain.

Above us, thunder roared and lighting clashed as the storm I summoned erupted into an orchestra of sounds.

That'll work, I smirked and lunged for the shifter.

My body slammed into it, pushing it back to land on its back. I twisted my legs from under me to straddle the tiger's thick chest and brought the dagger's tip deep into its heart. The creature roared as I twisted the blade, burrowing it further. I could feel its ragged breathing as it fought to free itself of my hold, but my dagger held it still in place. Its eyes flashed open, and I registered the rage in them, swirling amid bright hazel irises.

I reached for the amber crystal tucked into my shorts and slammed it down on the shifter's wide forehead. It growled and hissed, spit foaming at the mouth, as it kicked its legs beneath me. Nothing could help the shifter now. I had it beat.

On instinct, I twisted the dagger again and pushed it further into the tiger's chest until I heard something snap. The storm raged around us, and I had to slip and slide off the beast while its body thrashed on the driveway. My eyes widened as the shifter's limbs snapped into unnatural bends and I could hear the bones in its body break with each turn. Slack-jawed, I stared while the tiger shifted into its original form.

In mere moments, the tiger was gone and I was towering over a middle-aged man. His thick, red hair curled down to his shoulders and his deadened hazel eyes stared up at the sky that continued to blast us with rain. My knees shook as I stepped over him, snatching the amber crystal off his brow with one hand while pulling my dagger from his chest with another. As soon as the dagger was free of his body, I jumped back, widening the distance between myself and the shifter. The air that was heavy and warm before thinned out and a chilly breeze blew over the shifter's body. I watched in amazement while it dissipated into ash that fluttered off in the wind.

The vanquishing was complete.

My hands still trembled, but I managed to pull my cellphone from my jacket pocket and typed a message to Peyton.

Crystal Cauldron. Tomorrow at noon. We have work to do.

Sun beat down on us through the windshield of Peyton's car as we rounded the corner onto Main Street. My fingers brushed over my chapped lips while I retraced the events of last night in my head. River was a hunter and less than twenty-four hours ago, I was on a beach full of his hunter friends. How many of the kids at the quarry were actual hunters? I had no way to know without asking him and zero intention of ever talking to him again. He lied to me. Worse, he didn't even know how badly his lie affected what I had to do next. I needed to tell the High Coven what I found out and when I did, there would be hell to pay for him and his friends. How did this happen and why, even after all this, could I not forget that kiss?

River kissed me. He freaking kissed me.

And I liked it.

I felt like a traitor to my kind just for thinking it. The High Coven sent me here to stay out of trouble and here I was, kissing a witch hunter and liking it. I was no better than Beatrix at this point and it made me sick to my stomach. River was completely off limits and as soon as I got to the bottom of the murders, I was going to deal with him myself. No more crushes and no more staying off track. I had to get my life back in order. My head pounded to the sound of an off-beat drum, and I leaned my messy bun on the passenger window while Peyton tried to parallel park her beast of a car for the third time.

"Got it!" she exclaimed and shot a smile my way. "What are we doing here, exactly?"

I glanced out the window at the worn-out sign that hung above the shop. "Well, we're dealing with some serious paranormal myths here," I fibbed. "I mean, witch hunters? That's some creepy stuff even by Shadowhurst standards, no?"

"I guess..." Peyton nodded. "But why here?"

"Are you joking? What better place to dig up witchy dirt on the town than an occult shop?" I asked. "Plus, did you see that shelf of books behind the counter? Looked pretty witchy to me."

"Girl, you're turning into quite the detective. I love it!"

Peyton hopped out and slammed the door shut behind

her and we made our way into the shop. We marched in unison, our fingers wrapped around the ice coffees Peyton picked up on the way to get me and I fought the urge to smile. For the first time, I had a partner in crime. Not the high priestesses and not the witches in the coven that left me to my own devices. A *genuine* friend. Sure, Peyton did not understand what we were dealing with here but her eagerness to get to the truth was astounding and I couldn't be more proud to have her by my side through all of this.

The bell welcomed us in, and I bolted straight for the counter where Ms. Broussard was fumbling with a jewelry display. When I approached, her eyes snapped to mine and she parted her lips into a welcoming smile. Today, the shop owner let her hair loose and it hung in waves over her shoulders and down to her waist. It was so long that she looked like sea foam swallowed her whole, an ancient siren of sorts.

"Ah!" She clapped her hands together when we approached. "Welcome, girls!"

"Hi, Ms. Broussard." I smiled and leaned over the counter. "We were wondering if you might have some books on the town's history here? Maybe something on the founding families?"

Ms. Broussard arched an eyebrow. "If you're looking for history, the town's archives are a wonderful start," she said.

"We were hoping for something a little darker."

My friend winked at the shop owner, and I rolled my eyes. *Take it down a notch, P. We're not making a drug deal.*

To my surprise, Ms. Broussard winked back and stepped to the side to reveal the long shelf of books I spotted before. Their spines were empty, and I wondered how someone was supposed to tell the difference between the volumes, but the shop owner had no trouble picking them out. She rolled her fingers over the books, pulling out three and placing them gently on the counter. "These could help," she whispered. "Let me know if you need any others."

She slid the books toward us and disappeared through the doorway behind the counter. When she was out of sight, we exchanged shrugs and dug in.

Though I couldn't feel the same connection to these books as I did to the witch hunter tomes in the library, I could tell they were important. The pages were yellowed with age and as I flipped through one book, I spotted several diagrams and symbols that mirrored the ones I had in my grimoire. These definitely weren't a tourist attraction. Ms. Broussard's witchy book collection was the real thing.

My finger ran across the index of the second book I picked up and I tapped on a selection.

"Right here!" I yelped, leaning the book closer for Peyton to see.

"'Carriage Hill; a brief history'," my friend read, her eyes widening in excitement. "Yes!"

I flipped to the right section and read. My lips formed the words in silent and I had almost forgotten that Peyton was standing next to me.

"Hey!" She punched my shoulder. "Share with the rest of the class, please."

I sighed and skipped a few paragraphs before taking a deep breath.

"'After the discovery of witchcraft in Shadowhurst, they shunned all those deemed to be in tune with magic from the main society and directed them to move to a nearby village and away from prying eyes'," I read.

"Carriage Hill!"

"Looks like it," I continued. "'Though peace between the

members of Shadowhurst and those suspected of witchcraft was in place, it was short-lived. It was not long before the founding families gathered forces, determined to rid themselves of the infestation of the dark arts once and for all'."

Dark arts, my ass. These morons didn't even know what they were dealing with. Typical humans.

"'One by one'," I kept reading, "'witches were snatched from their homes and dragged back to Shadowhurst to burn at the stake in the center of town'."

"The bell tower," Peyton whispered and I nodded.

"'Of the ten founding families, five banded together to form a united front from any further magical threat to their lands. They trained in secret, growing in numbers as each new member of the families was introduced into the clan'." My hands shook and I had to take a few deep breaths to calm down. This was it. "This has to be how the witch hunters started," I said.

"So those books in the library were theirs?" Peyton asked. "Wait, you don't think River and Savannah knew about them before we told him?"

"Probably not," I lied.

Why am I lying to her? I had no clue, but somehow, I knew I was not ready to let her in on River's nasty little secret just yet.

"Wait!" Peyton furrowed her brow and tapped her finger on a passage. "Look at this."

I scanned the page she was pointing to, and my eyes landed on four words that stood out. "'Founding families, complete genealogy'," I read aloud. I flipped the pages to the index shown, landing on a large family tree that spanned several generations. I spotted the line for the Hunting family, River's ancestors, and next to them the Michaels'. So, he wasn't lying, and he and Savannah were part of the sordid history of this town. I read off the names, trying to remember the last names of River's friends, but I drew a blank.

"We were right," Peyton said pointing to two last names at the lead of the family tree, "Lacey and Grady were both part of the founding members. That's some freaky coincidence."

"Yeah." I nodded, even though I knew it was no coincidence at all. My suspicions were correct after all. The witch was targeting the families from this tree. "What does *this* mean, though?"

I nudged Peyton's attention to a line drawn across the page—separating the founding families in half. River and Savannah's names fell on the left while Lacey and Grady's on the right. My eyes traveled up the list, landing on the top of the tier. Both Grady and Lacey's great, great grandmother's names were listed but there was a blank spot next to the space where their partner's names would be. There was an asterisk next to the empty slots and another index sign. I rummaged through the pages to find the correct number association and my heart sank.

"What?" Peyton asked, registering my pale face. "What's it say?"

I swallowed the lump in my throat and shook my head before reading aloud.

"'Though not much has been uncovered as to the whereabouts of the first arrivals on the land that was later crowned Shadowhurst, it is believed that they were of non-human descent'."

Peyton's eyes widened and she yanked the book from my hands. "What in the actual hell does that mean?!?" she yelled.

"I think..." I swallowed again. "That whoever found this town wasn't Euro like we thought."

"So they were, what? Witches?"

I shook my head. "I don't think so," and pointed my finger on one word that clashed amongst the rest of the paragraphs that followed.

"Fae?" Peyton asked. "What does that mean 'fae'? As in fairies or some shit?"

As I opened my mouth to speak, the door behind the counter swung open and Ms. Broussard walked out holding a tray of tea and macaroons. "You girls hungry? I thought you might want a snack?"

She slid the tray across the counter and closed the book in front of us, pushing it out of the way to nudge the teas closer. Her gray eyes twinkled, and she winked before urging us to pick up a cookie each. My arm shook as I reached over, forcing myself to take a bite of the pink macaroon I picked up.

This was completely insane. There has not been mention of the fae in any of the texts in the High Coven's collection. In fact, the only other time I've heard the name was when I was still a kid and Beatrix told me fairytales of the magical beings that created my kind. I remember being in awe of the stories and forcing her to tell them to me repeatedly every night before bed. But the fae have been extinct for eons and, from what I knew, there was only a handful of them to begin with. As far as the stories went, the fae were once free to roam the earth and delight in its magic. They drew from the energy of the elements, using their power—that no one conveniently knew anything about—to replenish the magic in the earth. According to myth, it was the fae that created the first witches by teaching plain old humans their magic. It all sounded like a crock of crap to me, even as a kid. Witches were powerful and strong, not some byproduct of fae intervention.

Yet no matter how much I tried to fight it, there was no denying what Peyton and I just saw. The fae once lived in Shadowhurst. They not only lived here, they created the place. What was worse is that, according to the family tree in that book, they stayed long enough to have kids with some of the founding members.

The macaroon I stopped chewing formed a sticky mess in my mouth and I forced myself to gulp it down.

Things just got so much more complicated.

Chapter Sixteen

Ms. Broussard let us borrow the book for the week, which was a relief because my original plan was to break in after hours and snatch it up. Relief pummeled over me when she handed it over without question. There was no need to add any more indiscretion to the already massive list of wrongdoings my past carried. Plus, I couldn't imagine the disappointment the Chandlers would have felt if I went through with it and got caught. Somehow, I doubted they signed up for housing an unreformed felon under their roof.

"Where are we going?" I asked as the car's wheels screeched while Peyton took another aggressive right turn. "This isn't the way back to the Chandlers."

My friend pumped the gas and sent us flying again. "Quarry," she said matter-of-factly. "River wants to meet."

Blood rushed to my neck and my lungs collapsed. I couldn't breathe and I couldn't think. Staying away from the witch hunters was tough enough as it was in a small town like this, I would not be purposefully putting myself in their path, no matter how much I wanted to see those full lips of his again. I curled my fingers around the spine of the book in my hand. "Uh uh!" I yelled out. "No way! I'm not going back to the quarry."

"Cool your panties." Peyton laughed. "Savannah won't be there. He says he's coming alone."

That's not the problem, I wanted to yell but stayed quiet.

Peyton slammed the brakes before veering left and my heart leaped into my throat, though this time, I had the feeling it wasn't her reckless driving that made my skin itch. I couldn't get River out of my head. How was I supposed to be around him now that I knew what I knew? More than that, how could I explain to him why we could never be together despite the super hot kiss we shared? Without making him drag me to the bell tower to burn me to oblivion, that is. My head spun and I wanted to toss the macaroon I ate at the Crystal Cauldron all over the car.

"Hey." A thought brushed over me. "Has Ms. Broussard ever seemed strange to you before? Stranger than usual, I mean?"

Peyton's eyes narrowed my way and she shook her head no. "Nope. No way! Wait," she asked, "you're not thinking she's the killer, are you?"

"Maybe," I whispered. "She does have a *lot* of information on the founding families. And she fits the profile."

"What profile?"

Shit! I can't tell Peyton I think Ms. Broussard is a witch or I'll never hear the end of it from Sebyl. "Oh, just, you know..." I thought of a cover. "She stands out like a sore thumb around this place."

"Ha!" Peyton exclaimed. "So do we, and I don't think you killed anyone."

She had a point.

"So, you've never heard her mention Grady or Lacey? Or the founding families before?"

"Nope." Peyton shook her head. "And I've known her since I was a kid. She's an oddball, sure, but not dangerous. At least, I don't think so. Besides, last year when I went out with her niece visiting for the summer, I got to spend some time in her house and there was nothing strange that I saw."

Yes, but was there something witchy? I wanted to ask but didn't. *Wait, did Peyton just tell me she dated Ms. Broussard's niece?* I felt like an idiot. Peyton was into girls, and I didn't even notice. Not that it even mattered, but that seemed like information that a friend should have. It was looking like I was an even more crap friend than a crap witch these days.

I cleared my throat and wiggled my eyebrows. "You're into chicks?"

"Obvi." Peyton smirked. "Everyone knows."

"I didn't."

"Well, you do now. Why?"

I smiled. "No reason. I feel stupid for not catching on, though, in my defense, you did make a lot of inappropriate comments about River."

"Girl!" Peyton chuckled. "I'm gay, not blind. That boy is a fine piece of man. You should totally go for it!"

Already did and no, thank you...

"I'm off guys for a while," I breathed out. "I had a nasty experience with the last one."

Peyton pulled the car in reverse, and I realized we were about to park in the quarry's parking lot. "What happened?"

Turned out he's a witch hunter and would likely want me dead. "Long story," I choked out and climbed out of the car.

River's silver Tesla was already in the lot, and I followed

Peyton down the trail to the quarry. When we reached the beach, I spotted him in the water. His white slacks were rolled up at the ankles and he waded through the crystal clear blue like an old-time sailor. River's shirt was scrunched into a ball and tossed haphazardly on the sandy shoreline behind him. Of course, he had to be topless.

I rolled my eyes and waved to get his attention.

When he saw us, River bolted to shore, his eyes focused on only me as he ran. Every muscle in my body tensed until I felt like a statue of myself. Stone and cold and empty. My heart sank at the sight of him, and I couldn't help but mourn what could have been if things were different. There was only one other time in my life where I wished I wasn't born a witch, and this felt even worse than when Beatrix got caught. River's big green eyes searched mine and I forced myself to look away. He was the enemy.

"Hi," he said in that deep, sexy voice of his, "thanks for coming. I thought after last night—"

I held my hand up to stop him from talking.

"What happened last night?" Peyton's ears perked up.

"Nothing," I answered. "We hung out then River left. Nothing happened."

Beside me, River's shoulders rose and fell as he took a breath and his brow furrowed. There was a flash of pain across his eyes, and I had to bite the inside of my cheek and look away before I said anything else to hurt his feeling. Why did I even care about his feelings? *You think he'll care about yours when he ties you to the stake? Stupid.*

My hands fisted and I leered in River's direction. "Why are we here?" I asked with as much venom as I could muster.

His feet kicked sand and I could feel his eyes on me in my peripheral.

"So?" I hissed his way without looking over.

When he finally looked away, I shivered, letting the pieces of my heart attempt to sew themselves back together. This was the boy I let kiss me, the boy whose lips I couldn't stop thinking about even when I knew what he was. River looked up at Peyton, daring to sneak one more glance my way before answering.

"I want in on whatever project you're working on," he said.

"Nope!" I yelled out, shaking my head. "No way! Not having it!"

"Whoa, B, it's cool. Calm down." Peyton nudged my side. "Why are you so interested?"

River closed the distance between us and himself and the smell of his cologne dropped me on my butt. "Because I don't think it's a project at all," he arched an eyebrow, "and I think I can help."

"And what makes you think it's not a project?"

"You're trying to figure out who killed those students," River said, his tone aggravated. "I want in."

"I said no. No means no, trust funder."

"Trust funder?"

In a flash, Peyton stepped between us, her arms out to the sides. "All right! Cool it, both of you! I don't know what *this* is..." She waved her hand between us dramatically. "But I want to find out who's killing students before someone else dies. The cops seem to be dragging their heels and this town has always had each other's backs. So, you two need to figure your crap out so we can sort this out."

I cursed through a clenched jaw and River grumbled something under his breath.

"So?"

Beside me, my friend looked as annoyed as ever, but maybe she was onto something. I may not trust River, but I had a piece of information that could help the High Coven. Sebyl did say that they wanted me to infiltrate the hunter group and report back. What better way to do it than to use River to get to the rest? Could I do that? I wasn't sure, but that wasn't the point. I had to. And perhaps, if we let him in on our search, he'd open up and lead me to the rest.

"Fine." I rolled my eyes. "Whatever."

"River?"

"Yeah, okay," he mumbled.

Peyton patted me on the shoulder and flashed her teeth our way. "Perfect! One big, happy family!"

"So..." River arched an eyebrow our way.

"...What?"

"What have you got so far?"

A knot formed in my stomach, and I pulled my lips into a tight smile. This would definitely be harder than I thought.

"B thinks whoever is behind this might be targeting the founding families," Peyton said.

"Hmm..." River turned to face me, and the golden tan of his skin made my mouth dry up. *So much harder.* "You could be onto something there."

"Thanks," I growled, "but I didn't need the reassurance."

"Awesome, well, I think I found something you'll want to see," he said, brushing my attitude aside. "I took some of those books from the library home and I might have found a clue."

Of course, you took them home. Because they're yours, witch hunter! I wanted to scream. "What clue?" I asked instead.

"There was a reference to the original founders of the

town, so I ended up reading all night and found that whoever was here first might have left something behind."

"Fae," I thought aloud.

"Sorry, what?" River asked.

"The fae, or whatever," Peyton answered before I could stop her. "Billie found mentions of them in some book in the Crystal Cauldron. Probably just an urban legend, but both Grady and Lacey had ties to them, so it might be worth looking into."

"Were there any other student names that had the same family lines?"

"None that we could spot," Peyton said, "but there were five blank spots at the top next to some female names. I didn't recognize any of the last names though."

I sighed, my face caught in a permanent frown. "We need to see those books you have."

"Sure thing!" River grinned. "Let's go."

"Excuse me?"

He reached out for my hand but stopped himself before making contact. "They're at my house, remember?"

Lovely.

"You guys go ahead. I told my dad I'd be home for dinner."

There were no words to describe how deeply I wanted to slap my friend at that moment. Was she bat shit crazy? She couldn't leave me alone with a witch hunter! *Breathe, Billie, she doesn't know he's a hunter and she has no clue you're a witch. Let it go and get the job done.*

"Ugh, fine," I murmured. "Let's go."

Peyton flashed us two thumbs up, turned around, and bolted up the trail. Her gladiator sandals kicked sand up as she ran, and she was out of sight in seconds, leaving only me and River on the beach. My palms clammed and I fought the urge to run after my friend. *I can't do this. I can't do this. I CAN'T DO THIS.*

"Ready?" River asked, nodding to his car in the parking lot.

I peeled my gaze off him and glared at the trees, anything to avoid looking into his brilliant emerald eyes. "Let's just get this over with."

Chapter Seventeen

ulling up into River's driveway was like entering the Secret Garden. The foliage lining the winding road that led to his home was so thick and wild, I could barely see through it. Flowers of every color sprouted from the ground and the trees, large and old, intertwined their branches into a formidable fortress of green and yellow. My jaw unhinged and I stared in abandon at the three-story house that unfolded before us when we drove through the main gates. It was like something out of a picture book.

Unlike the Chandler residence, which was modern despite a few detailed finishes, River's house looked like a dollhouse. It had the same Victorian architecture as the other homes in Shadowhurst, but different somehow, more gothic. Intricate woodwork stretched around every window and door, and the porch that sat at the front was sprawled with climbing vines that reached all the way to the attic's windows. Much like many of the homes in Shadowhurst, River's house was a vivid bright blue with a shingled roof in a more pristine condition than some new builds I saw back home. Around its wide base, an array of flowers spread from the grass and reached their colorful petals to the sun.

"Wow," I whispered, mouth still gaping. "Your house is intense."

Beside me in the driver's seat, River chuckled and unbuckled his seat belt. "It's... different. Ready for the tour?"

I was ready to get the hell out of there, but I guess it couldn't hurt to look around while I was here. I mean, I had to get information on him somehow, so I had *something* to bring back to the High Coven.

My eyes lit up and I jumped out, eager to see what this fairytale wonderland offered.

I followed River up the bend in the driveway and to the front door with a hop in my step like a kid that just got the video game she wanted for Christmas. All around me, the elements of the garden blasted through, seeping into my body, and riling my magic. Their sharp scents intertwined into a mixture unlike anything I've experienced before. It was like being in a department store's perfume section but magnified tenfold. I breathed in, my senses locking on the lilacs to my right. My magic snapped to attention, reaching for the flowers' element with such fury, I thought I might implode. The air shifted and solidified over my palms and tears pooled in my eyes as I blinked away the bright lights that flooded my vision. The energy in the garden was so strong that I couldn't decide what element to pull from first. The flowers, the earth, the cool breeze that whipped my hair back and forth? My body froze as I swallowed them whole and let their power flow through me. I wasn't sure how much more teasing I could take and when River unlocked the front door, I almost ran him over in my urge to get inside. My skin tickled from the power I sucked in, and I was so rejuvenated that I completely forgot whose house I was in.

One look around and I was back to my moody self.

The front hall was a complete opposite to what I had grown used to at the Chandlers'. It was tight and cozy, with picture frames lining the walls in random patterns. Each one featured River at different ages of his life. My eyes locked on a photo of him as a baby in a toddler bath with foam standing upright on his head and I stifled a laugh.

"Ugh!" He grimaced. "I told her to take that down a million times."

"Why?" I asked. "It's cute."

His face lit up and I fought the blush that crawled up my neck to my cheeks. *It's not cute, you moron. Witch hunters are not cute.*

"Thanks." River smiled, that damn dimple blocking my senses. "Come on, my room is this way."

I froze. *His room? We're going to his room?*

"Smooth..." I tried to joke but my nerves read through every word.

"It's where the books are." He arched an eyebrow and sneered. "Unless you're thinking something else?"

"Just show me the books."

I pushed past him and marched up the stairs to the second floor even though I had no idea where I was going. When I reached the landing, I scanned the hallway but all I could see were locked doors. *What did you expect? A sign with his name on it? Maybe a little dinosaur picture to match? He's not five.* I groaned and turned back to him, shrugging my shoulders to let him know I had no time for games right now.

"One more floor," he grumbled and led me to a spiral staircase at the end of the hall.

Step by shaky step, I followed him up, my eyes staying on the tips of my boots so I didn't have to look up at his behind and pass out. It was a harder task than I imagined and by the time we reached his room—which I quickly realized was the attic—I had ground my teeth until my jaw hurt.

The room was smaller than I expected, and I wondered why he chose this space over all the other rooms I knew were available in the house. It was just him and his mom living here, why not take a proper bedroom? When I looked around, I saw why. The attic was more what I would imagine a teen boy wanted for a hideaway. It was tucked away and out of sight. Forgotten. There wasn't much in the way of decor and unlike the rest of the place, River's room left little to the imagination. All it housed was a bed, a small mahogany desk that perched under one of the three circular windows, and a red beanbag chair covered in wrinkled shirts. *Who even has beanbag chairs anymore? This guy is hopeless.*

My ears perked up as the woodsy scent that was so River engulfed me. The entire attic smelled like him, and I was having trouble keeping my thoughts together.

River threw himself on the queen-sized bed that still had tossed sheets from the night before and reached around to the nightstand. His shirt rolled up and I jerked my eyes to one of the round windows. *Don't think about his abs, don't think about his abs,* I recited and forced myself to inspect the garden below.

"That's quite the backyard you have."

Behind me, River slammed something on the floor next to his bed. "Yeah, my mom is into all that nature stuff, I guess. She spends every minute in that garden."

"I can see why," I murmured and turned to face him. "That the book?"

River nodded and scooted to the floor before patting the spot next to him. Hesitantly, I wavered over and sat down, making sure there was at least a foot of air between us. Even from the distance, I could smell his cologne and my toes curled just thinking about it. Oblivious to my torture, River flipped the pages of the book until he found what he was looking for. "This part here, see?"

I followed his finger to a passage that talked about creatures that stalked the humans in the dark. My eyes narrowed as I read over the paragraph a few times. *Shadowers!* This book referenced shadowers. My heart raced and there was so much spit gathering in my mouth that I had to swallow several times just to keep from drooling. So, the witch hunters didn't just want *my* kind dead. It relieved a part of me. At least now I knew they weren't prejudiced against my people. These assholes wanted everything dead that wasn't like them.

It was an odd stance to take, I knew that. Witches hated shadowers just as much and I never had a problem with that. But I didn't want to have anything in common with River and the rest of the hunters. Not after everything they've done to my people.

"You think this is about the fae? Like in that book you read?" River asked.

My face snapped up and I shot a confused expression his way. He had no clue that shadowers existed, which meant there was a lot more he didn't know. "Could be," I lied and pulled the book into my lap. "I don't see what clue you were talking about though."

"Well, when I read this, it got me thinking. What if, back

in the day when the..." He paused and shifted his weight. "When the first hunters killed all those witches," he continued and I swallowed the nausea that crept up. "What if they didn't get them all?"

They obviously didn't, you prick, or else I wouldn't be here.

"Huh?" He nudged my side.

Shit! Did I say that out loud?

"What do you think?" River urged.

I breathed out in relief that my mouth hadn't betrayed me like the rest of my body tended to do when he was around. "I mean, maybe. So what?"

"I was thinking that if that's the case and there were witches that were left undetected, they must have had kids. What if this killer is a hunter or something, trying to finish the job or whatever? It would explain the empty spots you saw in Grady and Lacey's family trees. Maybe those spots were there for the witches?"

I turned his words around in my mouth before shaking my head. "No, those were fae. I just know it."

"You think the fae exist?" he asked, baffled.

"Why not? You think witches exist," I fired back. "Enough to learn to hunt them."

River's lips pressed together, and he leaned his head back on the mattress. His wide chest rose and fell as he thought over what I said. "Yeah, well, the jury's still out on that."

"Meaning?"

"This whole hunter business, it's kinda stupid. My mom pushed me into it since I was a kid and I hated it. I mean, it seems impossible to believe something like that, but she was so insistent. Honestly, I think that's why my dad left. They always fought about it. Sometimes, I could hear them yelling in the kitchen even from all the way up here. Dad hated that she pushed me into it, but she was adamant about it. She used to say 'it's good for a young boy to have hobbies'. I wanted to tell her that most guys my age played sports, but after my dad left, I was all she had left. So, whether I liked it or not, I had to keep doing it. Anything to keep her happy. Plus, it was kinda fun to learn all that stuff. And the physical training was a good workout."

"Physical training?"

"Yeah. I guess hunting witches is hardcore exercise. Whatever that even means."

"So, you're what? Some kind of ninja or something?" I laughed but my insides hurt just thinking about what he was saying.

River's eyes met mine and for a second, I thought I saw him blush. "Sort of, I guess. I've been training to fight for so long, it's almost second nature by now. You know, I used to try and show off my moves to my dad when I was a kid 'cause I really wanted him to be proud of me. Didn't work. He left anyway."

Just like that, I forgot who I was sitting next to. I couldn't see the hunter, or the person raised to want me dead. All I saw was a sad boy with a broken family and my heart tore for him. He didn't choose this just like I didn't choose who I was. I shook my head, forcing myself to snap out of it. No, we didn't make the choice to be who we are, but that changed nothing. It's where life landed us, and I had to deal with that.

"You know, you're right," I whispered. "There might be something here. Fae or witch, real or not, something is hunting these kids. And I think we're on to something following the family lines. Even if we don't believe in the magic nonsense, the killer might, so we have to think like them."

River laughed. "Someone's been watching too much CSI..."

I was about to snap back with something clever when a head of blonde hair popped up through the attic's small door. "River, honey, I was about to make—"

The woman that barged in on us straightened her back and eyed me suspiciously. From the protective glare behind her eyes, I knew without a doubt this was River's mom and she was wondering what the weird girl was doing in his bedroom.

"Hey, Mom!" River said. "This is Billie, we go to school together."

Mrs. Hunting fumbled with a pearl button that held her prim, white suit secure. Her deep, brown eyes rolled over my slight form, and I could see the wheels turning in her head. After a few long—and excruciating—seconds, she tossed her mid-length wavy blonde hair to the side and walked over, hand outstretched toward me.

"Hello there," she purred.

The room closed in on me and I could feel every cell in my body screaming for me to run for the door. I had never met a boy's parents before and I had no clue how to act. *Do I shake her hand? Do I bow?* My thoughts jumbled. *Do you bow? Are you serious? She's not a queen. Geez.* My jaw clenched and I stretched out a hand to shake hers. "Hello, Mrs. Hunting."

"Oh, my," River's mom said, her tone sugary sweet. "Evanora is fine."

She twirled around the two of us and positioned herself

close to the window, eyes never leaving me. "I haven't seen you before, are you new in town?"

I nodded.

"Where from?"

"Oh my God, mom! What's with all the questions? We're studying."

"Actually," I grumbled and jumped to my feet. "I forgot I left my house keys in the Crystal Cauldron, so I should go get them."

Beside me, River stood, but I waved him down. "I can drive you there," he offered.

"That's okay. You should stay here. I can walk, it's not that far."

My intentions were faster than my legs and I tripped on my boots as I bolted for the doorway. "Nice to meet you, Evanora!" I yelled over my shoulder and ran down the staircase.

It took me a good few minutes to regain my balance but once I did, I spiraled down the stairs like I was trying to win a gold medal. My legs pumped as I ran through the house and back to the front door. Each step that took me further away from River and his mom felt like a tiny piece of freedom. Sure, she seemed nice enough, but this was the same woman who forced River into witch-hunting. Which meant she knew about witches and I would not stick around until she figured me out. Fooling a hormone-filled teenage boy into looking the other way was one thing, but a grown woman that spent her entire life prepping her son to be a killer? I was not ready to take that on.

As I ran down the driveway, I could feel eyes on my back but after turning around several times and seeing nothing, I shook the feeling off. My magic gnawed at the back of my mind, and I wanted to put some distance between River's house and myself as soon as possible. Something about this place gave me the chills. It could have been the overabundance of elements that gravitated toward my magic, but I had the good sense that more likely than not, it was the house of hunters I left in my wake.

Something flashed in my peripheral and I spun on my heels. The trees that lined the driveway rustled their leaves and the low glow of twilight settled around me. My eyes tightened as I searched the driveway when I noticed a shadow zoom behind the tree line.

You've got to be kidding me!

I took off after it, chasing in the direction I saw it move. It zigged and zagged, so fast, I couldn't make out its form, but I didn't have to see it to know what I was chasing. A shadower. Something quick and small. A coyote? I didn't have time to guess as I ran after it down the sloping streets of River's neighborhood. The shadower was impressively fast, but I had no trouble keeping up. All those years of training with the coven was paying off.

It zigged to the right ,and I followed, pumping my arms to pick up speed. When it disappeared from sight, I traced its path, my eyes widening over the familiar parking lot I found myself in.

The creature led me straight to Shadowhurst Academy.

Chapter Eighteen

The shadower lunged for my throat and I kicked my legs back, my head hitting the legs of a library table with a loud thud. I cursed under my breath and pushed back again as I tried to wrestle the beast off me. I still had no idea what kind of shifter I was dealing with, but it was for sure bigger than a coyote. Whatever it was, it was damn impressive and had me locked down in a brutal hold on the floor. I kicked its side again and twisted my body. My fingers stretched in the direction of the dagger it knocked out of my grip. I inched them closer to the hilt.

Above me, the creature growled, its warm saliva dripping on my face.

"Ew! Gross!" I yelled and kicked again.

This time, my fingers made contact and I could feel the cold of the silver in my grasp. I tightened my grip around the dagger's hilt and flipped it to point. I had no time to change my position as the shifter threw its jaws my way. Without thinking, I pointed the dagger up, burying the tip into its collarbone.

The shifter screeched and loosened its hold on me, and I took my chance. My hand reached for the amethyst pendant around my neck, and I tore it off, looping the chain around the shifters neck and pulling its ugly face away from mine. It thrashed above me, the bones of his hind legs punching my shins. Everything on my body hurt, but I couldn't stop.

I had to vanquish this bastard and get back to the body of the student that lay only a few feet away from us.

My eyes jerked to the girl, and I shuddered at the sight before turning my attention back to the shifter. In one swoop motion, I pushed it away and twisted to the side. Scrambling on the floor, I beelined for the amber crystal that rolled under the table. Close to me, the shifter screeched again, and I could hear its claws rip at the wooden planks of the floor as it charged for me once more.

I turned and let my magic guide me.

My eyes closed and I forced every source of magic I had in me into the crystal. Fire burst from my hand and when I looked up again, I could see confusion roll over the shifters wolf-like face. I didn't hesitate.

Swinging my hand forward, I blew at the ball of fire and pushed the flames its way. They spiraled from my hand, twisting and turning at a furious speed before crashing into the beast's chest. The shifter flew back, knocking into the case of books behind it and sinking to the ground. It rolled on the floor in a pathetic attempt to put out its burning fur. My face darkened and I crouched halfway before shooting the dagger into its chest.

My eyes followed the blade as it tore through the air and impaled in the shifter's heart. On impact, the creature's eyes met mine before it let out an agonizing scream and fell motionless to the floor. I ran toward it and yanked the silver from its chest before backing away to let nature run its course. Bones snapped and limbs thrashed but I didn't stick around to see who the shifter would turn into. Its human form was of no interest to me.

My heart was elsewhere.

With more speed than I thought I had left in me, I ran to the girl that lay motionless on the ground.

"NOOOOOO!"

This was all wrong. There was too much blood. *Why is there so much blood?*

I dropped to my knees to inspect her body and my head swam. Peyton said the other students were mummified, not brutally torn apart. Could it be that this was the act of a shifter and not the witch I've been looking for? There were cuts all over the body—some deep and some superficial—but all looked awful, nonetheless.

It wasn't until I wiped some blood off the girl's face that I saw it. Beneath the pool of deep red were glassy eyes; eyes that were once the brilliant color of the ocean. The girl couldn't have been older than me, but her skin was that of someone who had been dead for ages. Mummified.

The walls closed in on me and my knees buckled under my weight. I fell over the girl, my loose hair dragging in the blood that covered her chest. Tears fell from my eyes and crashed unto her dried-out skin. I swatted them off, forgetting the blood was still on my own hands. The smell of iron reached my nostrils and my stomach turned. It was as though my body was fighting against me and I couldn't keep myself from turning around and retching on the floor.

That definitely didn't help.

With blood all around me and a pile of puke on the side, I was sicker than ever. My fingers reached for the girl's jeans, and I pushed my hands into the pockets to see if I can find something that would tell me who she is. *Was.*

I felt the edge of something hard and pulled it out. A cell phone. Shaking, I pressed the home button and a picture of what I was sure was this girl and her boyfriend popped on the screen. She looked so different, blonde hair pulled back into a ponytail and a full face of makeup on. I traced my finger over the screen and let out a sob before swiping to unlock her phone.

"Goddess help me," I whispered as the fingerprint protected password screen came on.

I took a deep breath and reached for the girl's hand. "I'm so sorry," I choked out and pressed her index finger to the home button. The phone's screen lit up and I dropped her hand with a thud on the floor. Crawling back, I put some distance between me and the body and flipped through her contacts. Names I didn't know flashed through the screen until I spotted the *Facebook* icon on the bottom right corner. I pressed it and read the name in her profile.

"Ariana Willard Stameson."

Arrows shot through my heart as I realized that Ariana would never post on *Facebook* again. She would never see that hunky dude from the picture again. She'd never see her parents. My eyes flooded with tears, and I gagged on my spit, tossing her phone to the side and reaching into my jacket pocket to pull out my cell. I had no clue who I could call or what I should say. I couldn't call Peyton; not like this. Not until I cleaned myself up from all the blood that dried on my clothes.

My brow furrowed and I pulled up my text messages, tapping on the only other name I could think of. *Something happened. I need your help.* I typed and waited for the three dots to appear in my conversation thread with River.

Where are you? he responded and my heart sank.

School. It's bad. A girl was killed. Please, come quick.

I bit my lower lip and typed out another message. *I'm scared, River.*

How many more kids had to die like this until this bitch got what she wanted? I couldn't let it go on. I had to stop her! I had to—

Sirens echoed outside and my eyes snapped to the library windows. There were lights everywhere, dancing across the glass until it looked stained in color. I didn't have time to move when the library's door burst open, and I was met with a bright, white light shining into my eyes. I shielded my face with a blood-covered hand, my heart racing. Around my finger, my moonstone ring dug into my swollen skin and for a moment, I swore I saw it light up. *What the—*

"Stay right there!" a deep voice shouted from the doors.

My gaze snapped in its direction and my eyes widened as I took in the four uniformed policemen lining the entrance to the library. They pointed their flashlights my way like they were trying to burn me with them. I lowered my hand from my eyes and tried to stand.

"I said don't move!" the same officer shouted, cocking the trigger of the gun he pointed at my head. "What's your name?"

I strangled on my tears and swallowed hard. "Billie," I answered, my voice trembling. "Billie Stonewall."

The officer looked from me to his three partners and lowered the flashlight. He made his way toward me, and I didn't fail to notice that the gun was still pointed right between my eyes. "Billie Stonewall," he said when he reached me. "You're under arrest."

Chapter Nineteen

Shouts and screams echoed down the corridor from the cell they tossed me in, and I tried to muffle them with the sleeves of my jacket. It had been hours since the police pulled me out of the library, slapped me in cuffs, and took my information before leaving me alone. I stared at the bars that lined the cell, fighting the urge to lie down on the stained, thin mattress of the cot I sat on. These suckers would not see me relax, not if I could help it.

Thank the Goddess, there were no mirrors in the cell, not that I expected any. But regardless, I was relieved that I didn't have to see the state I was likely in. The girl's blood had already dried on my clothes and skin, but at least, I scored a bottle of water to rinse the taste of puke from my mouth. The cop that made the arrest was nice enough and I could tell he felt sorry for me even though I couldn't understand why. I was the prime suspect in a murder. I was found with blood literally on my hands, for Goddess' sake! My fingers reached for the moonstone ring, and I gasped when it wasn't there before remembering where I was and what landed me here.

My head throbbed and since they stripped me of all belongings when they booked me, I had no way of using magic to relieve the tension. *Shit! My dagger!* I cursed under my teeth as my hand reached for the empty slot in the hidden compartment in my boot. I left it at the library, not that it mattered now. That dagger was locked into evidence by now, just another thing to make sure I get locked up for good.

How did I let this happen?

I was an idiot to follow that shadower and not leave as soon as I found the girl's body, but I couldn't just run away. This was my job. It was what I was born to do, and I had to vanquish the beast before it hurt anyone else. Still, it was way too coincidental that a shadower showed up when it did and led me to the body, even by my standards of weird.

Out of all the times it could have attacked me, why did it choose then to do it? And why bring me to the library?

Things weren't making sense. There were pieces of the puzzle missing and I kicked myself for not knowing what they were.

Something clattered in a cell next to mine and my ears perked up. I wasn't alone in here. I wondered who else shared the agony of this space with me and if they too were innocent of their crime.

The holding cell was small—and smelled like mildew and piss—and it made me want to retch all over again. The walls, all concrete, were covered in stains and I tried not to think about what they might have been from. This was actual Hell, with a capital freaking H.

My thoughts landed on Beatrix, and I couldn't help but

picture her sitting somewhere in a place just like this at that moment. A heavy pain tugged at my heart as I considered how ironic it was that I should end up just like the woman I swore to leave behind. Yet, here I was, the spitting image of her, behind bars like an animal awaiting their death. Except there was one thing that separated me from Beatrix. I was innocent. At least, I liked to think so. What the police had in mind was a whole other can of worms.

Someone coughed and cursed down the corridor and I hunched myself over my legs, resting my head in my hands. My long hair was a matted mess and it hung over my face like car-wash curtains. I could see black streaks of blood in the blonde locks that reminded me of Peyton. Knowing my friend, she'd like this fresh look of mine. I had to admit, this was pretty badass. Jailed and covered in blood. it was like something out of a movie.

I groaned into my palms and tried to retrace the events in the library. *Might as well make the most of your time here. It might be a hot minute.*

Instantly, my mind replayed everything I saw. Flashes of my memories snapped into my thoughts, and I tried to reel them in and focus on the important things. The girl's body and how it was left. What did I remember that could have been important? There was blood, lots of it. *Yeah, okay, good. We know that already, think bigger.* I urged myself to dig deeper and see the details. Something was off and I couldn't quite put my finger on it. *Was it her clothes? No, that wasn't it. What was it?*

I rubbed my eyes and sat up. *Think, Billie, THINK!*

Then it hit me. I knew something was wrong as soon as I walked into the library, but I didn't know what it was at the time. Peach wood. I could smell it all around me, but I was too busy with the shadower to notice. This was the work of a witch and, judging by the girl's mummified body, it was a powerful witch who knew what she was doing. But why would a witch drain the energy of a student and why leave them in the library for anyone to find? *Unless...*

Horror struck me frozen, and my mouth dropped.

Unless she wanted me to find it.

It made perfect sense and I couldn't believe I didn't see it sooner. The cops showed up way too quick. Like they knew the body was there. Like they knew *I'd* be there. Their scapegoat.

I didn't know how, but the witch had somehow got the shadower to lead me to the library, just in time for them to make their arrest. It was planned. It had to be! There was no other explanation. My temples throbbed as the dots connected.

The witch knows I'm in town and she knows I'm just like her. Worse, she's using me as a decoy to buy her more time.

It was a good hypothesis, and I was pretty proud of myself for reaching it, but it still didn't explain what the killer wanted. I had to figure it out, but I couldn't do it from inside this cell. I wished Peyton was here so I could bounce these ideas off her, that girl was made for mysteries. Maybe the cops would let me call her if I asked nicely?

Wait, wasn't I supposed to get one phone call or some crap like that?

I tried to remember what I knew of law enforcement, but I limited my knowledge to what I'd seen on TV or overheard the high priestesses discuss.

Shit!

I tilted my head back and it banged on the cold concrete

of the wall behind me. How was I supposed to explain this to the High Coven? Our entire race depended on secrecy and staying under the radar and here I was, getting myself arrested on my first week undercover. This was such a disaster!

In my defense, I didn't even want the job, so they can suck on that while they figure out how to get me the hell out of here.

Whoever shared this row of cells with me coughed again and I almost lashed out at them. My hand pressed over my lips to stop myself from getting into a fight I'd likely later regret and I choked on the smell of dried blood that flooded my nostrils. The High Coven will figure something out and when they do, I'll be free to go. This wasn't the first time a witch had a run-in with the law, and it wouldn't be the last. Our job wasn't exactly clean-cut and there were protocols in place to handle situations such as this. I had no clue what those protocols were, but I knew they were there to protect me and my people. The High Coven will help, I was sure of it.

I dug my nails into the mattress and took a deep breath as I forced myself to count back from a hundred. A nifty trick I learned from Theodora. She used to use to calm her nerves before going on stage back when she still had time to perform, but it should work just fine for the situation I found myself in.

I was down to thirty-nine when heavy footsteps boomed down the hall and I stared at the officer who so eagerly snapped the cuffs on my hands hours ago.

"Miss Stonewall," he said after clearing his throat. "You're free to go."

I knew it! Those magnificent, magical bitches!

Not missing a beat, I jumped off the cot and met him by the barred doors that held my freedom. "Can I ask why?" I asked.

"Someone came forward with your alibi," the officer answered, his eyes never meeting mine. "But I wouldn't leave town yet, if I was you."

He turned the key and swung the enormous door open to let me through and I plastered a blank expression on my face. I was not about to let him see me smile. He didn't deserve it. As I followed him down the corridor, I kept my eyes forward, even when my cough-infested cellmate yelled profanities in my direction. Nothing would ruin this moment for me. I was free and now, I had something the witch didn't expect. I knew what I was looking for. *Don't worry, officer, I'm not going anywhere anytime soon...*

Chapter Twenty

My excitement was momentary as the officers processed me out, handed me my belongings, and handed me off to the person who helped secure my freedom.

River's face was impossible to read, but I wagered it was somewhere between irritation and confusion. I shrank in my spot before slipping the moonstone ring bank on and tightening the clasp of the pendant Ms. Broussard gave me over my neck. My eyes met River's and blood rushed to my cheeks as I let the embarrassment take hold of me.

In my haste to figure out what happened in the library, I had forgotten that I texted him. Now, I was stuck having to be grateful to the hunter for rescuing me like I was some damsel in distress. Nothing could be worse than this.

River tapped his driving moccasins on the cement and arched an eyebrow my way while grinning. *Nope, that's worse. Cocky bastard!*

I cleared my throat and walked over. "Thanks, but you didn't have to do that."

"Kinda did. But if you'd rather, I can go back and tell them I haven't seen you all night and that I lied when I told them you were with me."

I rolled my eyes. "I had it covered."

"Yeah, looks like it..." He unlocked the car and gestured me inside. "Come on, I'll take you home."

"Shit!" I screeched. "The Chandlers!"

River laughed. "Don't stress, I took care of it. Told them we were studying and lost track of time. There's a change of clothes for you in the back seat."

A cruiser pulled up beside us and I took that as my cue to get in. My hands reached around back to pull out a small paper bag that held a pair of black leggings and a tee with the logo of a band I've never heard of. As soon as River ducked into the driver's seat, I shot him a glare that meant I had questions that needed answers.

"Peyton put it together for you," he said and motioned to the clothes. "She said it's the only thing she had that looked like what normal people wear."

A laugh escaped me as I looked over the rips and safety pins that held the tee together. My friend sure had an interesting idea of what normal meant.

The drive back to the Chandler home was silent and I found myself constantly distracted by the slight noises River made. Every grunt and sigh as he swerved the Tesla down the gloomy streets sent shivers down my legs and I had to dig my ring into my thigh to keep myself together. *We hate him, Billie. Remember that we HATE him. Please!* But I couldn't, at least not really. I did not understand what these feelings were, but hate was not one of them. He came through for me and I couldn't wrap my mind around that. A witch hunter saved me, and I didn't even have to ask him to do that. Well, I sort of did when I texted him but still, it was a friendly gesture. And now, because of him, I didn't have to deal with telling the High Coven about my brief run-in with the police and could avoid the boring lectures that would likely follow that.

River slowed down when we reached my street and cracked open a window. Frosty air rushed the inside of the car, forcing the scent of his cologne into my throat. The hair on my arms rose and my body shivered as an image of his lips on mine flashed before my eyes. I shook my head, clearing my throat several times just to snap out of it.

"You okay?" River asked and pulled into the driveway.

From this angle and with the darkness of the evening spread across the yard, the Chandlers' home looked a lot less obnoxious than I remembered it being. The wraparound porch that I considered hideous and over-the-top was welcoming and I was relieved to be back. I tucked a hair behind my ear and blew out a breath, clutching the clothes Peyton lent me to my chest.

"I guess I should change before they come out here and find me looking like a murder victim."

"Um, yeah, okay." River nodded and opened the car door. "I'll wait outside."

He got out of the car, a little too slow if you ask me, and turned his back to me. *Wait, is he serious? He wants me to change here? NOW? In front of him?!? No, no, NO!* I kicked the seat then looked back to the house. I couldn't very well stomp through there covered in blood and running behind some random bush to change was just going to get the motion-censored floodlights going. I was doomed.

"You done?"

"Not even close!" I snapped and checked to make sure he wasn't looking. "Keep your eyes closed, pervert!"

I could hear him chuckle through the window and my blood roiled at the sound. *Stupid, hot, idiot.* My hands moved to rip my clothes off so I could wiggle into whatever Peyton put together. The top was easy to maneuver but changing into the leggings was a feat unlike any I faced before, and I've once vanquished four shadowers in one go. My knees hit every hard surface and I felt like a deer trapped in a clown car. As soon as I got the torture chamber that was the leggings Peyton provided on, I glanced over myself. This was not good. The rips in the tee were scandalously positioned to reveal every bit of cleavage my chest offered, and I could already see my boobs trying to make an appearance. I had half the mind to put my bloodied leather back on but thought better of it, choosing instead to flip the top over backward. It wasn't much better but at least the holes on this side went up higher. When I managed to get everything more or less in place, I knocked on the window to let River know it was safe to come back inside.

His eyes drifted over me so slowly that I had to check if I missed a hole and my boob wasn't hanging out or something. It wasn't, thank the Goddess. River gave me another glance and his cheeks flushed. "Looks good on you," he whispered.

"Uh, thanks?"

Why was that a question, Billie? Just say thank you. What is wrong with you?

"I mean, thank you. It actually fits. Sort of," I added.

"Sure does..." River purred.

The leather seat cushion swelled around me, and I could feel myself sink back, ready to disappear in its hold. He reached a hand over to rest on the back of the passenger seat and leaned in. *Is he going to kiss me? Oh, sweet mother of fae, he's going for it!* I closed my eyes and breathed out as the space between us closed and River was inches away. He shifted in his seat and reached for my face. My lids tightened and I tilted my head to get closer to him but before I could lean in, frigid air hit me smack on the forehead. I opened one eye and found River holding a small branch in his hand.

"This was in your hair."

Oh. OH! My cheeks reddened and I snatched the branch from his fingers. "Thanks, I forgot where I left that."

I only got a half-smile for that. Made sense, a half-smile for a half-assed joked.

"Billie, seriously," he scolded. "Are you okay?"

I nodded then shook my head no, then nodded again. "I don't know."

"That text you sent," he whispered. "I was terrified. I was going crazy when I showed up and saw the cops taking you away. I seriously almost tackled them right then and there, but I figured both of us getting locked up was not the best play. If something happened to you... I don't know. It really shook me seeing you like that."

"Something did happen. Just not to me."

He furrowed his brow and turned to look at me. *Really* look at me in a way I can't remember anyone else looking before. Like he was trying to understand who I was. We had that in common. "I can't imagine what it must have been like to find the body. I'm sorry I wasn't there with you. I should have been. *Someone* should have been."

The concern in his voice was so real and so touching that I found myself wanting to wrap my arms around him and never letting him go. In my entire life, no one had ever asked me if I was all right. They just assumed I would be because they trained me to do what I do. The closest I ever got to genuine concern was when Luna found me behind a dumpster with a broken leg after a particular gruesome shadower attack and even then, I felt nothing this close to happiness. River cared for me. Not the hunter or the hot boy with the killer V at his waist, but him—the real River.

Tears pooled behind my lids, and I blinked them away.

"It's fine. I'm a tough cookie, I can handle it."

We were silent for a few moments, staring at each other like this was the last time we'd get to be this quiet for the rest of our lives. River breathed and I found my own lungs matching his pace. My heart ached with every intake of air, but I didn't look away. I couldn't.

"I have something to tell you," River said, breaking the silence.

Oh, Goddess, what now?

"My friends found something else, something that ties the murders together. And..."

"And?" I pressed.

"And it's not what we thought. At least, not what I thought. It's not a hunter."

I leaned into him. "Then who?" *Or who do YOU think it is?*

"They got a hold of the police files, don't ask how. There were things at the crime scenes that the cops wouldn't have looked for but obviously, we would notice them because—"

"Because you're hunters."

"Yep." He nodded.

"What did they find? Your friends, I mean."

"Magic," River whispered. "They found magic."

What in the actual Hell? I arched my eyebrows so high

they almost kissed my hairline. "What do you mean they found magic?"

"I mean they found evidence of magic use. Same ones at each crime scene. Like someone performed a ritual before they killed the students. I'm willing to bet that girl you found had the same things around her."

"Peach wood, amethyst dust, salt," I whispered in between clenched jaws.

"Yes! How did you know?"

"I, uh..." I peeled my gaze off him. "I saw the same thing. In the library before the cops got there. And you're right, it's ritualistic, at least from what I know about this stuff."

"See!" River pushed my shoulder and smiled. "This is why we need you! You and Peyton have a knack for this stuff. I know you said you were into all this paranormal stuff."

"So? Lots of people are."

"Yeah, but lots of people don't know about my extracurricular activities." He wiggled his eyebrows in that cute way I couldn't resist. "We could really use your help on this."

"No freakin' way! I am not getting in the middle of—Wait, are you saying I get to meet the other hunters?"

River nodded and my stomach did somersaults, and this time, it wasn't from the way his pecs tightened under his thin cotton shirt when he moved. This was what I had been waiting for; a chance to find out who his friends were.

"So, you in?" River asked.

I looked him up and down, my eyes spending a little too much time on his chest area. "Hell, yes! I am one hundred percent in!"

Chapter Twenty-one

 *D*ragon's blood smelled like an actual heap of steamy garbage when mixed with eyebright and I had to pinch my nose shut as I dabbed the compact mirror in my hand with the paste. I damn near retched four times before I had the mirror covered.

I had woken up several hours before I needed to get ready for school to teleport my dagger from the evidence locker and perform a scrying spell on my bloodied jacket, hoping to have it lead me to the witch responsible for the murders. So far, all I had was a mess on the floor of my bathroom and a dirty mirror that smelled like crap. *Excellent start.*

I grimaced and rolled the pearl I purchased at the Crystal Cauldron between my fingers. Despite its small size, it had enough water element locked inside that I knew it would do the trick for the spell. Pearls were notorious in power containment for anything water-related, which made them an ideal gemstone to use in a scrying spell. If I could get my head to stop spinning long enough to perform it, of course. Last night still shook me and I barely got a wink of sleep before the alarm blared in my ear at four in the morning.

The pearl rolled over my palm, and I shut my eyes.

Around me, the room grew quiet, and I perked my ears to listen to the distant sound of the ocean that emanated from the stone. It was faint and light and I swayed to the hum of the waves crashing to shore. My lids fluttered and I breathed into my magic, forcing it to accept the offering of power in my steady hand. Waves clashed in my mind as I connected to the element and grabbed hold. I fisted my hand around the pearl and squeezed until I could feel my palms grow wet with magic. Arm outstretched, I held my fist sideways over the mirror and let a few drops of water drip unto the surface. The mirror buzzed and shook, levitating off the floor to creep closer to my hand.

My eyes snapped open, and I smiled before yanking it from mid-air.

As carefully as I could manage, I tilted the mirror to face the stained jacket I laid out next to me and waited. In my hand, I could feel the mirror fight against me and it shook under my hold. I grit my teeth and push more magic into it, stretching it closer to the jacket. A bright, blue glow surrounded the mirror and my lips curled into a smile. *Got you, sucker!*

My fingers tightened on the sleek surface, and I laid the mirror on the floor, crouching over it like a spider. My eyes narrowed and a breath of air jammed itself deep in my throat. Any minute now, the mirror should reflect the face of anyone that had been in contact with my jacket or the blood spilled over it. *Any... minute...*

I waited two more minutes and groaned before cursing under my breath. *Why didn't it work? WHY?*

Jaw-clenched, I raised the mirror to the jacket again and shook it. "Hello? Anyone there?"

The mirror shivered and the blue glow intensified but nothing appeared.

"Damn it!" I cursed and kicked it to the side. I glanced at the dagger that was still sealed in the evidence bag with yellow tape plastered across the Ziplock. *At least the retrieval worked without a hitch.*

This witch was better prepared than I thought. She must have known I'd try this and blocked herself from the spell. My hands reached for the grimoire, and I ran my fingers over the yellowed page, scanning the steps I had written to make sure I missed nothing. There were no mistakes made. The spell didn't work which meant I was blocked from using it. *Now what?*

There was a knock on the front door. "Ms. Stonewall?"

Silas' voice boomed on the other side, and I scrambled to stand, tucking the remnants of the spell under a towel. I walked out of the bathroom and shut the door behind me.

"One second!" I yelled out and dashed to the sock drawer of my dresser.

Pushing aside the top layer of bunched up socks, I pulled out the box of herbs I hid in the drawer and grabbed a piece of lotus root before tossing it under my tongue. On tiptoes, I walked back to the bathroom door and gripped the handle, pushing a gust of magic into the metal. The lotus root melted in my mouth in seconds, and I swallowed its bitter taste. My fingertips tingled and a pale yellow powder spread over the handle.

Better safe than sorry, I thought and wiggled the handle to make sure it remained locked.

The spell drained my body, but I bolted for the entrance, brushing out the knots in my hair with my fingers. When I opened the door, Silas stood before me, a cup of coffee in his hands. He pushed the cup my way and I jumped for it, breathing in the sweet aroma. *I need this bad right now!*

"Everything okay?" I asked after taking a big gulp of coffee.

He nodded, his eyes blank behind his glasses. "Your caseworker is here to see you. She's in the living room. Follow me."

With a nod, I followed him out, locking the door. I had gotten used to leaving my grimoire in the guest house, but even with the hiding spell I placed over it, it still made me nervous as hell to leave it unattended. Granted, walking around with a giant, old book around the house was bound to make me look like a total weirdo so for now, it was staying put in my dresser drawer.

"Everything all right, Billie?" Silas asked.

"Um, yeah, I guess."

He stopped to rearrange the glasses on his long nose and peered at me over them. "How do you like it here so far? With the Chandlers?"

"I love it, actually," I answered, blushing. "They're really nice. You too."

"Well, thank you for the kind words. Imala and Thomas can be difficult to get to know, but I am certain they cherish having you here. I wanted to make sure you knew that."

I smiled and gave him an awkward thumbs up. "Thank you. And they're not so bad."

Silas chuckled and gestured for us to keep walking.

The cup shook in my hand as we rounded the main house and dipped inside through the backyard entrance. A high priestess was here? Why? I steadied my hold on the coffee from fear it would go flying all over the mezzanine rug in the living room that must have cost more than I was worth. As I stepped into the airy space, two familiar black eyes burnt into me, and I stopped in my tracks.

"Sebyl!" I exclaimed and tried to hide the nerves in my words. "What's going on?"

Sebyl waved her gloved hand across Silas' face, and he turned on his heels, marching out of the room without so much as a good bye to me. The high priestess grinned, and I noticed the red of her lipstick was a few shades darker today. It was so dark, it looked deep purple and matched her suit perfectly. Sebyl brushed a hair off her face as she often did despite it being not out of place at all. Her gaze shot to me, and I jumped back.

"It seems you've been keeping secrets," she hissed.

Shit! Shit! Shit! SHIT!

"Language," Sebyl warned, and my cheeks blushed. *Of course, I said that out loud. Of course.*

"Sorry," I whispered.

My head was spinning, and I tried to figure out how much she knew. Had she felt me using magic just now and if she did, how pissed was she?

Sebyl curled a finger to gesture me toward her and I hesitated before moving closer. I have known this woman my entire life and I still feared her wrath. Sebyl was by far the most powerful witch I've met and the fact that she was a high priestess only added to my fear. I tried my best to stay on her good side but sometimes, there was no telling which side you were on with Sebyl. Judging by the look on her face as she glared at me, I'd have to wager I was on the wrong one.

"When were you planning on letting us know about the students?" Sebyl asked sternly. Her index finger twirled a loose strand of my hair like a cat playing with a string. "Important information for the coven to have, wouldn't you agree?"

I nodded. "Yes, I'm sorry. I was going to tell you, I swear! I was just waiting for the right time."

Sebyl's finger dropped from my hair like it burnt her. "No time better than the present."

I nodded again and took a small step back in case she smote me with her magic.

"I'm sorry. I was trying to understand it, so I had something more concrete to tell you."

"And what do you have to tell me?"

I bit my lower lip and swallowed. "That students are being killed and it involves magic?"

"We already know that, child," Sebyl hissed. "What have you been able to find out?"

"Uh, well..." I choked out. "Just that whoever the witch is that's responsible is powerful. Like crazy powerful. The students were all drained of their energy, so I know she's taking their life force, but I don't know why. Oh, and there was another shadower attack, but I handled it."

Blood rushed to my neck, and I rubbed at my chest with my trembling fingers. There was no point telling her about the cops, at least not yet. Sebyl was pissed as it is, and I didn't want to get into more trouble. I had the distinct feeling that wherever they shipped me off to next wouldn't be as luxurious as the Chandlers' place.

"Have you tried scrying for her?"

"I have."

"And?"

"Nothing. She blocked her magic from me, I can't get through."

"Interesting…"

Sebyl shifted her weight in her four-inch lilac colored heels and looked past me. Her gaze lightened and I felt my shoulders drop in relief.

"There's something else," I said and gnawed on my lip again. "I found some information that leads to a fae bloodline in this town. Several of them. I think the students were all of fae decent."

"Impossible!" the high priestess screeched. "The fae are extinct!"

The growl in her voice stopped me dead. Why was she this upset about it? Knowing the fae may have survived whatever drove them from Earth was a good thing. Fae strengthened the Earth's elements and we needed that to feed our magic. *This is excellent news, right?* Was I missing something here?

"What if they're not, priestess? Wouldn't that be something to look into?" I asked. "If fae bloodlines survived, we could use that to our advantage. We can get stronger!"

Sebyl shook her head and lowered her gaze to the floor. "How much do you know of the fae, Wilhemina?"

"Literally nothing," I snapped back.

It was the truth. Much like everyone else in the coven, I knew very little of the beings. There was nothing in any of the texts in the coven's library and what there was spoke of the fae as more of a fairytale than something real and concrete. Mostly, and as far as the witches were concerned, the fae were extinct or a complete myth. When I was a kid, I always wanted to meet them. If the tales were true, the fae were the strongest magical beings on the planet and their connection to the elements was out of this world. Unlike witches, the fae didn't need to have hold of an element to wield their magic. They were in tune with it. Like the five elements, there were five fae lines, each one holding a stronger hold on the element they were a part of. They were powerful and strong, and I knew nothing about them at all. What a piss off.

"Yes. Most modern witches do not. And with reason."

"But what reason? Why can't we know more?"

"The fae," Sebyl started, "were not a kind race. They were power hungry and arrogant and if they were still around, it would only be a matter of time before the humans found out. The fae dislike keeping their magic hidden."

My eyes narrowed. *Why did she use the word "like" in the present tense?*

"But their magic helps the elements be strong, and we need the elements."

Sebyl grimaced. "While that is true, they are much too unpredictable to be useful."

Present tense again...

"The fae may have taught us their ways and created our kind, but they were never our saviors."

"Wait, what?" My eyes widened. "The fae made us?"

"Taught," Sebyl corrected. "They *taught* us how to use the elements of the earth to wield magic. We were never made by anyone, no human was."

Stars glimmered in my vision and my knees buckled. "Hold on one second, you're telling me that witches were just regular humans?"

"Upon a time, yes."

"How is that even possible?"

"Wilhemina, darling, you of all people should know that everything is in this world is possible," Sebyl whispered. "The original witches were humans taken under the wing of the first fae. They were taught the ways of magic, pushed to their limits until they could wield it themselves, but only with the help of the elements. I doubt the fae would have it any other way, they love control a little too aggressively."

I shook my head. "Does that mean I'm human too? And you?"

"Not anymore, I'm afraid." Sebyl sighed and closed the distance between us. "Magic has a funny way of seeping in and taking hold, it shapes you until you are nothing but its vessel. Over time, the first witches paired off with others of their like, and their children were born with magic already in their blood. The circle of life and all. As the stories go, and it is up to you whether you choose to believe them, the fae created our kind to further their hold on Earth's elements. But power is power, and it wasn't long before witches wanted to free themselves of the dependency they developed on their teachers. They severed ties with the fae and lived life to the fullest. Right here in Shadowhurst, in fact. Soon, our kind grew confident in their magic and humans began to take notice. The repercussions were dire and many of our kind were destroyed in the process."

What. The. Shit. How was this not regular knowledge in the coven? My head hurt just thinking about it.

"What happened to the ones that survived?" I asked, still pissed this was the first I was hearing about such an integral part of our history.

"They fled to Stamwick, which is exactly how the High Coven came into existence. The witches banded together, forming a society that had to stay hidden from the human eye. Unfortunately, without the interference of the fae, our magic seeped out and well, you already know about the outcome of that horrid affair."

"The shadowers," I whispered. "So that's why we vanquish them?"

"Precisely," Sebyl noted. "The shadowers are foolish and short-sighted. Their hunger for energy and the kill overpowers their rational thinking and if we don't stop them, the humans will take notice again. We simply cannot afford that. Our kind has worked too hard to get where we are, and nothing can risk our safety."

"But why not teach this freely in the coven?"

"Who said we do not?" She arched an eyebrow and grinned. "Every witch that reaches a higher status in the High Coven is introduced to the full history. Once we are certain her loyalty to the coven is greater than her need for magic and power. We cannot have a repeat of the past on our hands."

I guess that makes sense. Still pretty shit though. "So why send me here?"

"Wilhemina," Sebyl said. "We have an innate trust in you and your abilities. Sending you here was not simply a punishment for what you did. I hope you understand that any other witch in that position would have been imprisoned without any questions asked. We have hopes for you and your future in the coven. *I* have hopes for you. We chose Shadowhurst as a test, to see how you react in certain situations."

"And?" I asked. "How am doing so far?"

Sebyl's eyes pierced mine. "Surprisingly well."

Okay, my mind was officially blown. This was crazy.

Don't get me wrong, I was extremely proud of the fact that the High Coven trusted me enough not to just lock my ass up next to Beatrix, but all the lies and secrets did not sit well with me. Our history was so much darker than I knew, and I didn't understand why it wouldn't be public knowledge. It seemed too important to keep quiet, so why did I not know about this before? And what else was the coven keeping from me and the rest of the witches?

"Was there anything else?" Sebyl asked.

My lips drew into a line, and I averted my eyes from her. I should tell her about the hunters and River. *I should, right? RIGHT?* But I couldn't. For some reason, I couldn't bring myself to betray him, not yet. And not when I wasn't sure if I could trust Sebyl not to blow up the entire town just to get to the hunters. "That's all I got so far. But I'm getting close to finding out the names of the hunters," I lied.

I could give her that much at least.

"Excellent work, Wilhemina."

"So what should I do now?"

Sebyl's fingers curled, and she grabbed hold of my chin to bring my eyes to hers. "You follow the blood," she whispered. "And if I find you're keeping things from the coven again, there will be consequences."

With that, the high priestess stormed from the living room and slammed the front door behind her. My lungs collapsed and I hit the rug with my knees, holding my chest and fighting for air. I just lied to the high priestess. What the hell was I thinking? But I knew what I was thinking. I was thinking that I couldn't trust anyone. Every door I opened led to more secrets and even more questions. And I was trapped in the middle of it all. All the secrets led straight back to me, and I hated it. I hated lying and I hated hiding things—from Sebyl, from the coven, from River. I was lying to all of them and eventually, those lies would catch up with me.

I had to ease some tension. I had to do something before the guilt ate me alive. If not for any other reason than to get my head back in the game. There was no way I would find this killer witch if I preoccupied my mind with keeping my lies straight. I was tired of keeping secrets and living in darkness and I knew that if I kept this up any longer, that darkness would swallow me whole. No matter how hard I tried, I couldn't be what the High Coven wanted me to be. I couldn't continue playing the part of a witch in the shadows, not when there was an entire world out there waiting to be explored.

There was only one thing I could do, and my body shook just from thinking about it. I had to let some lies go. Someone had to know about who I truly was, and it had to be someone I trusted.

I pulled out my phone and typed out a message. *We need to talk. I'll come to you.*

Relief washed over me as soon as my fingers pressed 'send' and I sunk back on the floor, my back resting on the couch's leather. I was about to break the coven's number one rule and I didn't care. If they had their secrets from me, I was sure as hell going to repay the favor.

Chapter
Twenty-two

"You're a WHAT?" Peyton screeched so loud, I had to cover my ears.

I had just finished telling her everything, well, almost everything, and she took it surprisingly well. If you don't count her saucer-sized eyes and open mouth the entire time I was speaking. But I had to admit, as soon as I told my best friend I was a witch, I felt a million times better.

"A witch," I said, "and please, stop screaming."

Peyton paced the long width of her room for the trillionth time and shrugged. "Sorry, this is like, mind-blowing news."

"I guess..."

"You guess? B, this is huge! You sure you're not just screwing with me?"

"Pretty sure." I rolled my eyes. "So, you got anything else to say except the yelling?"

My friend scoffed and ran to the small table tucked in the corner of her room to rummage through the stack of books atop it. While she searched for whatever it was her crazy mind locked on, I scanned her bedroom. For someone who hated the trust funders or anyone else with money, Peyton sure didn't live like a squatter. Her bedroom was twice the size of the one I had in the guest house, with exposed barn slabs across the ceiling and wall-to-wall windows to match. The rest of her house was no different and I could tell as soon as I walked in that whatever business her father was in, he was doing well for himself. But somehow, I didn't feel uncomfortable in their house. At least not as much as I did at River's. Though I had a feeling that had a lot to do with the decor of the bedroom I now sat in, which was done in typical Peyton style and the fact that there were no witch hunters in sight.

The bed was a canopy bed—much like mine—but instead of the exposed wood frame, Peyton had hers covered in twinkle lights and a sheer purple gauze that draped over the sides. The bedding was multi-colored and there were so many cushions on top of her skull-printed duvet that I wondered how she had enough space to sleep in there. On either side of the bed stood two small tables, both a bright purple with hand painted black flowers lining the legs. Across from the bed sat a comfy black sofa that I now perched in, and next to it was a giant statue of a giraffe with Peyton's clothes draped over its neck. The room was a mess and I loved it!

"Yo, you done in there?" I asked just as Peyton tossed a book in my lap.

She flipped through the pages and pointed to a drawing of a cartoon witch pointing her wand at an angry looking man. In the box next to it, the same witch was drawn smiling and the man next to her was now a nasty, looking rat. Above the drawing, the words "Smite Your Enemies" were sketched in.

"Can you do that?" Peyton asked, wide-eyed.

I laughed and closed the book with a thud. "Not exactly how it works."

"How does it work? Tell me EVERYTHING!"

My brow furrowed and I rearranged my legs to fit under me. I've never had to explain magic before, and I wasn't even sure if I knew how it worked.

"Um, well," I started, "it's weird."

"Go on…"

"It's like something that's a part of you. Like the air in your lungs or the blood in your veins. It's always there, just at the edges, but when I'm close to objects that have strong elemental power, my magic kind of sucks that in. Sometimes, it's only a little at a time and I can't do much with it, but sometimes, when the elements are strong, I can use their power and it strengthens me."

"What type of objects?" Peyton cocked an eyebrow. "Magical objects?"

"No, nothing like that," I smirked. "More like natural things. Herbs, crystals, things you can find in nature. Like water and earth and fire and stuff. Elemental things."

"Uh-huh, uh-huh, uh-huh." Peyton nodded like she was taking notes in her head. "What else?"

"I don't know. I guess when I'm upset or angry, the magic gets stronger because my emotions are so wild, and it becomes easier to use it. Like if I'm pissed, all I have to do is hold a crystal and I can make shit happen."

"Like what?"

"Lots of stuff," I answered. "Water, fire, that kind of stuff.

I can control the weather too, but I have to have a lot of elemental pull to do that and it wipes me out. The more magic I use, the weaker I feel, so it's kind of a catch twenty-two."

"So, if you use too much, you can what? Die?"

I chuckled. "Not die. You're so extra! But I get wiped out and have to rest before I can use it again. Since it's a part of me, when I get tired, *it* gets tired. And vice versa."

Peyton was quiet for a long moment and stared at something past my shoulder. Her eyes were wide again, and her breathing slowed so much, I could barely see her chest move. I was scared I broke her when she spoke again. "Show me."

"Show you what?"

"Magic."

Cool air wrapped around me as Peyton ran to snatch something from her desk before jumping on the couch next to me. She held her hand out and nodded to the smokey quartz crystal resting in her palm. "Show me."

Hesitantly, I reached for the crystal and sighed. *No turning back now.* My fingers curled around the crystal and my blood boiled. The familiar tingle of magic rushed over my skin, and I tilted my head back to take a deep breath. In my mind, an image formed as clear as though I was looking at a photograph. My lips curled in satisfaction. Next to me, Peyton giggled in excitement as I squeezed my fist around the crystal before uncurling my fingers. She gasped.

In my hand, sprouting from the crystal's center, was a beautiful white lily. Its petals fluttered as Peyton's breath washed over them and she let out another excited giggle before yanking the crystal out of my hand. As soon as her hand touched it, the lily burst into a white powder and disappeared.

"What the hell?" my friend asked, her eyebrows kissing.

I shrugged. "You scared me, so I dropped my hold on it."

"B! That was so freaking cool!"

"You're taking this all pretty well..." I said.

"Are you kidding?" Peyton screeched. "This is like the weirdest thing that ever happened to me!"

"Well, technically, it's happening to me, but okay." I locked my eyes on hers. "So, I didn't freak you out?"

"Girl, are you kidding? I live in Shadowhurst! I'm just surprised you're the first witch we had around here."

I bit my lower lip. "Yeah, about that..."

"Oh, God! Don't tell me, there's more of you."

"No, I mean, yeah, but that's not what I'm saying. The murders, I'm pretty sure a witch is killing these kids."

Peyton's gaze darkened. "How do you know?"

"Just the way the bodies were left and then when I found that girl in the library, I could smell peach wood everywhere."

"And peach wood is bad?"

"Peach wood is very, very bad. Whoever this witch is, she's trouble and she's sucking the energy from these kids. But I don't know why. And then River's friends found the same hints of magic in the other crime scenes, so I know it has to be—"

"Wait one minute!" My friend held her hand up to shut me up. "River knows about this?"

"Um, actually..." I breathed out. "Good thing you're sitting, 'cause there's more. River and some of his friends are witch hunters."

"SHUT THE FRONT DOOR!" Peyton screamed and jumped up. "There are witch hunters?!?"

"There's lots of things," I sighed. "But that's not the point. The point is that he confirmed my suspicions about the bodies being related and that magic is involved. I need to find this witch before she hurts anyone else."

"Wait, are all witches chicks?"

I smiled and nodded. "Always have been. No clue why, so don't ask."

"Noted. So, River is a witch hunter and you're a witch. You haven't told him yet, have you?"

"Obvi not!" I hollered. "I'd be tied to a stake by now if I did. Though, I'm not sure that's how they would even kill witches these days. From what he told me, the whole hunter thing sounds like an after school club for him and his friends. I doubt any of them would know what to do with a witch if they met one. My kind has done a pretty decent job at staying off the radar, so whatever River and his friends know, it's what they could find from those books their ancestors left behind. Which isn't much, you've seen them yourself. Anyway, no, I haven't told him and I'm not going to, so you have to keep your mouth shut. About all of this."

Peyton made a crossing motion across her heart and lowered to sit next to me. Her eyes sparkled in excitement, and I could tell she was not done quizzing me about magic and my people just yet. "Wow. A witch and witch hunter. You guys are like a modern day Romeo and Juliet!"

"Yeah, no. No, thanks. I have no interest in River Hunting."

"Ha!"

"Oh, shut up!" I pushed her over and shot a death stare.

"No, that's not it," Peyton chuckled, getting back up. "Just you know, River Hunting is a hunter. Kinda funny. 'Cause of his last name."

I grimaced and fisted my hands. I could see where she

was going with this, but it wasn't funny at all, at least not to me.

"And don't think you have me fooled with your 'no, thank you's' and your 'I don't like him' garbage. You totally have the hots for him."

"I can't, Peyton. He is the *last* person I should have any kinda hots for."

"I get it, B. That sucks."

She crossed her legs in her lap and inched closer to me. Her hands reached for mine and she squeezed them so tight I started to sweat. "I got your back, B. No matter what, we're friends."

Tears burnt at my eyes, and I did my best to smile. Across from me, Peyton smiled from ear to ear and her excitement made me want to wrap her in a hug so tight, she'd burst. Correction, I did that exactly. I squeezed Peyton so hard that I could feel her heartbeat against my own. A sob choked deep in my throat, and I cursed the High Coven for making me live with this secret for so long. Humans weren't as judgmental as they made them out to be and Peyton was proof of that. They weren't scared of the unknown, some of them embraced it with excitement and open arms. All the worry I had about telling my best friend the truth melted away and I smiled like a psycho while pulling her closer.

After a few minutes too many, Peyton shifted in my embrace, and I let her go. She wiggled her eyebrows. "So, show me more of this badass magic you got in them veins!"

Chapter Twenty-three

Sweat beaded on my forehead and poured down my neck and chest as I ran laps around the never-ending track that circled the baseball field of the academy. I have spent my fair share of life running, both in coven training and during shadower patrols, but I surprised even myself by how much stamina I still had left. This was my first gym class at school and to my relief, I was in decent enough shape to give the rest of these girls a run for their money. I had already run circles around Savannah, whose eyes shot daggers my way each time I passed her. Not far behind me, Peyton moaned and shouted obscenities as we sped by the TA who seemed to be more interested in his phone than making sure none of us passed out from exhaustion. He was older than me by only a few years, but the stubble on his pointed chin and the grease in his hair suggested those few years meant everything to him. This guy was the type of dude I avoided back in Stamwick and unfortunately, the kind that gravitated toward me like a bug to a net. The TA looked up from his phone as I jogged by and flashed me a sleazy grin.

Ew. Uh-uh. Keep your eyes to yourself!

I rolled my eyes before turning to run back to face Peyton. Her face was puffy and heavy breathing replaced her usually perky attitude. My smile widened and I gave her two thumbs up, which were reciprocated with yet another curse word, this one louder and directed straight at the TA.

A laugh escaped me, and I turned back, sprinting to the finish line.

My legs pumped faster than my speeding heartbeat as I jumped over the line and skidded to a stop. Wiping the sweat off my brow, I waited for Peyton to catch up, which took an unbearable amount of time. Pretty much everyone got there before my best friend.

By the time she made it, I had already cooled off and was downing my second bottle of water.

"Thanks for joining us," I teased when she approached.

Beside me, Peyton looked destroyed. She bent over her thighs and heaved so loud, it sounded more like growling. Her hand shot up when I opened my mouth to speak, and she took a few more deep breaths before peeling herself up to face me. "That was brutal. That guy is a total dick, by the way." She shot a side-eye in the TA's direction. "Yeah, I'm talking about you, Warner! Don't think I won't remember this!"

"Okay..." I wrapped an arm around my sweaty friend and pulled her away. "Let's kick it down a notch before he makes us do another lap."

"I'd like to see him try!" she shouted.

We'd only taken a couple of steps when someone's shoulder knocked against mine and I turned to see Savannah and her two hyenas, Abigail and Morgan, glaring at me. As always, Savannah's gym outfit looked more like something you'd see in a club than on the field and I didn't fail to notice that half her ass was hanging out of her high cut shorts.

"Watch where you're going, new kid!" she scoffed and turned away from me.

"Cool, cool, cool," I said, glowering at her exposed flesh. "Careful you don't miss the corner calling you when it's time for your shift."

"What did you just say to me?" Savannah flipped on her heels and marched toward me. Her curls bounced behind her back and I could see the lines on her forehead deepen when she approached. I shot her a death glare, but Savannah's useless expression made me quickly realize that the idiot wouldn't get my point if it fell on her face, slapped her raw, and shaved off her eyebrows.

Behind her, Morgan flipped her long red ponytail back and forth. "I think she just called you a hooker... Epic burn!"

Savannah hissed at her friends and the hyenas scurried away to join the rest of the class by the water coolers. "Watch yourself, new kid. River's not around to back you up over here."

Peyton chuckled. "Girl, if you think she needs backup, you're in for a rude awakening!"

My eyes narrowed at my friend, but I kept my mouth shut. Something I was hoping Peyton might do sooner rather than later.

"Run along to your little friends, Savannah. No one has time for your bullshit right now."

She opened her mouth to speak, but I turned away, smacking her in the face with my braid as I did. I reached for Peyton's hand and stormed off, racing to the bleachers that spanned around the field a few feet from us. When I was sure we put enough distance between us and the Queen of Hell, I let go of Peyton's hand and slowed down.

"Yo," my friend said, "not that I don't want that fool to know what's what, but we kind of have to get back to class."

She nodded in the direction of the other girls who had already started stretching for whatever torture Warner had in store for us next. My lips tightened into a line.

"You go ahead," I said, "I need to catch my breath for a minute."

"You're not letting her get to you, right?"

"Are you kidding?" I exclaimed. "That girl has no clue who she's dealing with."

Looking around to make sure we were alone, I dug into my shorts pocket and pulled out a small garnet cluster. My hand fisted around it, and I brought my other hand in front of her face. My best friend gasped at the compact ball of fire that danced along my skin. Peyton's eyes sparkled and she slapped her hands together in glee.

"That's my girl!" she yelped and turned to run back to the group.

I sucked in air until I couldn't breathe in anymore then blew it, willing the fire away. My skin felt hot to the touch, and I shook my hand in the light wind that blew over the field before stepping into the shade the back of the bleachers offered. The sun was beating down on us for the entire duration of the class and as soon as I rounded the tall rows of seats, I felt my body relax. I rested my head to lean back on the wooden planks of the bleachers and closed my eyes.

Something about telling Peyton the truth yesterday changed me. Maybe not as dramatically as I had hoped, but I felt lighter. Less in the shadows somehow, which was ironic since I was literally standing in darkness.

"Mind if I join?"

I jolted my head straight and turned just as the familiar smell of wood attacked my senses. Beside me, River stood looking as beautiful as ever. His hair was tousled in just the right way and his green eyes tore into me. The shadows the bleachers cast danced across his tanned skin and I found myself unable to look away. *Say something...* I growled at myself. *Say SOMETHING!*

My lips parted and I choked on my spit. "Hi, stranger."

Anything but that... Who even am I right now?

"Sorry to interrupt. I needed a break," he said and peeled his gaze off me.

"Me too," I agreed. "That TA sure is something."

"Who? Warner?" River ducked to peak through the seats. "He's not so bad. You get used to it."

"There seems to be a lot I have to get used to around here."

River looked at me through thick eyelashes and took a step forward. His long legs carried him to me until there were only inches between us. He leaned his elbow on the plank behind me and my toes curled. I could feel the heat rush from his body, finding all the right places on my skin.

"Hey," he said so quietly I had to lean in to hear, "I wanted to talk to you about what happened after the quarry."

Oh, Goddess, no. Okay, Billie, be smart. Say nothing, just keep your mouth shut.

"Did you now?" I purred.

Magnificent job.

"Yeah." He narrowed his eyes my way.

"Which part?"

Ew, what? Why are you still talking???

"The part where I kissed you and you told me to leave. Did I do something wrong? I mean, I know the whole witch hunter thing is a lot to take in, but it's not really a big deal."

Not a big deal? You must be joking! It's like the biggest deal ever!

I wanted to get out of there, STAT. But I also didn't. His body was just so damn close, and he smelled so good that I couldn't force myself to move. Instead, I shifted my weight and leaned in closer. "It's a little bit of a deal."

"Something you don't want in your life?" he asked.

Think, Billie! You can't say no because then he'll leave, and you'll kill your only chance of getting to the other hunters. My mind raced as I tried to think of something to say that would encourage but discourage him at the same time. This was an impossible situation and I felt like I was trying to solve a *Rubik's Cube* with missing pieces.

"I'm," I said, "I'm not sure yet. It's heavy."

"Take all the time you need. I can be patient." He brushed the braid over my shoulder and traced the side of my neck with his finger. "But not too patient. I really like you, Billie."

My entire body exploded. His fingers hovered over my skin, and I purposefully leaned into them until his hand cupped my neck. His body tensed and mine followed. As River pressed his hand to the back of my neck, I felt myself move toward him. My chest pressed against his and I rose on the tiptoes of my sneakers until my lips were perched just above his chin. River breathed out and my skin tingled as the warmth of him spread over me. My hands pressed to the wood plank, fingernails digging in to keep me steady. Every inch of my body wanted him, and I couldn't think of one good reason to pull away.

"Yo, B! We gotta go, it's— Oh! Oh, sorry! I... uh..." Peyton's wide eyes stared us down. "I can come back?"

"NO!" I yelled out and pushed myself away from River. "I mean, it's fine. We should go. We have that thing!"

"What thing?"

"A thing, just a thing. Right, Peyton?"

Peyton looked between me and River, nodding and shaking her head 'no' at the same time. "Right... our thing... A very important thing!"

My best friend snatched my hand and pulled me away from a very confused River. As soon as we were back on the field, I felt like myself again. My skin cooled off and I could form complete sentences.

"Dude! What was that?"

"I honestly don't know," I sighed. "He has some freaking pull on me I just can't shake."

"Told you." Peyton winked. "Star crossed lovers."

"Okay, enough. Let's just get out of here before I do something else I regret."

We beelined for the class and snuck in between a group of girls before Warner, TA douche, could notice us missing. I spent the rest of gym class trying to pay attention, but my mind would not let go of River. *As soon as I get home, I need to do a repelling spell to get that guy out of my orbit.* The problem was, I didn't think I wanted to, which only made my stomach turn more. The High Coven sure made a colossal mistake when they sent me to Shadowhurst. Bigger than I wager even they imagined.

Chapter Twenty-four

"Earth to Billie!" Peyton yelled out over her shoulder.

Rapidly blinking my eyes, I looked around to see she was a good ten steps away from me and looked as annoyed as ever. Her hair was tied into a miniature topknot with only her bangs covering her face and it did wonders to bring out the cross expression on her face. She tapped her purple Vans on the sidewalk and continued to glare at me, her arms out wide. "Did you hear anything I just said?"

I shook my head. "Sorry, I think I zoned out there."

That was the understatement of the century. I didn't just zone out, I spent the last ten minutes she was talking picturing River's biceps. What the hell was actually wrong with me? My heart tightened in my chest as I tried to remember what Peyton might have been going on about, but I drew a complete blank. All I could see was River and his frustratingly perfect chest. Somehow, I landed myself in the worst case scenario. Knee deep into a hunter.

"Ya think?" Peyton rolled her eyes and ran back to where

I was standing. Her legs sliced through the cool evening air like an ore through water. "I was saying, we should hit up those books River has and cross-reference them with the ones we got from the Crystal Cauldron."

"Oh, yeah," I agreed. "That's a good idea. You sure you don't think Ms. Broussard is in on it?"

"Not sure, maybe."

"So shouldn't we check her out more?"

Peyton smacked my shoulder and flashed her teeth. "Already one step ahead of you! I got her to invite me over this weekend. I'm going full undercover to see if I can find something in her house that'll give her away." She looked at me. "What?"

"Nothing," I sighed. "It's an excellent plan. It's just dangerous. I mean, if she is the killer, I don't think you should go alone."

"Well, I'm not taking you with me! You said it yourself, this witch is dangerous. And you will be in deep shit if she's on to you like you think she is."

"I guess..." I took a deep breath and straightened my shoulders. "But I can't let you risk yourself for this. It's not fair."

"Girl, calm your tits. I'll be fine."

"Peyton!" I snapped. "There's a witch on the loose that's draining the life from students. What makes you think she won't hesitate to do it to you?"

"Trust me, I'm not her type."

"What does that even m—"

My voice caught in my throat as an eery sense that we were no longer alone washed over me. My head jerked from side to side, scanning the small side street we were on, but I couldn't see anything around. Shadows crept over the houses that stood on the horizon, and I tried to pinpoint our exact location with relation to Peyton's house. I couldn't see it from where we stood but at the end of the street towered a massive church, which I remembered being just around the corner. We had to be close.

"We should move," I whispered, eyes still narrowed to the side. "I don't think we're alone here."

"What?" Peyton's eyes widened and she hooked her arm under my elbow to pull me toward the church. "We can cut through there, it's right next to my backyard.

Around us, the evening settled into shadows, and I could sense the hairs on my arms rise. Something wasn't right. We were being followed. We jogged down the small street and I could see the church grow as we approached it. The stained glass windows stared back at me and the large mahogany doors formed a large open mouth.

Just then, footsteps echoed behind me, matching the pace of our own. My mouth opened to match the church and I stopped in my tracks, yanking Peyton back with me. The steps behind me skidded to a stop.

"Don't... move..." I instructed through clench teeth.

Peyton nodded and I saw her face pale. My best friend was already as ashen as snow, but standing here in a dark, empty street with my threats in the air, she looked like a Peyton-sized statue.

I dropped her arm and kicked my boot up to snatch the dagger from its core before looping around to turn back. My breaths hung heavy, and I could see it linger in the frosty air before disappearing. I curled my fingers around the dagger, not worrying about showing it off to the stranger I faced. It was a man in his late twenties with long blonde hair and the rigid body of an athlete. He wore a knee-length overcoat and his eyes glowed in the threatening darkness, lavender orbs pointed straight at me.

"Witch," he hissed and curled his lip to reveal a row of teeth sharpened into points. "And you..."

His bright eyes trained on Peyton's back and I could see my friend grow rigid at his words. I peeled my gaze from him to stare at Peyton, but she didn't acknowledge my presence. Her eyes were locked on the church doors just steps ahead. I could smell her fear like it was my own.

"What do you want, mind reaper?" I shouted and felt Peyton's shoulders rise next to me.

"You," he growled, and I rolled my eyes. *Why do the shadowers always have to make everything so extra?!?*

"Well, you got me. Now, run along before we have a problem."

I had no intention of fighting a mind reaper right now. Not with us this out in the open and Peyton here. The last thing I wanted was to put my friend in danger. Unfortunately, the mind reaper made my mind up for me.

Before I could blink, he lunged for me, his hands outstretched to grab hold of mine.

My training kicked in and I shoved Peyton out of the way to send her tumbling off the sidewalk and unto the grassy area behind us. She scrambled on the ground, pushing herself back and dragging her ass across the grass, her eyes locked on the man. There was something different in her expression that I couldn't place. Something akin to recognition. I shook my head and turned back to the mind reaper that stood inches away from me.

He moved fast, his fingers reaching for me until he was so close to my neck, I could taste his breath in the air. Without hesitation, I dropped to the ground and spun sideways, slicing my dagger at his shins. The blade cut through the thin fabric of his slacks and the smell of iron filled the air. The mind reaper cursed and jumped back, his eyes jolting from me to the cut on his leg.

"I will have you," he whispered, and my heart leaped in my throat.

He jumped and though I tried to swerve out of the way, I was too late. The mind reaper pummeled me to the ground, and I could feel the cement of the sidewalk tear at the exposed flesh of my forearms. I cringed, biting my bottom lip to keep from screaming.

"BILLIE!" Peyton shouted behind us and got up.

"Stay back!" I warned her and dug into my jeans pocket for the hand held mirror I had stashed there. "I got this!"

The reaper went for my throat, but before he could make contact, I flipped the mirror and pointed it to the moon. The light reflected off the surface and I titled the mirror toward the reaper's eyes. He yelped, shutting his lids and freeing me of his evil glare. I kicked his stomach, sending him flying backward, and jumped to stand. My eyes met Peyton's for a moment before I tightened my grip on the dagger's hilt and rushed for him.

Close to me, Peyton's cries echoed, but they didn't reach me. Everything around me grew still until all I could hear was my heavy panting. My legs pushed off the sidewalk and I leaped in the air, landing with one foot on the ground and one on the reaper's chest. His breath burst from his lips, and he coughed as my boot kicked him again. I lowered my knee to his cheek and pressed it down to hold him in place as I pushed the dagger into his heart. The sound of ribs breaking screeched in my eardrum and I dropped the mirror on the ground to pull out the amber crystal I had stashed in my jacket. After the first shadower attack, I didn't leave the house without it.

Fire burst from my fingers as I slammed the crystal to the reaper's forehead. I could feel him writhe under my hold as he squirmed to get away. His arms jerked and he kicked his legs back but between my dagger in his chest and the crystal ripping his mind apart, I had him trapped. I stood up, forcing my magic into the crystal as I let go. With a swoop motion, I lifted my boot and smashed it into the dagger's hilt to drive the blade deeper into the reaper's heart.

Behind me, Peyton gasped.

The reaper let out an agonizing scream as flames burst from his body, burning him into oblivion. My eyes widened and I watched the man's skin turn to ash and his lavender eyes become vacant. He let out a last breath and I pulled the amethyst pendant off my chest and threw my magic outward. A gust of wind engulfed the reaper, twirling like a small tornado and dispersing his ashes around me. My hair whipped over my face, and I closed my eyes, breathing to pull the magic back.

The wind settled and when I looked down, the reaper was gone, and my dagger and crystal lay on the cement.

It was done.

"What...in... the... actual... Hell?" Peyton breathed heavily behind me.

I turned to my friend and ran to scoop her into a hug. My arms tightened around her shoulders as I squeezed the living daylights out of her. "Are you okay?"

"What the hell was that?"

"Mind reaper," I whispered.

Peyton pushed away from me and walked to the empty

spot where the reaper just lay seconds ago. "Okay, you really need to fill me on this crap," she said, her face still ashen.

"I will. Let's just get to your place now. Hey, why did that guy look at you like you've met before?"

Peyton shrugged and arched her eyebrows. "I've seen nothing like *that* before. Let's get home, I'm freaking out over here."

I nodded and intertwined her fingers in mine. We walked the rest of the way in silence, zigging and zagging through the church's grounds as I let Peyton led the way to her backyard. My lungs burnt and my hair was a matted mess of sweat and knots. When we got to a large fence that encased the yard, I stood back while my friend fumbled with the lock to let us through. My gaze watched her as she cursed before finally getting the back gate to open. Even with the shadower gone and both of us safe, I couldn't get my heart to stop racing. That mind reaper knew Peyton somehow, I was sure of it. But why? What did my best friend have to do with the lavender eyed monster I just vanquished? More importantly, why was she pretending like it didn't happen?

Chapter Twenty-five

There is no way Peyton could be involved in the weirdness happening in Shadowhurst. No freaking way!

I recited the thought like a mantra as I walked through the halls of the academy the next morning. With everything going on, it was becoming harder and harder for me to concentrate on the classes. How was I supposed to think about velocity equations right now? I wanted to skip the day and take time to dig into my lead on the fae families, but I knew that wasn't an option. Missing class meant word would get back to the Chandlers, who would no doubt contact my fake caseworkers and I did NOT want the High Coven to butt in. At least not until I can figure out why that mind reaper knew Peyton and if she was involved in these murders.

My body vibrated from thinking about it. Could my best friend—my only friend—be a part of this somehow? Could she be the witch I'm looking for?

I didn't sense magic off Peyton in the entire time I've known her, but this witch was more powerful than I gave her credit for. If she could block herself from being scried, she probably had no trouble blocking her magic from me. But could Peyton be this evil and cruel as to kill all those students? I couldn't picture it. Then again, I couldn't picture River being a witch hunter, and yet, here we were.

That's it! As soon as school's over, I'm going straight for the books. I didn't care if that meant spending time with River, all I wanted was to find out who the next target was so I could catch the witch in action. *What if it's Peyton?* My head wanted to explode and my mouth dried. What would I do if my plan worked, and it *was* Peyton who showed up for the kill? Could I surrender my best friend to the High Coven?

"Focus, moron," I cursed myself.

A student from one of the junior classes locked her gaze on mine and I smiled before mouthing "sorry" and scurrying off. I was starting to lose it here.

I ducked past a group of students huddled outside the music room and turned the corner. I had taken the long way to second period, knowing Peyton was likely late as usual so I had no chance of running into her. I felt bad avoiding her and not responding to the gazillion texts she sent me this morning, but I really did not know how to face her right now. Something about the shadower interaction I witnessed wasn't right and I couldn't talk to my friend until I had some answers.

Putting some weight into my steps, I zoomed by an open classroom door when a hand reached out to tug me inside. My breath hitched and I pushed whoever grabbed me, following with a swift punch.

"OUCH!" River yelled, rubbing his elbow. "Morning to you too."

"Oh my God, River!" I gasped and brought my hands to my mouth. My eyes landed on his and I licked my lips before crossing my arms over my chest. "What's with the assault?"

"I called your name like three times." He shook his head. "Had to get your attention somehow."

"It couldn't wait till after class?" I snapped.

River stepped to the side, and I gasped when I saw we weren't alone in the room.

"Told you I'd let you meet the other hunters."

The air thickened around me, and I had to dig my heels into the floor as my gaze rippled over the other people in the classroom. Directly behind River, at a table, sat Tyler with Abigail perched like a spider monkey in his lap. Abigail's mini-dress was bunched up so high, I could see where her legs started and her hands were dug into the front of his button-up. Neither of them bothered to look my direction. Next to them, Morgan and Jayden argued over something I couldn't hear. As always, Jayden sported his academy varsity jacket and Morgan had on yet another version of the floral tanks she seemed to be obsessed with. She glanced up at me and winked before returning to the argument. With difficulty, I tried to force a smile, but my face froze when I turned my head to the last person in the room.

Sitting cross-legged on a classroom table in leather leggings and a crop top was Savannah. Her eyes pierced into me, and a snarl formed on her lips as our eyes met. She shook her curls and leaned back on her hands like she was trying to make herself look less intimidating. It did not work. At all.

I swallowed and turned back to River. "So, these are the hunters?"

"Yep!" he announced. "Well, most of them."

"Who's missing?"

River cleared his throat and his eyes darkened into a deeper shade of emerald I've seen.

"Grady," he said before facing me again. "Welcome to the team."

Morgan smiled and Jayden gave me a thumbs up. Abigail still refused to look at me, but I noticed Tyler glance over her exposed shoulder and grin. To my left, Savannah murmured something nasty under her breath.

I wasn't surprised to find out River's closest friends were the hunters. Of course, they were. It made sense now why someone as nice as him would hang out with the hyenas.

"Um," I choked out. "Hello. Again."

"This is a mistake, River," Savannah snapped.

"Cool your jets, girl," Jayden said. "If River says she's cool and can help, then it's totes fine with the rest of us."

River turned to his friend and nodded. "Thanks."

"I got you, bruh."

Morgan turned to face me, and it surprised me to see a smile on her face. "So, Billie. Why don't you fill us in on what you dug up so far?"

Before I could answer, Savannah hopped off the table and made her way toward me. Her eyes darted between me and River and when I followed her gaze, I realized that I had been holding his hand the entire time I was in the classroom. My cheeks flushed and I unwound my fingers from his just as she approached.

"I don't trust her," Savannah hissed. "She's not one of us. You should have checked in before you went blabbing all our secrets to the new kid."

"She has a name," River said. "And the others don't seem to have a problem with it."

The queen snapped her neck to look at her friends, who all looked away in unison to get back to what they were doing before. "This is some serious bullshit, you all know that, right?"

I stepped closer to face her. "Hey! I'm here to help. So, deal with it."

She was in my face in seconds. The curls of her hair brushed against my cheek, and I uncurled my spine to meet her eye to eye. Savannah's face was grim, a shield of rage and hatred. She pointed a finger at my chest, her arm shaking. "You," she growled, "don't belong here."

Without thinking, I slapped her hand away.

"Get off your high horse, princess. You're not the boss of anyone here."

Behind us, Jayden whistled. "Whoa! I like her!"

"This won't end well, River," Savannah said but kept her arms at her side this time. Her eyes jerked back to me, and she sneered. "He's waaaaaay out of your league."

Heat filled me from head to toe and my vision blurred. If I thought I was fed up with Savannah and her holier-the-thou attitude before, I was definitely over it now. My teeth ground against each other and my jaw tightened as I fisted my hands at my side. On my finger, the moonstone ring felt cold against my burning skin as my magic rushed to the surface. I could feel its power and energy flow through me, begging me to act. Shaking, I brought my hand to the amethyst at my neck and pulled on its element. Energy soared from the crystal, shattering my bones into pieces. If I acted quickly, I could make this girl drown right in the classroom.

My lids fluttered and I tried to push the magic away, but it was too strong and too wild now. My entire body shook with its hold on me, and I had to bite the inside of my cheek to keep myself from lashing out. *Why am I trying to control this? She's a hunter, they all are. I should hurt them. I should kill them right here and now.*

Beside me, River moved to stand between us, and the smell of wood and earth surrounded me. My eyes blinked as I tried to focus on his face and not on Savannah's spiteful insults. She was yapping so fast, I couldn't make out the words, but I knew that everything she was saying should hurt me somehow. River grabbed my hand, yanking it away from the crystal and looked at me through those beautiful, thick lashes of his. My breath quivered and I found myself limp in his grasp, unable to follow through with what my magic wanted me to do. His thumb drew circles over my palm, and I counted them as I took deep breaths to calm down.

"You're not here for her," he whispered. "You're here for those students."

Sixteen circles.

My heartbeat slowed and I swallowed his words like they were a life-raft, clinging to every syllable to keep from going under. He was right. I had to calm down and follow through. I needed the hunters to understand all this. *Follow the blood.* Sebyl's words flashed in my mind, and I buried the heels of my boots into the floor. I had to follow the blood. Grady's blood, Lacey and Ariana's blood. Fae blood.

I peaked over River's shoulder to scan the hunters. Now I got why they were so dead set on finding the killer witch. She took their friend from them. I almost felt sorry for the group until Savannah rolled her eyes and groaned. Infiltrate the hunters, use them to lead you to the witch, then call in the High Coven to deal with them. The plan wouldn't change no matter how many damn circles River drew into my palm. *Twenty-seven.* I ripped my hand away from him and stepped around his wide shoulders to face the hunters.

"So," I said and half-smiled. "Who's ready to help me catch a witch?"

Chapter Twenty-six

"Yo, B! Wait up!" Peyton yelled out as I marched down the path leading to the bike locks.

I cringed at the tone of her voice before turning around. My eyes narrowed, but I slapped a smile on my face to not give myself away. I still had no clue if I should trust her, but as instantly as I turned to my friend, I was filled with worry instead. Peyton's hair was a hot mess, and her eyes were puffy like she'd been crying all night. I furrowed my brow and waited for her to catch up.

"Crazy busy day." I shrugged. "You okay?"

Peyton spat out the string of hair she was chewing on. "Yeah, yeah. Couldn't sleep last night. I found something. A name."

"Huh?"

"Girl, catch up! I found another name! Like the..." She lowered her voice. "Fae."

Oh. OH!

"Holy crap, for real?" I asked, my fake smile warping into a genuine one.

"Sure is! After you left, I spent all night searching the web for original families that could have married outside of Shadowhurst."

"Why?"

Peyton shook her head and rolled her eyes. "Because of this petty thing called vows and how women fall for that stereotypical bullshit of giving up their entire identity to take on the man's name?" My friend's face looked disgusted as though the thought of changing her name made her want to tear her eyes out. "Anyway, there was a ton to go through, but I was able to track one of the last names from the book Ms. Broussard gave us to a family living at the edge of town."

She paused and I bit a loose cuticle from my thumb. "WHO?" I half-shouted.

"Drumroll, please..." Peyton made an air drum motion with her imaginary sticks. "The Claytons!"

"Who the heck are the Claytons?"

"No one important. Man, that came out wrong. I meant no one we run with."

"Run with? Who *are* you right now?" I laughed.

Peyton shook off her shoulders and beamed a smile my way. "Sorry, I had like twenty capps this morning so I'm totally vibing. The Claytons live about fifteen, twenty minutes from River. Normal peeps and they have two kids."

"So, two kids could be in danger?"

"Not exactly," she said. "Jillian is away in college, but Clay is a student here in Shadowhurst. First year."

"I'm sorry, his name is Clay Clayton?"

My friend's grin widened, and she chuckled under her breath. "Yep. You can't make this shit up."

A group of girls pushed their way past us, and we backed up to the grassy knoll to give them a wide berth.

Peyton shrugged and rubbed the back of her neck with her hand, the loose lace fabric of her seventies-inspired rocker shirt rolling up to reveal a bluish bruise. The closer I looked, the more I realized it looked like a hand-print. Like someone had grabbed her too hard and didn't let go.

"Peyton! What happened?" I shrieked and pointed to the bruise.

Without meeting my eyes, Peyton lowered her sleeve and brushed it down. "I'm an idiot is what happened," she answered, still refusing to look at me. "Walked into my dresser last night."

Her eyes shifted from side to side and a knot formed in my stomach. She was lying.

"Um, 'kay..." I whispered.

I had no clue why my best friend had to lie about a bruise. If someone hurt her, I'd be the first one she should be telling. The idea of someone hurting Peyton made my blood boil and I imagined myself letting my power loose on whoever it was and returning the favor. *Which is why she didn't tell me, right? RIGHT?* I couldn't tell. Whatever reasons Peyton had for lying, she clearly thought it was best I didn't know. Maybe she was trying not to worry me or maybe—

My head pounded and I had to suck in a sharp breath. Maybe whoever hurt her was someone she knew and was trying to protect.

I was yet to meet Peyton's parents but just thinking that one of them could have done this made me sick. Peyton had always spoken so highly of them, her father especially, but what if that was just a coverup?

"You sure you're okay?" I asked again.

"Yeah, girl. Totally cool. Nothing to worry about." She smiled, but it didn't reach her eyes. "So?"

"So what?"

"What do you think about Clay?"

I peeled my gaze off her arm and forced myself to face her. "Oh, right. Yeah, good catch! I'll tell River and the others."

"Sorry, what?"

Peyton's face scrunched and I remembered I haven't talked to her all day, so she didn't know that I met the other hunters or that I was on my way to River's house right now. "I met the other witch hunters," I admitted.

"SHUT UP!" My best friend slapped my shoulder, her eyes wider than oceans. "Tell me everything!"

"I will," I said and turned to walk away. "I promise I will, but not right now. I have to go meet them and I don't want to be late."

Before I could rush off, Peyton grabbed my hand and placed something inside. It filled her eyes with worry, and she looked everywhere but at me. When she pulled her hand away, I saw a braided, pink bracelet resting in my palm.

"I made you this. It's like a friendship bracelet or whatever."

My heart exploded as I ran my finger over the pink threads. It wasn't anything special and not as expensive as the jewelry most of the other girls wore around school but to me, it was perfect. I've never had an actual friend before and definitely not one that made me a friendship bracelet. "I love it," I said and tied the strings into a knot around my wrist. "It's beautiful."

"Girl, you a savage!" Peyton laughed. "It's literally string. Don't act like you've never seen string before."

My eyes watered and guilt enveloped me in its agonizing cocoon. This was the same girl I had doubted and despite the sweet gesture she just made, I knew I couldn't fall for it. Not yet, at least.

"Thanks, really," I said. "But I'm super late. I'll call you later, 'kay?"

Without looking back at her, I bolted for my ride. There was still so much about Peyton I didn't know, and I couldn't risk telling her anything I might regret spilling later. My friend was keeping something from me and until I found out what it was, I had to keep her at an arm's length. My feet hit the pedals and I zoomed out of the parking to River's house. The wind hit my face and sent chills down my spine as I rolled down the streets of Shadowhurst to my first witch hunter meeting. Never in my life did I imagine this would be where I ended up but somehow, it felt like where I belonged.

Cars lined the curved driveway in front of River's house by the time I pulled my bike in. I tossed it to the side of the house, not bothering to lock the chain, and sprinted for the front door. As I reached my hand to ring the doorbell, the familiar pull of the garden rocked me gently. Under my skin, my magic blossomed, and I stood still for a good few minutes before shaking it off.

The doorbell echoed through the house, and I stepped back from the porch, shielding my eyes from the sun to see inside the attic windows.

"You made it!" River said from the doorway.

I jerked my eyes to him and cleared my throat. "Yeah. Looks like I'm late."

River looked around the driveway and smiled. His green eyes twinkled, and his full lips curved into a half-smile. My body roiled with excitement, and I took a few brave steps to close the distance between us. *I could seriously jump his bones right here on the porch.*

Ew! WHAT? Why are you like this?

"Everyone's already in the kitchen. Come on."

He tugged at the sleeve of my flannel shirt, and I followed him inside. We walked past the pictures in the hallway and my eyes latched onto the one of him in a bathtub. Choking down a laugh, I sped up to catch up.

River led me through the living room, which looked as cozy as ever with the plush sectional positioned in front of a massive stone fireplace in the center of the room. The mantle was full of more picture frames, and I didn't fail to notice the few crystals carefully arranged around them. My magic reached for their elements, and I had to shake my fingers to keep it in check. Thank the Goddess, the crystals were too small to make a dent and those damn lights stayed hidden so I could keep my balance. Behind the sofa stretched a wall-sized bay window with a variety of planters full of every kind of flower I could imagine. It looked like River's mother liked the garden so much, she brought it indoors. My smile widened and I turned back to River, my face colliding with his back. I was so in awe of the living room I didn't notice that he stopped in his tracks.

In front of me, River cleared his throat and chuckled before stepping aside.

"Told you she'd make it," he said to the rest of the group.

I looked around the triumphant island that sat in the focus of a French-inspired kitchen and counted off the hunters in the room. They were all there, including Savannah, who sat with her arms crossed at the far end of the island. She tapped her long, light blue nails on the quartz countertop and scowled.

"Lovely," she breathed out. "Can we start now?"

Morgan and Tyler's eyes snapped my way and I breathed in deep before shaking off Savannah's annoying attitude to join everyone in the kitchen.

"So, what do we do?" I asked, genuinely interested. I had no reference to witch hunters and was eager to get as much information on their dealings as I could.

"We follow leads," River answered.

My shoulders dropped. "That's it? We sit around and go through notes?" I looked over the stacks of file folders and books spread out on the table. "Isn't there like training or something?"

Everyone laughed. Everyone except Savannah, of course.

"I don't think you're ready for our training yet." Morgan smiled. "Think of this as initiation. If we like what you offer, we might let you play."

The way she said the last word made me shiver. I could only imagine what kind of playing they'd be up for if they found out who I was. Probably something involving a lot of blood and torture. "Training?" I asked, raising an eyebrow.

"Yeah, dude," Morgan said. "You don't think we just sit around reading all day, do you?"

I kinda did, but kept my mouth shut.

"So, bring us something good and you can come to the farm."

The way she said it made me think of some old mafia movie and I suddenly had an image of being buried in cement at said farm. "What farm?"

"Savannah's place. It's perfect for training! Right?"

Morgan looked to her friend but got nothing but an icy glare in return. "It's all right. I guess."

"Stop underselling it," Abigail piped in. "Your place is bomb! Plus, your parents never being around is perfection. Too bad their wine cellar is locked down like a freaking vault or I'd never leave!"

Beside her, Savannah's smile dropped, and she folded her hands into her lap. Something about what Abigail said snagged a cord and her body grew as rigid as stone. "Whatever. It's a house on a farm, no big deal." Her eyes found mine. "You said you had something?"

"Oh, right," I said, cluing into the topic change a little too slow. "I found something that can help. Or my friend Peyton did."

"Oh, God," Savannah growled, "now she's bringing more people into this."

Beside her, Abigail looked up from the notebook she was doodling in and met my gaze. "Actually," she said, oblivious to her friend's glare next to her, "I want to hear this."

I shot a smile her way and let my jaw relax. This might not go so badly after all. Abigail has not spoken a word to me since the first day we met, so for her to be interested in anything I have to say was a monumental step in the right direction. I might get these jerks on my side sooner rather than later. Sure, Savannah would always be a problem, but she could be the High Coven's problem as far as I was concerned.

"We think we know who the next target is. Clay Clayton?"

"Clay? Really?" River asked.

"*That* guy?" Jayden added.

I nodded. "Turns out he could be one of the fae families we found before."

"I still can't believe this town has fae ancestry," Abigail said.

"Girl, be more worried about the fact that fae exist," Morgan exclaimed. "'Cause that's the part that's blowing *my* mind!"

She brought her hands to her flaming red hair and made a bomb motion before grinning from ear to ear. I liked this girl. Something about her was fun and easy and I could see her and Peyton getting along.

My fingers twirled the loose strings of the friendship bracelet on my wrist.

As soon as I thought of Peyton, my mouth dried, and my vision blurred. I couldn't shake the feeling that something was wrong with my best friend, and I wished I could help her. More than that, I wished she'd be honest with me and tell me what was going on. Why would she tell me about Clay if she was the witch? It made little sense. Unless it was a trap, and she was trying to steer me away from her next kill. My stomach turned and I was very aware of how hot it was in the kitchen. Sweat poured down the curve of my lower back and I had to pry my shirt away from my skin to cool off.

"I'll be right back," I said and backed up into the living room. "I left something in my bike basket."

Turning to leave, I heard Savannah make a crack about my ride, and River snap at her to stay quiet. Her words never reached me, and I was on the front porch before I knew it. The air outside wrapped itself around me and I breathed it in, letting the elements of the garden's florals invade my senses. My eyes opened and closed as I counted to ten while forcing any thoughts of Peyton being the killer from my mind. At my chest, the amethyst cooled and sent calming vibrations into my heart.

Something moved in my peripheral and I snapped my head in its direction.

I was met with nothing but trees and bushes, but I could tell that I wasn't alone. There was someone else here and whoever it was, they had magic. I could feel their energy in the surrounding elements. It was faint, but it was definitely there. I stepped down from the porch and followed the tingle that grew over my skin. Each shaky step I took made me want to turn around and run back. This was dark magic I could feel, so dark I couldn't breathe.

"You coming back?" River yelled out and I jumped at the sound of his voice.

My neck turned from him to face the scuffle I heard but I still couldn't see anything. What was worse, River's presence seemed to have scared off whoever was there, and I could no longer sense their magic in the air. I looked around once more to make sure before running back to the porch and into the house.

All of a sudden, being locked in a room full of witch hunters wasn't the worst thing I could imagine.

Chapter Twenty-seven

Meeting the hunters was surprisingly useful. Tyler's dad was a police officer and got him copies of all the case files on the dead students without so much as a hassle. I started to understand that most of the hunter's parents were just like River's mom, pushing their kids into the role mercilessly. As Abigail and Tyler counted off the possible magical items in the crime scenes while the other hunters took notes, I let myself drift off. The group I was smack dab in the middle of seemed like regular kids. They joked and teased each other, and I often found myself laughing along without having to force it. I wondered how much fear someone had to have to push their children into something as dangerous as witch hunting and hated the hunters' parents for putting that pressure on them. Then again, it likely never crossed Beatrix's mind the dangers she was putting *me* in when she first started training me as a witch. And the High Coven only quadrupled that danger when they put me on patrol.

Perhaps the hunters' parents were not so different from everyone else in my life. We were all just scared in the end.

After a few hours of explaining to everyone what I knew about ritualistic magic such as the one at the crime scenes, all under the guise of an overactive imagination, we could put together a plan. We decided it was best not to warn Clay since he had no clue of the danger he was in. Instead, each hunter and I would take turns keeping a close eye on him. We paired off into groups of two and I tried to hide my excitement from ending up with River. Without surprise, Savannah complained the entire time, but finally let it go, stating she didn't need a partner and wasn't a scared little wussy like the rest of us. Her words, verbatim.

Out of all the hunters, I found Jayden to be the easiest to be around. He didn't give off the same privileged attitude as the rest and it surprised me to find out that talking to him did not leave a nasty taste in my mouth. The entire time we were in River's kitchen, Jayden must have made me laugh at least a dozen times and I had to accept that I was enjoying his company.

He had just finished telling some dumb joke about a rabbi and a priest that sent me into a whirlwind of laughter when River pushed his way between us. His eyes were darker than usual, and I could see his nostrils flaring when he stared Jayden down. *Wait, is he jealous?*

My stomach flipped and my cheeks flushed at the thought.

"It's getting late, y'all," Abigail announced and collected her sparkly pink notebooks off the counter. "I don't know about the rest of you, but I have plans for this one tonight."

She brushed a finger over Tyler's lips, and he grunted in approval. I was getting the impression that since Tyler was the quiet, brooding type, Abigail took full advantage. There was no question in anyone's mind about who wore the pants in that relationship. Or in Abigail's case, the barely-there mini skirt.

Her finger traced down his chin and around his chest and Tyler growled and kicked his leg like an excited puppy. Most of the hunters groaned and rolled their eyes. Jayden made a barfing motion with his finger before turning to wink at me.

"Get a room!" he shouted. "Ain't no one here that needs to see your foreplay right now! Gross!"

My eyes watered and I let out a loud belly laugh that soon spread around the kitchen island. Tyler blushed but Abigail seemed oblivious to the other people in the room and fondled his pecs some more. *This girl is something else!*

I was still smiling like a tool when River leaned on the counter next to me. "Mind sticking around for a bit?" he whispered.

"Uh, suuuuurrrreeeee..." I said in more of a question than a statement.

"We're first to watch Clay tomorrow so I want to make sure we have our ducks in a row."

"Bruh! Who talks like that?" Jayden chuckled before fist bumping River and heading out. "Watch out for this one, B!"

As the rest of the hunters cleared out of the kitchen, I could feel Savannah's glare on me. Though this time, instead of brushing her off like I normally would have, I inched myself closer to River. I arched my back and leaned into him before aiming a smile and a wave her way. Behind us, Savannah cursed under her breath and stomped out, slamming the front door behind her.

"That was vicious," River noted.

"Ha! Just a little revenge for how she's been treating Peyton and me."

I winked and backed away to put some distance between us and missed the warmth of his skin immediately. River's eyes clouded with confusion, but it only took him a second to rebound and he was back to his usual, calm self.

"So, how do you feel after your first hunter meeting?" he asked.

I thought about his question. How *did* I feel? I wasn't sure anymore. I expected to have spent the evening trying not to reach for my dagger and slice their throats, but it turned out not to be as bad as I imagined. In fact, I even enjoyed myself a little.

"It wasn't bad," I answered truthfully.

"I knew it!" River exclaimed. "I knew you'd like being a hunter!"

A bout of nausea engulfed me, and I tried not to throw up on his lap. Did he seriously just call me a hunter? What a joke! If he only knew the truth, he wouldn't be making those wild accusations. But...

"So, I'm a hunter now, am I?" I asked.

River smiled and reached over to brush a hair off my forehead. "Through and through, Goldilocks."

"Oh, ew, no. Uh-uh!" I shook my head. "We are not doing nicknames!"

"We are now, Goldilocks!"

I slapped his chest and laughed into my hands. "You'll regret this," I hissed.

"Already kinda do." He snickered and then his eyes darkened again. "Hey, can I ask you something? You ever feel, I don't know, out of place or something?"

You have no idea, hunter! "I guess. Why?"

"I don't know. Just that sometimes I get this feeling that I'm different somehow. And not because of the whole witch hunter thing."

"And you think I feel that too?" I asked, arching an eyebrow. "Why?"

"Not sure. Something about you is different. I can't explain it, but you're not like the other girls I know."

"Well, the other girls you know are tools, so that would explain it."

River smiled, but something in his eyes told me to worry.

"What's wrong?"

He rubbed the back of his neck and looked up at me through dark lashes. "Sometimes, when I'm by myself, I get this weird feeling. Like I'm different. Dark."

"You feel dark?" I tried to make his revelation sound like a ridiculous notion, but I understood what he was saying. I felt that darkness myself from time to time, more so after a particularly gruesome vanquishing. Perhaps River was reacting to his own life in the same way I reacted to mine. Like it was a duty more than a choice. I thought back to the times our skin touched, and the dark energy escaped him, and it all made sense. Somehow, I could feel his emotions as though they were a tactile thing. It was super weird and totally freaking me out.

"You're right, it's stupid," he said and lowered his gaze. "Forget I said anything."

The sadness in his voice broke my heart and I reached for his hands. I wrapped my fingers over his fists, barely covering them. River's eyes met mine and I breathed out, placing a palm across his chest. "It's not stupid," I whispered. "And I feel it too sometimes."

His heart raced under my palm, and I pressed down,

wishing I could use my magic to calm him. But for some reason, I wouldn't allow myself to do it. I wanted his emotions to flow through me. I wanted every wild thought he had, and I wanted to swallow them whole. I wanted it to be *me*—not magic—that relaxed him.

I took a deep breath and locked my eyes on his.

Everything happened so fast. Before I knew it, River's hands were free of mine and he cupped my face with one while pulling me in with the other. His lips crashed to mine and I moaned against him. The sound River made in response made my knees shiver and I raised myself from the slender stool I was on to hop on his lap. His back hit the counter and he winced, but his arm wrapped around my waist to pull me closer. Closer. Closer. My legs hooked around his waist until I was straddling him like a show pony. His tongue pushed my lips open and my breath quickened. Every part of my magic screamed in my head, and I tried to keep it locked away when our tongues touched. River pulled on my hair to tilt my head back and deepen our kiss. I nipped at his bottom lip and River growled against my lips. His woodsy scent invaded my scenes and I moaned again before nibbling some more on his lips.

This was Heaven. This moment right here was everything I've ever wanted. This—

"River Hunting! What the hell is going on here?"

My back froze and I jumped off River's lap to find his mother standing in the kitchen doorway. Her mouth was wide open, and I could see the anger roll off her as she crossed and re-crossed her arms. My face was on fire, and I tried to straighten the knotted mess that my hair had become with little success.

"Mrs. Hunting!"

"Mom!"

In front of us, Evanora shot daggers with her eyes and each one pierced my flesh with their bite. "Explain to me what I'm looking at, please."

"Mom, it's fine," River said as calmly as he could manage but I could hear his breathing was still heavy from our out-of-this-world make out sesh. "We were just—"

"I don't need the details, River!" Evanora snapped. "I'll show you out, Miss Stonewall."

Her voice was ice cold and it sent goosebumps down my arms, but I followed her to the front door, flashing an embarrassed smile at River before ducking out of the kitchen. When we reached the doorway, I laced my boots and dared to sneak a peek at Evanora. Her hazel eyes narrowed, and creases ran up and down her forehead.

"I'm sorry, Mrs. Hunting. We shouldn't have been doing that in your kitchen."

Evanora's lips crashed into a line as she stared me down. "You shouldn't have been doing that at all."

"Excuse me?"

"Billie, dear," she growled. "I will make this very clear, so I need you to pay close attention. My son is many things but unkind is not one of them. He has a big heart—something he gets from his father—and often, it steers him wrong."

"I don't understand," I whispered.

"River has a future and a bright future at that. I have worked very hard to make certain that my son is on a specific path that will allow him to achieve that future. Girls like you are simply not part of the equation."

"Girls like me?"

"Yes, Billie. I mean no disrespect, but I believe we want what's best for River. Am I correct in thinking that?"

I nodded again because my damn mouth forgot what it was there for.

"Very good. And what's best for him is to be with someone more in tune with our ways, someone more in his league. Someone like..."

She didn't have to finish her sentence, I knew what was coming next. "Savannah Michaels."

"Perhaps, yes," Evanora agreed. "I'm glad we understand each other. You can, of course, stay friends, but I would appreciate it if you did not get yourself involved with my son. I would hate for him to have his feelings crushed when this," she waved her hand over me, "little tryst did not work out."

With that, she gave me a wave good bye and closed the door in my face.

Frigid air slammed into my face, and I hugged my arms closer to my body to keep from shaking. My senses dulled and big, sticky tears burned the back of my lids. I blinked and they rushed down my cheeks, drawing dark lines of melted eyeliner over my face. I was hollow and afraid and not even the magic I pulled from Evanora's stunning garden could make me whole again.

My heart was completely and utterly shattered.

Chapter
Twenty-eight

The energy of Main Street on this warm fall afternoon, completely opposed my own. After a million attempts, I managed to convince Imala to drop me off instead of joining in for a shopping spree. There were many things I wanted to do with my free afternoon and going shopping was not one of them. I could tell she was disappointed and promised to make it up to her by letting her take me out for a girl's brunch tomorrow. It was surreal to deal with affection from the adults around me, but I refused to let Beatrix's actions jade me. If Imala wanted to play mom, I was sure as hell going to let her. Just not today.

Today, I needed space.

"You sure you don't want me to come with?" Imala's soft voice filled the car. I swear, sometimes the woman sounded like she was auditioning for a Snow White remake and I expected birds to fly through the window and perch on her shoulder.

"I'm sure," I answered. "But I promise, tomorrow, it's you and me!"

Imala widened her smile and unbuckled her seatbelt to reach over. Her arms wrapped around me and before I could hold myself back, I inched closer to her. She smelled like coffee and Coco Noir, and I inhaled her with a sharp breath. I slouched and my lips curled into a childish grin as we parted. *Is this what having a mom feels like? Super weird.*

I stared at her like a weirdo for a few minutes then unbuckled my seatbelt.

Voices invaded my senses as soon as I hopped out of Imala's Porsche and waved good bye. The street was full of Shadowhurst residents and tourists alike, all bumping into each other as they chattered away about whatever items they could snatch up in the stores. Unlike the other times I've visited, Main Street was an exploding ball of energy and I tried to stick close to the shadows falling from the canopied roofs as I made my way through.

A group of students gathered in front of the ice cream shop a few feet past me and I crossed the street before anyone could recognize me. Not that it was such a strenuous task to go unnoticed. Even after all these weeks here, I doubted most of the kids at school even knew who I was.

My phone vibrated in my pocket, and I turned it to airplane mode without reading the message. There were only two people that could have been messaging me and I had no interest in talking to either of them. My mind still reeled from thinking Peyton might be involved in the killings and after my unfortunate and rude AF talk with River's mother last night, being around him today was out of the question.

Rounding the corner, I almost knocked over a postcard stand from one of the corner shops and had to apologize fifty times to the owner before rushing off. I sped my way past a few bespoke clothing stores and skidded to a stop. Above me, the worn-out sign of the Crystal Cauldron swayed in the breeze, and a knot formed in my gut.

I knew why I came here today. To prove Ms. Broussard is the killer witch and clear Peyton's name. But now that I stood in front of the dusty glass entrance, my body refused to enter. Was confronting the witch that was killing students the smartest play here? Probably not, but I knew I had to try everything. Peyton was going to Ms. Broussard's house tonight and if she was the witch I was after, I had to warn my friend before it was too late.

Blowing off the hair that fell over my eyes, I straightened my back and turned the handle.

As soon as the bell rang, I was attacked with the familiar scent of the Crystal Cauldron. Hints of myrrh and chamomile pushed their way into my throat, and I had to fight to keep the tingle in my fingers in check. I stuck to the center of the shop, refusing to let the siren calls of the crystal-lined shelves overtake me, and marched to the back counter where Ms. Broussard was writing in an old notebook. Her hair was back up in that messy bun she fashioned the first time I met her, and I could see her frustration as she crossed out something she wrote seconds ago.

"Ms. Broussard?" I asked as I approached.

The shop owner's eyes snapped to me in surprise. "Billie! Hello."

"Hi." I swallowed hard. "Is this a bad time?"

"Not at all," she said and slammed the notebook shut. "I'm trying to get ahead on tax season, but I have to tell you, numbers are not my strong suit."

"What is?" I blurted out before I could stop myself.

Ms. Broussard narrowed her eyes then tightened her lips into a thin line. "Why, magic, of course!"

She chuckled and spread her frail arms wide to present the shop to me.

"Ha, right." I tried to smile but failed.

"Anything I can help you with today, Billie? And where is that perky little friend of yours?"

"Who, Peyton? Oh, she's busy," I answered. "I'm here alone."

Excellent work, detective. Tell the suspect you came alone. Stellar work.

"Well, you are just in time for my tea break, dear," Ms. Broussard said and waved me behind the counter. "Do me a favor and flip the open sign?"

My body tensed but I did as she asked before joining her behind the counter. Ms. Broussard led me through the back door of the shop with a smile and I reached for the amber crystal in my back pocket as a precaution. The last time she came through this door, she was holding a tray of snacks and tea, but knowing my luck, I was marching to my death here. I strolled behind her, my eyes scanning the tight corridor we passed for escape routes. I cursed under my breath. There wasn't even a window I could crawl through.

At the end of the corridor was another doorway and my gaze drifted over the intricate carvings that marked its frame. Some lines and symbols sat tightly packed next to each other, and I didn't have to look for long to know what they were. Protection runes. This made no sense. No witch in her right mind would display protection runes like this. The whole point was to hide them from intruders until it was too late.

"Um..." I grimaced, running a finger over one rune.

"Oh, these?" Ms. Broussard's gray eyes twinkled. "I told you, dear. Magic is my strong suit."

Not really, I wanted to say but kept my mouth shut.

The shop owner unlocked the door with a key hanging from a long chain around her wrinkled neck and led me through. As I stepped over the threshold, my heart lightened. The air seemed to separate around me as I walked into the tiny room and my feet felt like they were floating. All the negative energy I had before walking in was replaced with something different, something I haven't felt in ages. Satisfaction.

Correction, not protection runes. Mood alteration. Interesting...

Ms. Broussard gestured to the red velvet sofa that sat opposite a wide-screen television and turned for the small kitchen to my left. Despite my better judgment, I followed her lead and plopped myself to sit. The smell of paprika pounced at my senses and I felt my shoulders drop and my ears perk up. Everything about Ms. Broussard's tiny hideaway behind the Crystal Cauldron was relaxing. My eyes jumped around the room, taking in every detail like a scavenger. Unlike the shop, the room I found myself in was full of light energy and it was then that it hit me.

She lives here!

I didn't know how I didn't notice it before. Between the walls lined with books and the beaded curtains that separated the living room and kitchen from what appeared to be a small bedroom nook, everything in this space pointed to someone's home. Freshly cut flowers in six different vases sat on the small windowsill close to me and framed pictures hung haphazardly on the walls. It seemed Ms. Broussard might have missed a few courses on interior decorating because this place had so many colors around that it made my eyes bleed.

"Peppermint?" the shop owner asked, shoving a teacup under my nose.

I jerked back in surprise and reached a trembling finger to clasp the handle. *This is it, Billie. She no doubt put something in this. Say your good byes now, you idiot.* Why didn't I ask Peyton to come with me? I was for sure going to regret this.

My nose wrinkled as I took a whiff of the tea, but all I could smell was mint and water.

"Oh, calm down, child," Ms. Broussard sang. "I didn't poison the damn thing. That was always your mother's forte."

A lump formed in my stomach, and I almost dropped the tea in my lap. My eyes widened and my jaw hit the floor. *What did she just say?*

"What did you just say?"

The shop owner laughed, and the sound echoed through the room. "My, my. You are just like her."

"You knew my mother? I mean, Beatrix?"

Ms. Broussard frowned. "I take it you never repaired your relationship."

"Hard to repair when she's locked up," I said and slapped my mouth shut before I could say anything else.

"Oh, yes. Such a shame. I heard about her dealings with the High Coven and was broken-hearted. I'm sorry, Billie."

"Don't be. She wasn't great even when she was around."

"Yes, well, Beatrix always marched to the beat of her own drum. Ever since she was a wee child," the shop owner said. "I have a feeling you're much the same."

"I..." I shivered. "I can't believe you knew her. How? When? And why didn't you say something before?"

Ms. Broussard settled her own teacup on the round maple coffee table at my feet and lowered to sit next to me. Her back rolled into the sofa cushions and she groaned as her old muscles worked to let her get comfortable. "I wasn't certain it was you at first. But then you came back and asked for those books, and I just knew! I knew you had to be Beatrix's girl. I mean, you look exactly like her. And most humans walk right by that shelf without so much as a second glance, but not you."

"So, you're what? A witch too?"

"No, no. Though I often wished that was the case." She smiled. "I am simply a conduit of information for your kind. A friend. One your mother trusted."

The muscles in my face tightened and I could feel myself try to speak, but no words came out. Beatrix was here and stayed long enough to make an impression. But for what purpose and why had no one at the High Coven told me about this? I knew why Beatrix wouldn't, I haven't spoken to the woman in years, but the high priestesses? They knew every detail of the lives of those in the coven and there was no way they didn't know about this. So why keep it from me? *Goddess, help me. What have I gotten myself into here?*

"Can you tell me about her?" I asked, eyes narrowed.

Ms. Broussard grinned, leaned deeper into the sofa, and gulped a big sip of the steaming tea in her mug.

"It all started when that little rascal stole from my shop..."

Chapter Twenty-nine

*H*oly *actual spitballs*. My mother, the Wicked Witch of the West herself, used to live in Shadowhurst. My mind was officially blown.

From what Ms. Broussard told me, she didn't just live here. She grew up here. My head was a mess of recent information that I refused to agree with, but I knew what the shop owner told me was true. Beatrix never talked about her past and now I knew why. She fled this place like it was a freaking plague and here I was, trolling around its streets like it was freaking *Disney World*. I felt so stupid.

What was worse was that my prime suspect in the killings was now mush. There was no way Ms. Broussard could have committed the murders. She wasn't even a witch.

Outstanding work, Sherlock. You're back to square one...

My mind was chaos and my pulse raced like a jackhammer as I let myself remember the conversation with Ms. Broussard. She didn't tell me much—and not for my lack of constant questions—but one thing was for certain, my mom lived here until she was about my age. Until she met my father. I pried for information on him, but Ms. Broussard assured me she had never met him, and my mother refused to speak of who he was. She said she got the sense that he was someone important, which would explain why it was so hush-hush. *Beatrix, did you sleep with a married man, you hussy?* I wouldn't be surprised if she did. Even as a kid, I noticed the way men gravitated to Beatrix. The way she lured them in with her charm and legs that went on for days. It would explain why she ran off so fast and left Shadowhurst in the dust. News traveled like wildfire here and a young girl getting knocked up by a wealthy married dude was a front-page story.

When Ms. Broussard first mentioned Beatrix's past here, I felt a ping of excitement at the prospect that I might have a family somewhere nearby. Grandparents or something like that. But my hopes died when she revealed that much like me, Beatrix was totally and completely alone. Apparently, she lived in the orphanage at the edge of town and hated her life. Guess we had something in common.

I despised that I had to find this out from a rando shop owner in a town I was just passing through. Would it have killed the High Coven to let me know? I mean, I couldn't count on Beatrix to tell the truth to save her life but the high priestesses? I trusted them! I thought of them as surrogate mothers for Goddess' sake!

OMG! What if my dad was someone I met already?

I was still running inventory of every well-to-do, middle-aged man I've encountered in Shadowhurst when an arrow sliced the air and landed in the ground next to my feet. My leg jerked back, and I followed the trajectory to Savannah's scowl in the distance. Her fingers were wrapped around the bow she held over her shoulder and her eyes burnt into me with rage.

Oh, right. I'm training with the witch-burning hunters. Got it.

My cheeks blushed and I reached to pull the arrow out of the ground before tracing it with my finger. We've been in the extensive field of Savannah's family farm for hours—because of course, she lived on four hundred acres of land—and they were yet to let me join them in training. It seemed my job in this group was to watch them practice their moves and get water when I was asked for it. I bit my tongue each time someone hollered for a bottle and tossed it their way. This was such a waste of time. I could kill them all right now, before they even had a chance to fight back.

Still, I had to say that the hunters were better equipped than I imagined. Most of them ran through drills and staged fights like it was second nature.

"You keep trying to kill me and we're going to have a problem!" I yelled out, eyeing Savannah carefully.

"Get over yourself, new kid!" she yelled back. "No one is trying to off you here."

"Could have fooled me!" I turned my gaze to the arrow at my feet. "Pretty sure your parents don't want to find a bleeding girl on their land."

Savannah's eyes turned somber for a split second. "They'd have to be around long enough to notice," she hissed before changing her features to the stone-cold bitch look I was very accustomed to at this point.

Hmm... Absent parents and a shitty attitude? I was starting to understand why Savannah was such a problem all the time. It almost made me sad to think we might actually have something in common. Almost. She was likely just as abandoned and as lost as me, but the main difference was that I didn't go around acting like a bitch every time someone wanted to play with my toys.

I stuck my tongue out at her and rolled my eyes before tossing the arrow over my shoulder. As she walked away with a huff, I leaned back in the tall grass and continued to study them.

They broke off into groups, some training in hand-to-hand battle and some picking up random weapons tossed onto a rolled out blanket in the field. It was no surprise to me that Savannah gravitated to the bow and arrow and her annoyingly perfect skill with it *was* impressive. She knocked another arrow and sent it barreling to the target board, firing the tip straight into the center. Bullseye. Beside her, Jayden and Morgan cheered before knocking their own arrows to try. Near them, Tyler was trying to teach Abigail the correct way to flip an opponent on their backs, but it was a wasted effort. All the girl could do was giggle and flirt before getting flipped over on her back. She made such a small effort to stay standing that I wondered if she was letting her boyfriend knock her around on purpose.

"Pathetic," I growled and sank deeper into the grass. The large cornfield behind me rustled in the wind and I pressed my palm to the earth to suck in its energy. My body shivered and I half-smiled at the warmth that spread through me as my magic connected to the elements.

"Don't let her fool you," River said and I startled, turning to see him towering over me. "Abigail is fierce, even if she won't show it."

My gaze turned back to Abigail, who was now inspecting a broken nail with a pout. "I find that very hard to believe."

"Watch this." River winked and snatched the small knife he had stashed in his back pocket.

He whistled in Abigail's direction and threw the knife without so much as waiting for her to notice him. The blade twirled through the air, slicing its way straight for her throat. I gasped and covered my mouth, ready to dial nine one one to let them know we had a girl bleeding out in a cornfield. To my surprise, Abigail's eyes snapped to the blade, and she yanked her arm up to snatch it by the hilt before it could impale her.

"Nice try!" she yelled out, and tossed the knife down, burying the tip into the earth.

River kicked my boot with his trainers and smiled. "Told you. Fierce."

"Wow," I whispered, picking my jaw off the ground. "That was... surprising..."

"We've been doing this since we were kids. Abigail is an oddball, but there's no one else I could count on more in a fight. Even after she had her nails done."

A loud laugh escaped me, and I leaned in to bring my knees closer to my chest. "So have you been in a fight before?"

"Assuming you don't mean just at school, right? 'Cause I've had my fair share of those. Football guys can be a bitch."

What a shocker, River's a jock. UGH. Gross.

"Obviously," I answered, trying not to roll my eyes.

My gaze narrowed and my neck felt tight like a noose has just been draped over it. We both knew what I was asking. I wanted to know if they've killed a witch before. If they've killed someone like me.

"Not yet," River sighed. "But better safe than sorry, right?"

I nodded despite the bile that crept up in my throat. "Your tricks are cool," I said and swallowed down nausea, "but I'm pretty sure you don't stand a chance."

River's brows arched and his eyes darkened as he stared me down. "You think you can do better?"

Not breaking a sweat, I hopped to stand. My eyes burrowed into his and I shook the inviting scent of his cologne off for fear it might break my focus. If he thought Abigail was fierce, he was about to get his ass handed to him. My hand reached around him, and I grabbed a fistful of his hair to pull his head back. My lips brushed against his and I turned my head to his ear. "Dare to find out?" I whispered and ducked down, spinning my legs from under me to loop around his shins.

River hit the grass and I could hear his butt smack the ground with a thud.

"Hope that doesn't bruise," I teased and buried my feet into the earth.

He was up before I could blink, kicking his legs forward and flipping like a freaking ninja. His hair swung over his eyes, and he shook it off, gaze trained on me. His lips curled into a sinister grin, and he waved me forward.

Oh, it's SO on, hunter!

I pounced for him. My fists colliding with his chest and sending him barreling backward. River regained his balance and chuckled, which only infuriated me more. His thin shirt emphasized every muscle in his abdomen, and I forced myself to peel my eyes off his stomach to glare back. Before he could come for me, I pounced again, this time kicking him in those panty-dropping abs with my boot. River rebounded and lunged. He was so fast, it was almost inhuman. His body soared through the air and before I could swerve out of the way, he was on top of me. My heart burst from my chest as my back hit the ground and his legs wrapped around my mid-section. Above me, River grinned again, but I knew I wouldn't let him win this. I turned under his weight, bucking my hips up to push him off. He flew back and rolled a few feet away from me. As he tried to get up, I ran for him, pushing off the grass to jump in the air. Wind whipped my hair around my face as I blasted toward him like a black widow in heat. My legs shot out from under me, and I buried my knees on either side of his face, squeezing hard to lock his neck in place.

River tapped the ground with one outstretched arm and smiled.

"If I had to pick a way to die," he said breathlessly, "this would be it."

Laughter and applause rose behind us, and I spun to see the remaining hunters watching with wide eyes. Jayden arched one eyebrow my ways before making a crude gesture with his mouth. Blood rushed to my cheeks, and I looked down to River, whose head was in the most inappropriate position right now with relation to my hips. *Get up, idiot!* I cursed myself, but all I could do was stare.

"Not that I'm complaining about the view," River purred and ran a finger along my thigh, "but I think Morgan is trying to get our attention."

I turned to see the redhead wailing her arms in the air like she was out at sea without a life vest.

"What's wrong?" I yelled out after climbing off River's neck to stand. "What happened?"

I held an arm out for River to pull him up and we ran back to the group. Their faces were pale, and they huddled around Morgan, reading the screen of her phone over her shoulder. Everyone was silent, even Savannah, and a cold chill rushed through my bones. "Guys, what's wrong?"

No one spoke. Behind me, River stepped closer so my back could rest against his chest and squeezed my shoulders. "What's going on?" he asked sternly.

"It's Clay," Morgan whispered. "Clay Clayton. He's dead."

She shoved the phone our way and tears flooded my vision. It was a newspaper article detailing the events surrounding his death. From the looks of the pictures, the reporter was on the scene before it could get cleared by the police. A gasp escaped me as I curled my fingers over her phone. My hand shook and I brought the screen closer to my face, blood cooling as I looked into the dead eyes that once belonged to Clay Clayton. His face was sunken in and mummified much like the other bodies, but it wasn't the state of his starved body that gave me pause.

The dead student lay in the middle of what looked to be an empty field. His hands out to the side in the shape of a cross and around him, salt formed a circle. My eyes drifted over the image, and I pinched my thumb and index finger to enlarge the remnants of writing around him. My vision blurred and I blinked away the tears that threatened to drown me as I focused on the symbols in the circle. Peach wood, amethyst dust, salt. But that wasn't it. There were runes engraved in the dirt at each of the five points of the circle; runes sketched in blood.

I slapped my hand to my mouth and closed my eyes.

I knew exactly what this was. I knew why the witch was killing these students.

Chapter Thirty

"No, no, NO!" I gasped and shoved the phone back into Morgan's outstretched hand. "This is a damn disaster!"

Beside me, River tensed while the other hunters stared like I was having a mental breakdown. Which wasn't far from the truth, I definitely, one hundred percent was.

"Billie, what's wrong? What do you see?" River asked.

"Yeah, girl," Abigail added, "spill."

The pressure around my eyes intensified and I had to reach for River's hand just to stay upright. He squeezed my fingers, rubbing those annoying circles on my palm again with his thumb. Except this time, they weren't annoying at all. This time, I craved his touch more than the air I needed to breathe.

"Here," he said and helped me down to the grass. "Sit. Breathe."

I forced myself to meet his eyes and took deep breaths while Savannah groaned next to us. Her bedazzled ankle-booties tapped the earth, and I could sense the vibration reach my body. Every tap sent me spiraling and I cringed at the sound. Noticing my discomfort, River shot her a side-glance, and she froze. I pulled my thoughts back and willed myself to calm down before daring to look up at her. Above me, Savannah's eyes widened as she registered the fear on my face.

"Holy shit. You're actually scared."

"We all should be," I whispered.

"Okay," Tyler said, and I was jarred by how deep his voice was. "Someone better tell me what's going on or I'm going to legit lose it."

I filled my lungs with air and ran my gaze over the hunters.

"We are in deep shit if this is what I think it is," I finally said.

"Dude, come on! You're killing us with the theatrics!" Jayden yelled.

Less than a second later, Morgan's slap echoed through the field and Jayden was rubbing his chest with a puppy dog expression on his face. "Give her a second!" Morgan snapped. "It's okay, Billie. Just calm down then tell us."

Her smile spread and it helped dislodge my heart from my throat.

"I read about these before. These runes," I said. "It's a ritual. A bad one."

"A ritual for what?"

"Energy collection."

River's brow furrowed. "So, this witch is stealing energy from these kids? Enough to kill them?"

I nodded.

"Well, no kidding," Savannah snapped. "We kind of

already got that from the fact that they're, oh, I don't know, mummified!"

"That's not it," I said and narrowed my eyes at her. "Not that she's taking their energy. It's what she's taking it for."

Everyone fell silent and I could feel all eyes on me. I shrunk in the grass, letting go of River's hand to hug my knees into me. Every sound and smell intensified, and I closed my eyes, wishing when I opened them, I would wake up from this nightmare. When I peeled my lids apart, nothing had changed. *Wonderful.*

"So, what's she taking it for?" Abigail asked.

"If I'm right..." I gestured for Morgan's phone, and she tossed it into my lap. I pinched my fingers to zoom and pointed to the runes I spotted earlier then waved the screen for the group to see. "She's targeting these students not because they have fae blood, but because they have *specific* fae blood. I can't believe I didn't see it before!"

"Hey," River whispered, "don't be so hard on yourself. No one even believed these fae characters were real."

I should have. ME! The freaking witch over here!

My gaze dropped to the ground and my face flushed. I hated lying to him, but they needed to know at least some truth if they were going to help me end this.

"I know. It's just that I've seen a ritual like this before, in books I read back in Stamwick," I lied. Well, half lied. I saw this ritual in a book, but they didn't need to know it was in Sebyl's grimoire when I stole it back when I was eight. "And from what I've gathered, not all fae are the same."

"Meaning what?"

"They all have unique elements they control, or unique powers, I guess. You guys know about the elements, right?"

The hunters looked at me like I was an idiot and

Savannah scoffed. "Obvi," she said and rolled her eyes. "We're witch hunters, remember?"

How could I forget, asshole?

"Anyway," I continued, "there are five fundamental elements. Fire, air, water, earth, and spirit. And there are fae that control each one. At least, from what I've read. These runes here," I pointed to the screen again, "are for each of the elements. And I didn't notice it because, well, I don't know why. But the bodies of the students were all positioned with their heads pointing to different spots. Like—"

"Arrows," River whispered.

"Exactly! She's picking specific students with bloodlines that date back to the fae of each of those elements. And that's not the worst part."

"Wait, what?" Tyler growled. "What's worse than this?"

My eyes burnt and I swallowed audibly. "She has four already. Fire, water, earth, and air. She's only missing one to complete the ritual."

I glanced back to the screen to double check and pressed my lips into a line. There was no mistaking this ritual now that I knew what it was for, and I kicked myself for not seeing it sooner. I should have looked into the fae as soon as Sebyl mentioned them. Hell, I should have asked more questions! Why did I even—

"Not to sound like a total moron," Jayden said, interrupting my downward spiral, "but what happens when she completes it?"

River leaned over me and put his hands over my knees. My pulse slowed and I found myself able to follow the conversation again without getting distracted. Mostly, River's unexplainable effect on me was frustrating but at that moment, I was glad to have him as a friend.

"We're screwed," I answered. "If whoever is doing this completes the ritual, she'll be more powerful than any witch who ever lived. At least, that's what I'm assuming would happen. I've never heard of anyone getting their hands on fae magic before. And trust me, I've read a lot of occult books back home. Like a LOT!"

The hunters broke off into arguments and their voices carried over me like an orchestra. Words blurred together and I couldn't make out a single sentence as they talked over each other. I couldn't blame them, this was a big bomb to drop and despite their knowledge of the occult, finding this out was shocking. Hell, it was shocking to me, and I've been a part of this world my whole life. I still couldn't believe it. No one had ever performed this ritual. Goddess, most witches didn't even believe the fae existed in the first place! But they did exist and after everything Sebyl has told me and the strange occurrences in this town, it made sense that their bloodlines were still coursing through the veins of their descendants. Sebyl said the fae were control freaks and dying off without so much as leaving a trace of power wasn't something that someone who loved to control would do. The fae left breadcrumbs in Shadowhurst. Pieces of themselves scattered across generations. Pieces of their magic. This witch found that out somehow and was trying to use it to get stronger. But for what? And why now?

I cleared my throat and the hunters turned to look at me.

"We need the name of the last target, and we need it yesterday," I announced.

Beside me, River shifted his weight uncomfortably. "But how? We don't even know what to look for and if it wasn't for you, we wouldn't have even known about Clay."

My spine uncurled and determination settled in my gut.

"I know just the person to call."

Three hours later we huddled in a circle around River's kitchen island again. My nerves were sky high and despite River reassuring me his mom was away for the day, I couldn't help but glance back to the front door from time to time to make sure. I needed another awkward exchange with Evanora right now like I needed a nail in the eye.

Across from me, Jayden tossed a chip into the air and caught it with his mouth before fist-pumping the air. Beside him, Morgan rolled her eyes and shook her head in my direction, to try making me smile. It sure as shit didn't work. These kids were something else. There was a killer witch on the loose and they were joking around like it was nothing. Their self-assuredness was exhausting, and I didn't understand how they couldn't see the gravity of the situation. If she gets her next kill, we're done for. Even the High Coven couldn't—

Oh, sweet mother of Gandalf. The High Coven!

In all my obsession with finding the witch, I completely forgot to fill them in on what I found out. I needed to call the high priestesses and I needed to call them now. My hands reached for the phone tucked in the waistband of my navy blue leggings but as I pulled it out, it vibrated in my hand.

My eyes snapped to the screen and Peyton's red-streaked hair and aggressive eyeliner popped into view. With a nod, I exchanged a glance with everyone at the table before answering.

"B!" my best friend screeched into the phone, and I had to lower the volume to keep my eardrums from bursting. "I don't know what's been up your ass with the disappearance acts but I'm glad you texted."

"Peyton." I squirmed. "You're on speaker. I got River and his friends here."

The other line went silent, and I had to tap on the screen to make sure we were still connected.

"Girl! The witch hunters?" Peyton shrieked. "Sweet!"

Next to River, Savannah cursed under her breath and my face grew beet red. I really needed to put a muzzle on my friend before her enormous mouth ruined everything.

"Speaker..." I whispered into the phone.

"Right, sorry," Peyton said. "What's up, peeps?"

The hunters grumbled hello and leaned in closer to the screen.

"Okay, Peyton, you're up. Tell me you found something."

"Um, excuse you! I'm like a freaking bloodhound. If there's dirt, I will sniff it out."

River chuckled. "We'll take that as a 'yes'."

"You can take that as a 'hell yes'!" my friend yelled.

"Wow, you two have this whole dramatic suspense down to a science," Abigail said and laughed. "Spill the tea already."

The screen flashed as a burst of texts came in from Peyton and I swiped them off-screen.

"I'm sending you the deets, but long story short, I expanded the search. I figured we were hitting a dead end here in Shadowhurst when it hit me! Carriage Hill!"

"What about it?" everyone asked in unison.

"Duh! It used to be part of Shadowhurst until, you know, the whole 'burn, burn witch' fiasco."

Knots formed in my stomach and my knees shook uncontrollably. I blinked and tried to keep my eyes on the phone so that the anger on my face didn't attract attention. "That's brilliant, Peyton. Did it work?"

"Oh, yeah. Totes. Looks like one of the so-called witches the original founders kicked out was part of a fae line. I found a name, but I don't know anyone in town that matches it. Graves. Anyone know it?"

We all shook our heads and exchanged looks. The name did not ring a bell to anyone but something about it clung to my mind. I felt like I've heard it before, but I couldn't place my finger on where or when. *Maybe back in Stamwick?* It sat just at the tip of my tongue, and I hated that I couldn't place it. This was important and I would let everyone down if I didn't figure it out.

"That's a 'no' on our end," River said.

"Cool, cool, cool," Peyton breathed into the speaker. "So, what's the plan now?"

Everyone looked to me, and I shrank in my seat. "Uh, we'll see what we can dig up on our end." I looked at the group. "You guys think you can hit the Google genie and see what you can find? Now that we have a lead, we should follow it. Peyton?"

"Yes, ma'am?"

"Are you home right now?"

"Yep. Dad has me jailed until I get my math grades up."

"Great, stay there. I'm coming to you. Let's see what else we can find from Carriage Hill on this Graves family in the books."

The group nodded in agreement, and I shoved the phone into my leggings before bolting for the door. I could feel River's eyes on my back as I receded but there was no time for good byes right now. We were so close I could taste it. Peyton found Clay and I knew my friend was the key to finding the next victim. She just needed a pair of fresh eyes, and I was happy to lend them. Every gut feeling I had about Peyton being involved dissipated as I hopped on my bike and peddled out of the driveway. There was no way she was the witch and I felt stupid for ever thinking it. She was kind and smart and quirky, and she was my best friend. I pushed the pedals and sent the bike rolling down the steep slope of River's street to Peyton's house. Whoever this killer was, I was coming for her with guns blazing.

Chapter Thirty-one

It was already pitch black by the time I got to Peyton's house. The street lamps illuminated portions of her street, making the surrounding trees look like they were on display in a museum. My legs were hurting from how fast I got there but when I climbed off my bike and hit the ground, I felt rejuvenated. Walking was a small blessing but one I appreciated at that moment.

I shook off the needles in my toes and made my way to the porch. As soon as I stepped in front of Peyton's front door, my pulse jumped to attention.

The lights were off in the entire house and even the small, antique lamp that hung above the door was dark.

Didn't Peyton say her dad was home? Or did I make that up?

My hand trembled as I reached for the handle and turned. The door swung open, and I was met with the night that had settled over the Ling residence. It was quiet. Eerily quiet. My gut told me something was wrong, and I snatched the dagger from my boot before bothering to turn a light on.

As I walked through the house, flipping switches in my wake, I realized that I was alone. My legs pumped as I raced to Peyton's room but when I burst in—expecting to find my friend lounging on her enormous bed—I saw only darkness. My heartbeat skyrocketed when I turned on her bedroom lights.

Peyton's room was a complete mess.

There were pillows thrown all over the floor and wind tore at the curtains through the open window. My eyes caught something sparkly, and I moved closer to the window to find shards of broken glass under my boots.

Something bad happened here!

I parted the curtains to peer out, but it was too dark outside to see anything. My head pounded and my mouth felt drier than bone. Where was Peyton? And what the hell happened here? Closing the curtains, I darted for her desk and ripped the friendship bracelet she gave me with one quick tear. The pink string lay flaccid in my palm, and I fought back tears as I fumbled to remove the amethyst pendant from my neck. I had to find her, and I couldn't do it without magic.

As quick as I could manage, I slid the amethyst off the chain and tied the torn bracelet around the small, silver loop at the top of the crystal. My fingers curled around the makeshift pendulum, and I pushed my magic into the amethyst to connect to its energy. Sweat beaded down my face and back as I closed my eyes and forced the pendulum to obey. If Peyton was nearby, I could track her. I just prayed she was close enough for the pendulum to pick up her energy through the bracelet.

Come on, Peyton. COME ON!

Tears streamed down my cheeks, and I wiped them

clumsily with my free hand before letting the pendulum drop from my fingers. It hung still at first but in moments, a dull purple smoke spread from my fingers and enveloped the crystal, forcing it to move. The pendulum swung in the window's direction, and I gasped.

"She's in the backyard?" I asked then cursed myself. Who was I even talking to right now? *Crystals don't talk, moron.*

I ran for the stairs, skipping two steps at a time to reach the bottom. My body burst through the front door, and I rounded the house to the backyard. It was so dark, I couldn't see a foot in front of me but the glow of my magic around the crystal illuminated enough of a path that I could run without tripping over something. The pendulum swayed aggressively forward, and I darted in its direction. My chest heaved as I ran around the massive swimming pool in Peyton's backyard, and I couldn't help but cock an eyebrow when I passed it. *So, she has a pool? Good to know.*

Cold air whipped around me, and I was about to stop to check the pendulum again when I heard voices rise from close by. Somewhere beyond the tree line that blocked Peyton's backyard from the rest of the world, arguing ensued. My ears perked up and I tried to focus on the voices. It didn't take me long to make out my friend's high pitched tone, but I couldn't place the others. There were three of them from the sounds of it.

I pocketed the pendulum and stepped into the foliage of the trees, eyes widening when I crossed to the other side.

There, in the middle of a small clearing, stood Peyton. She was still wearing her flannel pajama pants and her hair was a hot mess. Whoever dragged her out of bed must have been worth it because there was no way my friend would ever leave the house looking like that.

I wiped my brow and took a few more steps forward. "Peyton?"

My best friend's head snapped in my direction, and I saw her face pale when she spotted me. Her eyes were dark and though I couldn't tell from where I was standing, it looked like she was pissed I found her.

"Get back in the house, B!" she yelled, but I stood firm.

"Not until you tell me what's going on. Who are these people?"

I peeled my gaze off Peyton and trained it on the three strangers in the clearing. They were older than us by at least ten years and I could smell their rage from where I stood. Two men and a woman with hair so pale, it picked up the light of the moon.

One man shifted his weight, but his blue eyes refused to leave mine. He was slender in build but his white tank top clung close enough to his body that I could see every one of his taut muscles peek through. His hair was as dark as death, and it shot out from his head in every direction. The second man, crouching low next to the first, was shorter, but I didn't fail to notice that this guy was built like a refrigerator. His stumpy body was stacked with overgrown muscle and his bright blue hair hung down to his shoulders. He raised his head, and I noticed the distinct yellow glow of his eyes. My attention jumped from one man to the other as my pulse raced.

Shit! Shifters!

Night air wrapped around me, and I could feel the heat rise off the creatures to reach my body. *Peyton, what are you doing out here with two shifters?*

"Well, will you look at that, boys? We got ourselves a witch!" the woman growled and my eyes snapped to her.

She was tall, not as tall as Savannah but still impressive for a girl. My gaze drifted up her long legs, past the hem of her leather skirt and to her wild, pale eyes. Her white hair was pulled into four braids at the top then spread to flow down her back and she flicked the strands off her shoulder when she turned to face me head-on.

"Welcome to the party," she purred and patted the shoulder of the dark-haired shifter next to her.

"Get... in... the... house..." Peyton bit out through clenched teeth.

"Not... a... damn... chance..." I hissed back.

We exchanged glances and I tried to figure out where my friend's head was when stump-boy lunged for us. He barreled through the clearing, using his arms to push himself until he was flying right at me. The shifter growled and his bones snapped into a million agonizing sounds that echoed through the clearing. When he landed before me, the man was gone and a large, black wolf stood in his place.

I gasped and pulled Peyton back, stepping around her with my dagger pointing at the shifter. Spit fell down its snout as it breathed heavily, and its wolf eyes burrowed into my soul. Shivers ran down my spine, but I struggled against my fear and dug my hands into my jacket pocket. I fumbled around, digging deeper and deeper as realization crashed into me. *Crap! I don't have the amber.*

I cursed under my breath and dug my feet into the grass. The wolf snarled and stomped its paws in response.

Behind him, the second shifter grunted and in seconds I was facing not just the wolf, but a bear larger than Peyton's

Jeep. I chuckled nervously, still pressing Peyton out of the way.

Seriously? The scrawny guy is a bear? What in the actual Hell?

"You're outnumbered, witch!" the woman screeched.

And she was right.

Without the amber, I had no connection to fire, and taking down two giant shifters with just my dagger would be difficult at best. I've had worse odds before, but I still didn't like this. My thoughts jumbled as I tried to think of a solution. Before me, the shifters grew impatient and I could see them readying to charge.

Before they could move, I brought the tip of the dagger to my finger and sliced a piece off. I grimaced at the pain but as my blood streamed down my hand, a smile formed on my lips. I dropped to my knees, pushing my finger into the ground. My hands shook and the lines I drew resembled a kindergarten sketch, but it did the job. The shifters growled and I slammed my dagger into the earth and forced my magic out. Around us, the clearing shook and I could feel Peyton's hand grab my shoulder to stay steady. My lids fluttered as I continued to push my power into the runes I drew to form a barrier around us. Death spread from my dagger and the grass withered as my magic crawled toward the shifters' paws. Their wild eyes widened, and they hissed but took a few steps back.

"Clever girl," the woman purred, her eyes locked on me. "But those tricks don't work on all of us."

She walked toward me, not bothering to speed up her stride. Her self-assured grin made my heart race and I choked down the saliva that collected in my mouth. The woman reached me and I noticed she wasn't wearing any shoes. I stumbled back, dropping my magic, and locked eyes on her. Slowly and viciously, she reached out a single finger and inched it closer to my forehead. My body shook but I could not move. Sweat poured into my eyes and I blinked the sting away. My thoughts jumbled and nausea overtook me. *A mind reaper.* I grimaced and squeezed my eyes shut. My head spun, but I fought against her pull. I could taste her need for me and my thoughts on my lips and I wasn't about to let her succeed.

There was a loud yell behind me, and I snapped my eyes open to see Peyton jump over my crouched body to face the woman. My friend's eyes were darker than the deepest night and her short hair whipped around her face as she screamed. The woman's gaze landed on Peyton but before she could reach for her, my best friend crashed her palm to the reaper's chest.

"NOOOOO!" the woman shrieked and doubled back.

Her white hair turned even paler, and her eyes rolled back into her head. She fell on her back, wriggling in the dead grass. Her naked toes curled, and her fingers tightened into fists at her side. All around her, the air grew darker.

My eyes widened and my jaw hit the ground as I watched the reaper take her last breath before her arched back relaxed and she grew still. In seconds, her skin charred and withered into ash.

Peyton straightened her back and stomped a slippered foot into the grass. "Get the hell out of my yard!" she shouted.

At her command, the two shifters whined and took off running. Away from us.

"You're a…" My voice hitched and I couldn't force the words out. "A…"

"A soul sucker," Peyton finished for me. "Yep. Surprise?"

And just like that, the world crashed around me.

Chapter Thirty-two

Somehow, the night got even darker, and I couldn't focus my eyes. Peyton towered over me, whispering something but her words didn't reach me. My entire body was shaking so hard the ground beneath me trembled, sending jolts of energy into my blood.

Peyton was a soul sucker. My *best* friend was a freaking shadower.

Every muscle hurt and I tried to will myself to move but I couldn't even lift a finger and as icy air rushed by my face, I could feel every tear that streamed down my cheeks. What was happening to me? How did I let myself get into this situation? Peyton was a shadower and the guy I couldn't get out of my stupid head was a witch hunter. *Who have I become?*

Everything I've ever known shattered around me in pieces until I didn't know which one to pick up first. I had no idea how to put myself back together.

"Billie?" Peyton whispered and knelt next to me. "Talk to me. Please."

"I... I..."

"It's a lot to take in, I know. But you have to know, girl, I wanted to tell you. I just, you know, was waiting for the right time."

The right time? Is she serious? There was no right time to tell me this! She was something I hated, something I had to kill. My heart ached and I rubbed my eyes with my fists until the skin around them felt raw to the touch.

I have to kill my best friend. "I can't do this," I said and forced myself to stand. "Not anymore."

"B! Hang on!" Peyton shouted, but I was already gone.

Lights flashed in my peripheral as I paced the length of my small living area. My fingers twirled the moonstone ring, and I watched the fire burning in my left hand with rage and intent. The power I used in the clearing took a lot out of me and my magic was already starting to fade, but I wanted to hold on to what was left just a little longer. I wanted some kind of control for at least a few moments. The amber crystal vibrated in my palm, and I breathed into it, sending the flames higher and higher in my hand. My eyes twinkled as they took the fire's glare and if anyone was to walk in, I was sure I'd look like a damn psycho.

I inhaled the smoke and shut my fingers around the crystal to put the fire out.

Near me, my phone vibrated for the hundredth time, and I snarled in its direction. Peyton hadn't stopped trying to text me since I left but I refused to read any of her messages. She lied to me, and she did it in the worst way possible. Peyton knew I was a witch—I trusted her enough to tell her

—so she knew what I would have to do when I found out who she was. That was why she refused to tell me. Not because we were friends, but because we both knew what would happen if I found out. I would have to vanquish her ass into oblivion.

My chest tightened and I rubbed the spot closest to my heart until I felt my skin burn hot.

"What are you going to do?" I asked myself. "You can't actually go through with it."

My knees buckled and I dropped to the wooden floor with a thud. At that moment, my future wasn't looking so great. I went from being a coven witch to someone who developed feelings for everything my kind stood against, and it tore me apart. I wondered if anyone else in the coven had ever faced this impossible situation, but chances were, I was the only idiot in the bunch.

Knees dragging, I crawled to where my phone sat on the round coffee table and pulled it into my lap. My hands shook as I pressed the home button and swiped Peyton's messages from sight. Taking a deep breath, I scrolled through the contacts and hit dial.

The phone rang five times before a familiar voice sounded on the other end.

"Hello? Wilhemina?" Rhiamon answered and my heart dropped.

"Rhi," I whispered. "Rhi, I need your help."

"Honey, what's wrong?" the high priestess asked, panic rising in her voice.

"I can't stay here anymore. I can't." The line grew silent, and I sank to my butt, pressing the phone closer to my ear. "Rhi?"

There was a shuffle of feet and then Rhiamon was back on. "I'm here. Tell me what's wrong."

"Everything!" I screamed. "Everything is wrong. This is too hard! I can't do any of it. I'm not strong enough."

"Breathe, Wilhemina. You'll be fine."

Her words were stone, and I sniffled my nose, wiping the tears from my face. I shouldn't have expected anything else from her, Rhiamon was the fighter of the group, and I don't even know why I called her. Maybe I thought she'd care somehow but if I was honest, I was hoping she'd tell me to pack my bags and hightail it out of there to come home.

She didn't.

"Have you found out the names of the hunters?"

Bile rose in my throat as her question sat in. It was always about the job with this bunch and for once, I wished it was about me. I stayed silent, refusing to give her any information until she told me what I wanted to hear. "I want to come home."

"That," Rhiamon scolded, "will only be possible after we secure Shadowhurst."

"But—"

"Honey, I hope you understand that what we did was a direct result of your own actions. You used magic in front of humans, Billie. Witches have been caged for less. You get that, right?"

I nodded even though she couldn't see me.

"Now, have you had any progress in following the fae bloodlines?"

My teeth ground against each other and I pushed down nausea that overtook me. *You mean the fae you never told me about?* I wanted to demand. "The witch is using the fae elements to collect energy," I said instead. "I found signs that point to a Drawing Out Life ritual in all the crime scenes."

Rhiamon gasped. "How many has she been able to secure?"

"Four. She's missing the Spirit element. But I don't know who the target is yet."

"Very good," she whispered. "This is excellent work, Billie. But listen to me and listen carefully, you must find the last fae line before she gets to them. I don't think you understand the gravity of the situation."

No shit. Thanks for the stellar advice.

"I understand it better than you think," I snapped back. "I'm the one dealing with it."

"And you're doing a wonderful job. I'm just making sure that your head is in the game. Under no circumstances can we allow this witch to complete the ritual. It would be catastrophic."

"For whom?"

"For everyone. For the entire world. A witch with that kind of power is not to be messed with. It's unnatural. She would be stronger than the High Coven itself and if that happens, there would be no controlling her."

There was that word 'control' again. Hearing it made me want to smash my phone into pieces. Was that all the High Coven cared about? I knew we needed witches to protect the humans, but all the secrecy still made little sense.

"Why can't we just tell the other witches what's going on? They can help. I don't think I can do this on my own."

"You can and you will. And you will keep this to yourself."

"But, Rhi—"

"No 'buts', Wilhemina!" she snapped. "You will do as we instructed or Goddess help me, you will leave us no choice!"

I jumped back from the phone. Tears flooded my vision, and I could feel the blood rise to my neck. "I'm sorry," I whispered. "I didn't mean it. I'm just scared."

"It's all right to be scared, honey," Rhiamon said, her voice lighter. "But you need to remember that you have a job to do and trust me, we will all feel much better when you've done it. Now, with that said, I am not blind to your feelings. If you need me and other high priestesses to come there, we will."

"No!" I yelled out a little too fast. "I mean, it's okay. You're right, I have to get my head in the game."

The idea of the high priestesses coming to Shadowhurst made me uneasy. So far, I've been able to hide the wicked secrets I've been keeping without a hitch but with them here, everything would fall apart. Once they found out I lied about not knowing who the witch hunters were, I was done for. Not to mention the fact that I was hoarding feelings for one of them or that my best friend was a soul sucker. Uh-uh! No way could I let them come here. I made this mess and I had to clean it up on my own before I landed myself in a cell next to Beatrix.

"You're sure?" Rhiamon asked again.

"Hundy," I answered. "I can do this. You trained me well."

"That's wonderful! And don't worry, once we put this to bed, I'll talk to the rest of the coven and convince them to let you come home. We miss you, Billie."

A few loose tears escaped me, and I choked back a sob. "I miss you too."

"Oh! Luna is here! Let me get her on the phone!"

"No, it's okay!" I yelled out before she could pass the line. "I gotta go anyhow. The Chandlers are having dinner soon and I have to keep up appearances."

"They're treating you well?"

"Uh-huh." I smiled. "Great, actually."

"That's wonderful, Billie. And make sure to let us know as soon as you track down the last element."

"Will do," I said and pressed two fingers to my forehead in salute. "Tell Luna I said hi. See you guys soon."

The line went dead, and I had to close and open my mouth to release the tension in my jaw. In my hands, the phone vibrated again, and I rolled my eyes when I saw Peyton's name pop up. Before I could click the phone off, her message caught my attention.

READ YOUR TEXTS. THIS IS IMPORTANT!

Whoa! All caps. I sighed and clicked on the text thread. *This better be good.*

The first gazillion messages were all her asking me for forgiveness followed by prayer emojis and sad faces. I scrolled through them—refusing to let her get to me—when my gaze landed on a longer text.

Look, I know you don't want to talk to me, and I don't blame you, but you have to hear this. I know who Graves is.

My eyes widened and I sucked in a breath before reading the next bubble.

The Graves family moved to Carriage Hill before the burnings started as we thought. There were a few family members, but then the trail went cold. So, I did some digging and (fireworks emoji) it turns out that they killed the entire family for suspected witchcraft.

So far, this sounded like a dead end, but I read on.

No one survived but there was a name that kept popping

up, so I followed it. Turns out, there was one survivor. A girl. I dug up some old paperwork and this chick was adopted into another family. Then she got married and as per uzhe, she took her husband's name (barfing emoji).

Abigail was right, suspense seemed to be a strong suit of Peyton's. I scrolled through the next few texts that were all her railing about women taking on a man's last name until I saw one that piqued my interest. As I read, my hands clammed up and my stomach turned. The ring on my finger pressed into my skin as I squeezed the phone to my face. *This can't be right!* I reread the message and dropped the phone in my lap.

Graves became Stonewall?!?

No, no, no! How was this possible? I was this girl's descendant? I had to have read that wrong. I checked the text again, but it stared back at me with the same incessant declaration. A bomb went off in my chest and I felt myself roll onto my side, melting into the hardwood floors. Pulling my legs into my chest, I focused on my breathing for fear of tossing my lunch to the floor. I wasn't sure how many more surprises I could take. This day was already a shit-storm and it seemed to have just gotten worse.

My family was a descendant of the fae. Not just any descendant, the last one this damn witch needed complete the ritual. There had to be some mistake. I didn't even know I had a family, but not only was I way off base, I was also the witch's new target.

Tears stung at my eyes, and I blinked them away before peeling myself off the floor.

I had so many questions—more than I could list off the top of my head—and no way to get answers. The High Coven were useless, and it was looking like even if they knew about this, they wouldn't tell me the truth if I lit a fire under their asses. There was only one way for me to get the answers I needed and whether I liked it or not, it had to be done. I had to find out the truth about my past before this witch got to me.

I had to talk to Beatrix.

Chapter Thirty-three

The smell of mugwort and thistle drifted through the small waiting area I was dumped in while someone retrieved Beatrix from her cell. That was over forty-five minutes ago, and my patience was now about as thin as the chipped nail on my index finger. I was so nervous, I actually made myself nauseous. To make matters worse, there was nothing to do in this stupid room but wait. And chew my nails down to the cuticle.

The prison that held the witches who disobeyed High Coven rules was not what one would imagine. Aside from the concrete that made up most of the surroundings—seriously, it was everywhere—the prison itself was nothing more than an old iron casting factory refurbished to cram in as many holding cells as possible. The building was massive but there were enough concealment spells around the perimeter to keep the humans away and prying eyes back in their sockets. As far as everyone was concerned, the factory that now housed the magical prison of the High Coven was just that—an abandoned building that was deemed unsafe by the city. What made the prison such a hellhole were the spell blocks the High Coven put into the walls and flooring to prevent any elements from seeping through and, unless you had a bulldozer handy, you were royally screwed if you landed yourself here. Sitting in the waiting room, I could feel the pressure of the coven's magic all around me. It was heavy and thick, like a fresh coat of oil paint on a canvas, and it was everywhere. My eyes glanced around the dull walls, and I choked on my spit when I took a sharp breath in. Being here for a lifetime would be excruciating.

The thing they don't tell you when you're a young witch is how much you need magic to survive. Not just need it, but demand it, like the air you breathe. I didn't find out until much later in life of the repercussions Beatrix and other traitors like her had to suffer but when I did, I almost felt sorry for her. To rot in a ten by ten-foot cell with no access to the elements and no magic rushing through your blood did not sound like fun at all. In fact, it seemed almost inhumane. But after the crap she pulled to get locked up, I couldn't blame the High Coven for taking these measures. Every witch caged in this prison deserved what she got and seeing it first hand only confirmed my decision to stay on the coven's good side, no matter what it took.

I traced a finger over the armrest of the chair I nervously sat in, grazing the letters stamped into the metal. *Stamwick Metalworks.* The coven kept as much of the original building as they could in case a health and safety inspector showed up to check the premises. It rarely happened, but every once in a while, some overachiever came knocking and one of the warden witches had to tour them around. The story was always the same—the factory was bought by a wealthy investor who used it as a filming location for an upcoming feature film. It was a pretty decent cover, the place reeked of creepy energy that would have been an ideal setting for some B-rated horror flick. Too bad the horrors inside were very real and more gruesome than even Hollywood money could buy.

Footsteps echoed beyond the waiting area, and I jolted to attention.

The, not surprising, concrete door at the far end of the waiting room swung open and I was greeted by one of the witch wardens. She looked to be in her late thirties and her grim facial expression told me she was not someone I wanted to mess with. Her dark brown hair was tied into a low chignon and there was not a lick of makeup on her face. With a low growl, she trained her silver eyes on me, and I gasped before sinking into the metal stool I sat in. The witch had only one eye! Well, one eye and a black socket where the other one should be.

Bile crept up the sides of my throat and I gagged into my hand.

"Miss Stonewall?" she asked, arching one eyebrow.

"Y... yes," I stuttered. "That's me."

"Follow me," the witch said and gestured to the door. "The prisoner has been secured in the visitation booth."

I hesitated but forced myself to get up.

We walked down a narrow corridor with bright overhead lighting that pierced my vision and I cringed as our footsteps echoed behind us. For someone with only one eye, the witch was quick on her feet, and I had to run up several times to keep pace with her. When we reached the end of the corridor, she popped a piece of lotus root under her tongue and waved her hand over the door we stood before. There were a few clicks on the other side and then the door swung open to let us through.

I expected to see Beatrix chained to a chair with a muzzle over her face like that movie about the guy who ate people for fun. Instead, we faced yet another corridor, this one even more narrow than the first.

"Go straight through and knock three times on the door. You'll be let in."

"Wait, you're not coming with me?" I asked.

I turned, but the witch had already slipped through the doorway and slammed it shut behind her. My temples pulsed and sweat dripped down my neck, soaking the back of the new band tee I put on that morning. This was it. I was about to see my mother for the first time in Goddess knows how long and I didn't know how to react. Suddenly, I was a kid again, eager to gain her approval. Would Beatrix even recognize me? I knew I looked a lot like her, but it's been over ten years, what were the chances she knew who I was anymore?

Shaking, I raised my hand and knocked three times as instructed.

There were more clicks before the door opened much like the first and I felt myself waver. My hand pressed at the doorframe for balance, and I stumbled through, drunk on my own nerves and fear.

The room I entered was wide with no other entrance points besides the door I used to enter. As soon as I was over the threshold, the metal scraped against the concrete floor and shut with a bang. Trapping me inside. I pushed the mane out of my face and looked up. In the middle of the room was a large round table with two chairs, on one of them, a woman sat with her gaze downward. Her blonde hair was shaggy and looked like it's been cut by a blind person and the gray suit she wore was wrinkled so thoroughly that it resembled crumpled linen. There was a number stitched to the lapel of her left shoulder and I memorized the numbers. Prisoner fifty-seven.

The woman stirred in her seat and raised her pointed chin my way. Her hazel eyes met mine and my breath hitched. "Wilhemina?"

I cleared my throat and nodded before forcing myself to sit down in the empty chair opposite her.

"Hello, Beatrix," I choked out. "Long time."

"Long time indeed, baby," she smiled. "Goddess, how I missed you! You know, just the other day I was thinking about that time we got stuck in that elevator. After I vanquished a soul sucker, remember that?"

I scowled. "Not your baby and I'm not here for memory lane. Thanks."

Across from me, Beatrix's body tensed, and she stretched her hands over the table toward me. I instinctively pulled away, the chair creaking under my weight. Not that I was afraid she'd hurt me, she had no magic in this place and I was certain we were being watched, but I still didn't want to be anywhere near her.

"Then why did you come?"

My mother's voice grew sharp and serious, and her eyes narrowed to slits.

"I have some questions for you. About who we are, our family that is."

She laughed. "We have no family, baby. We only have each other." Her eyes drifted past me and grew darker like she was remembering something she'd have preferred to keep hidden.

"Stop lying," I snapped. "You've done enough of that to last a lifetime."

"I'm telling you the truth, dear. No one is on our side in this world. No one at all."

"Graves."

"I'm sorry?"

"I said, Graves." I sneered and leaned into the table, placing my palms on the icy surface of the concrete.

Beatrix widened her eyes and her jaw slacked. "How do you know that name?"

"I know a lot more than you think so you better start talking."

"Not until you tell me what you already know." She forced a smile, but it didn't reach her eyes. "No point wasting time since I doubt they'll let me talk for long after they hear what I have to say."

She gestured to the blinking red light in the corner of the room, and I nodded in recognition. So, I was right, we *were* being watched. Without thinking, I reached for my ring and felt instant disappointment when it wasn't there. I had to leave all my crystals and herbs with the wardens before I came in but not having my crutch nearby was debilitating. I don't think I realized how much I relied on the moonstone ring to calm me down until that very moment. My hands fisted and I squared my shoulders, gaze trained on Beatrix.

"I know our real last name isn't Stonewall. It's Graves, isn't it?" Beatrix nodded and a sense of resentment rushed over me. "I also know that we have fae blood coursing through our veins, spirit blood."

As promptly as I uttered the word 'fae', Beatrix's face dropped. Her eyes grew dark and pensive, and the two inner points of her eyebrows met until she looked like she only had one brow to begin with. The wrinkles in her forehead were so intense that I nearly started laughing while picturing her forty years from now as an old lady. *Get over it! You will never see her again, especially not forty years from now.*

"Wilhemina," she whispered, "you need to stop whatever it is you're doing. You can't go looking into the past. It isn't safe."

She leaned in and I followed her lead. As her hands reached further on the table, I inched my fingers toward hers but stopped before we touched. Tears were already starting to form under my lids, and I had to push them away. I couldn't let her know she got to me. "Why isn't it safe?" I asked and leaned back again.

"Our past is complicated. *Your* past specifically. Stop asking questions before you put yourself in danger."

"I'm already in danger, Beatrix!" I wailed. "So, you better help me. I know you don't care for me, and I know you never wanted to have me around, but you have to help me!"

"Baby," she said, "of course I care for you. I love you. You're my daughter."

"Didn't love me more than magic, I guess."

Beatrix cocked an eyebrow. "Is that what they told you? That I'm here because I misused magic? Figures."

"What are you talking about? It's the damn truth, Mother!"

"Baby," she whispered and leaned in, "there are two sides to every truth..."

Loud footsteps sounded in the corridor and worry flashed over her eyes. Her hands reached for mine and I let her snatch my fingers into a firm hold. My entire body vibrated and the tears I was trying to hold back were streaming down my face. I wanted to press her more, to find out what the hell she was hinting at, but the fear on her face stopped me cold. Whatever lies Beatrix spewed settled in my gut and I instantly hated myself for falling for her garbage.

"Listen, baby. We have little time left, but you have to promise me you'll stop what you're doing. Getting mixed up with the fae is a death sentence, just look at *me*!" She gestured to her gray uniform but her one hand stayed cradled on top of my own. "Do you still have that ring I gave you?"

I nodded.

"Good, that's good. Keep it close and never lose it! The only thing your father ever did right was give you that ring."

"My father? Who is he? Is he still around? How do I find him?" Questions poured out of me like a waterfall, but I couldn't stop myself from asking them.

"You must never look for your father, Wilhemina," she said, and her voice was stone. "Promise me!"

"I can't do that!"

Beatrix's lips opened but before she could say anything else, two witch wardens pushed into the room and grabbed her by the elbows. They pulled Beatrix to her feet, shoving her away from me. My mother's bare feet dragged on the cold floor, and she fought their hold, but her body was too weak. She'd been without magic for too long and it surprised me she could even walk anymore. Most witches that have been caged for this long were nothing but vegetables by now.

"Promise me, Billie!" she shouted before they shoved her through the door and into the corridor. "Promise me!"

Her screams echoed through the room, sucker-punching me in the gut. I bent over the table, breathing so heavily that my lungs felt like they would explode. My body shook and I scraped my nails over the table, breaking another one in the process. Why did I come here? Why did I think she would help me get answers?

My head pounded and I threw a fist down into the concrete, wincing at the jarring pain it sent up my arm. Beatrix was right about one thing, in this world, there was no one on my side. Not her, not my friends, and not the High Coven. If I was going to survive being the killer's next target, I had to do it myself and on my own terms. My spine uncurled and I clumsily shoved hair out of my face, scrubbing the skin clean of the tears that stained it. A plan formed in my mind, clearer than anything I've thought before. It wasn't safe and it wasn't coven sanctioned, but these were desperate times, and I couldn't wait around to get their permission. My days were numbered, and this was the best play I could think of. There was only one way to get to the monster that wanted me dead.

I'm going to bait the witch out by giving what she wants most. I'm going to give her me.

Chapter
Thirty-four

"You're the next target?" Savannah's face looked like I just ran over her puppy with a pickup truck. Why was this girl always making my life so hard? By the looks of her, you'd think she was jealous it wasn't her on the list of next to die in some creepy ass ritual.

I rolled my eyes and turned my back to her, facing the rest of the hunters. "*Anyway*, looks like my mom lied about our family history and I have fae heritage."

"Mind," Jayden said, "blown. Like totally. I'm speechless here, guys. For reals."

"You're spewing a whole lot of bullshit for someone speechless," Morgan teased and tapped her palm a couple of times on his cheek. "But you're lucky you're cute."

My gaze turned to River beside me. "Are those two a couple?"

"Ew!" Jayden and Morgan yelled in unison.

"Besides," Morgan added and waved her arm over Jayden, "I don't do whatever *this* is."

"Ouch! Shots fired!" Jayden yelped. They both laughed and I found myself more confused than ever.

"Morgan's into the ladies," Abigail offered when she noticed my blank stare. Beside her, Tyler growled in approval, and she smacked him on the shoulder. "No picturing my bestie doing her thang. We talked about this!"

Tyler's face dropped, but he still managed to fist pump Jayden when Abigail wasn't looking. Beside them, Morgan only rolled her eyes and continued to paint her nails.

Huh. Would Morgan and Peyton get along? I cursed myself for even thinking of Peyton right now, but the last couple of days without her were horrible. I reached for my phone every half hour to text her, but no words came out. There was no way to describe the loss I felt over finding out my best friend was a shadower, but the most confusing part was that I was starting to come around to it. Agony spread over my bones, and I groaned. Sooner or later, I'd have to tell the High Coven who she is, and they would swoop in to take care of the problem. My stomach turned just thinking about what that meant. River rolled his shoulders in my peripheral and my stomach turned. When the High Coven was done with Peyton, he and his friends would be next.

"Seriously, though, you?" Savannah sniped. "You're so... unimportant."

Maybe I'd be okay with her getting axed.

"Yes, me," I hissed. "And it's not some badge of honor. I'm going to die if we don't stop this witch, or did you forget that part?"

She flipped her curls and rested her head on Abigail's shoulder. "Yeah, yeah, whatever. Just get on with it. You had some plan?"

"And shouldn't Peyton be here?" Morgan asked.

Interesting.

"She's busy," I answered a little too quickly. "And she wouldn't like what I'm about to say, so…"

Everyone looked at me with wide eyes and I shifted my weight in the stool. As usual, we gathered in River's kitchen, which I was realizing was ground zero for the hunters. They all seemed so comfortable here, but that was likely because no one else had the pleasure of being told off by Evanora. Although, no one else was caught sucking face with River on this very counter, at least I hoped no one had. My arm brushed against his and I sucked in the familiar scent of his cologne before gritting my teeth. *Get a good whiff while you can.*

"We'll use me as bait," I said matter-of-factly. "This witch is gunning for me, so we present me on a silver platter and see if she shows."

"Then what?"

I haven't thought that part out yet, which was exactly why they were here. The witch was powerful, even more so now that she had four fae bloodlines coursing through her veins. I couldn't defeat her on my own and bringing in the High Coven was out of the question. Not until I was ready with whatever tale I would spin to convince them not to throw me in a cell for keeping the identities of the hunters secret for this long. Plus, if I took care of the witch myself, there was more of a chance they'd look the other way when I told them. The problem was that I didn't know how to proceed once I had her where I wanted her. Luring out the witch shouldn't be too difficult, but what's to stop her from killing me and completing the ritual before I dealt with her? I needed help and, as it turned out, my only lifeline was the group of witch hunters crowding the kitchen counter.

"You deaf or something?" Savannah asked and knocked on the marble to get my attention. "What do we do when she shows up?"

"I don't know yet," I answered. "You're the hunters here."

"Um, we haven't met a witch before," River admitted. "So, we're kind of rolling with the punches on this."

"What would you do if you have met one?"

I wasn't sure I wanted to know the answer, but they might think of something I couldn't.

"Chop her head off?"

Yeah, that's not going to work. "That won't work," I said, cringing at the thought.

Tyler leaned in, his face peeking through Abigail's long locks as he rested his head on her shoulder. From this angle, they looked like creepy conjoined twins in one of those old-school circus movies. "I'm pretty sure chopping anyone's head off is a sure way to get them nice and dead."

"Not this witch. She's too powerful."

"You got all that from some books you read back home too?" Savannah asked and her eyes narrowed my way. "No offense, but we've been training for this our entire lives. I vote for the chopping. Who's with me?"

She glanced around the table two hands popped up. Tyler and Abigail, no shock there. The other two kept their gazes down, except River—his eyes were only on me.

"You're sure it wouldn't work?" he asked.

I shook my head. "Think of it this way, she was already a powerful witch before she started this ritual because no way in hell someone can suck in that much energy unless they knew what they were doing. But now, she has four potent elemental fae lines running through her. She'll strike you dead before you even make do with this chopping you're so into."

Abigail and Tyler exchanged glances and shrugged.

"Fine, no chopping. What's the alternative?" Tyler asked.

This was the most I've heard him say to me since we've met, and it was refreshing to know he could string sentences together. What was even more exhilarating was that he was willing to go against Savannah's plan and side with me. It felt like I was justified somehow, like the hunters accepted me. A warmth spread through me, and I noticed myself unable to stop the smile that crept over my face. Was I happy that the hunters liked me?

Never mind, you can deal with your bullshit feelings later. Eyes on the prize!

"So, what's plan B?" Abigail asked.

I scrunched my nose and rested my chin in my hands. "I think we can use the ritual she was trying to perform against her. I'm still not sure of the details but I can hit the—" I stopped before the word 'grimoire' escaped my lips. "The books I saw at the Crystal Cauldron. There was a bunch there with spells and rituals, so I'm sure I can turn up with something."

"That's an excellent plan and all," Savannah purred, "but there's one minor problem."

"What?"

"We're not WITCHES!"

Ugh, right. As far as they knew, I was a regular human like them. I had to think of something to convince them to follow through with this. If I was going to use the killer's spell against her, I needed five points in the circle, which meant I needed five living bodies to fill the spots. Sure, they weren't witches, but energy was energy. They didn't need to have magic to stand in, they just needed to be alive. It was so simple, I couldn't believe I haven't thought of it sooner. I could recreate the Drawing of Life ritual the witch was using, but instead of fae energy, I use the hunters. If I could drain enough of their life force to strengthen myself, it should give me enough of a boost to knock the monster on her ass. *Shit!* This would go against so many coven laws, my head hurt just thinking about it. My mind raced as I thought of a plausible explanation and landed on keeping it as close to the truth as possible.

"As far as I know, magic is all about energy. This isn't Hogwarts. We don't need to perform any magic, but we need to convince the witch that we can and are going to. Then we keep her busy enough to knock her out."

"And then chop chop?" Jayden asked.

"NO!" I yelled. "Then call the cops and tell them we found the murderer. What is with you and the decapitation?"

"Meh." He shrugged. "Just would be cool to slay a witch like we're supposed to."

My shoulders dropped and I looked around the table. "How about this? If my plan to trap her doesn't work, you can chop her head off."

"Preach."

Everyone nodded and I felt sick to my stomach. I was teaming up with people who wanted nothing more than to kill a witch in the worst way possible. I could only imagine what they'd do to me if they found out I was one too. The hunters cheered before diving into a deep conversation about who would be in the circle and who was nominated for the kill if things went wrong while I closed my eyes, taking deep breaths like I was in a Lamaze class. Beside me, River cleared his throat and I turned to look at him.

"You okay?" he asked.

"Who, me? Yeah, super. About to lure out a powerful witch and hope she doesn't kill me. Couldn't be better."

"I meant because of that visit with your mom?"

Oh, right. I told him about that.

"I'm fine. I haven't seen her in forever, so it's not like she's my mom anymore." My heart ached from saying that even though I knew it was true. "Sorry I didn't tell you about her before."

"You mean the jail part?"

I nodded. "Yep."

"Don't sweat it. If it helps, I wish my dad was in jail so I wouldn't have to think about why he never bothers to come see me."

"You don't mean that."

"You're right." He sighed. "I don't. But it still feels like crap."

My hand reached for his under the table and our fingers intertwined. River's gaze found mine and I couldn't help but smile at the childish grin on his face. The pastel pink cotton tee he was wearing was doing all the right things to bring out the green in his eyes and the pressure between my thighs increased. For once, I was grateful to have the hunters there, or I might have pounced on him like a lioness protecting her cubs. I squeezed his hand and let the tension in my neck drift away.

"I get that," I whispered. "If anyone knows what it's like to have an absentee parent, it's *this* girl."

"Well, I, for one, like *this* girl." His smile widened and I leaned in, oblivious to the fact that we weren't alone.

River's hand squeezed mine harder and blood rushed to my face. *You hate him, you hate him, you hate him.* I recited to myself, but my stupid body had other ideas. All I could think of was his fingers around mine and the smell of his cologne in the air.

Something vibrated in my back pocket, and I jumped up. River's arms dropped to the side, and I grit my teeth as I tried to smile while whispering, "sorry," before pulling the phone out. My eyes were still on his yummy lips when I pressed the home button and Peyton's message popped into view.

I don't care that you're a witch. If you want to vanquish my ass later, I get that. But I sure as shit will not let you do whatever it is you're planning to do without my help. I have a particular skill set we both know about, and you need me.

River grabbed my arm and pulled me back down to sit. "Who's that?"

"Someone's that going to help." I scowled. "Whether I want her to or not."

Chapter Thirty-five

Freezing cold air nipped at my skin as I finished drawing the last rune in the circle. Around me, the cornstalks of Savannah's family farm whispered in the wind, their rustling deepening the uncontrollable nerves settled at the base of my stomach. Even though I hated agreeing with Savannah on anything, using her family farm as the spot to draw out the witch was an excellent plan. It was far enough out of the way, about a twenty-minute drive from the Chandlers, that we'd be well hidden from the human eye and the large cornstalks helped muffle any sounds that might arise should a fight break out. I was hoping it wouldn't come to that, but there was no actual way to know what to expect at this point. Lucky for us, Savannah's parents were in Costa Rica on vacation. So at least, we didn't have to worry about them interrupting our plans. I could see the enormous farmhouse that Savannah called home in the distance and even in the dark of night with most of the lights off, it still looked intimidating. I couldn't help but wonder if Savannah ever got lost in the halls when she was a child and if she was lonely growing up in such a sizable place all alone. As far as I knew, Savannah had no other siblings, which explained her mightier-than-thou attitude well. The one best thing to come out of the spoiled brat's upbringing was that we now had this killer spot to perform the ritual to draw the witch out.

I looked around and smiled. We couldn't have picked a better night to do this.

The full moon was high above, and its radiant light coated the field in shades of silver, the rays dancing along the treetops of the wooded area that sheltered the farm from the rest of the world. There was a definite chill in the air but at this point, I was so used to Shadowhurst weather that I didn't even bother zipping up my jacket. The amethyst pendant around my neck swayed against my skin as I drew the last rune and leaned back to inspect my work.

Since I couldn't very well bring my grimoire with me, I had to leave it back home, concealed with a spell, and work the ritual from memory.

Huh. Did I just refer to the guest house as home? That's weird.

I retraced the details of the ritual in my head and walked around the salt circle to make sure each of the five elemental points was correct. When I was satisfied, I looked to the hunters, and Peyton, and gestured for them to come forward to claim their spots.

As a group, we decided that myself, River, Peyton, Savannah, and Jayden were playing the parts of the elements while Tyler, Abigail, and Morgan hid in the cornfield to keep watch. It was a decent enough plan and if something were to go wrong, at least I knew I could trust Abigail to protect us with the knives she had already sharpened in preparation.

Hopefully, that wouldn't be the case, but who knew at this point.

"So, who's where?" Peyton asked, looking around the runes in confusion.

Her act of clueless human was convincing, though I knew better. Peyton was a shadower, not just any shadower, a soul sucker, and her knowledge of ritual and spell-work had to be better than average. The more I thought about it, the more her obsession with the occult made sense. I just wish I'd seen it sooner.

"Um." I cleared my throat and raised to standing. "Savannah should take the Fire spot. River can take Water, and Jayden should be in the Earth spot. You can stand in the Air position, and I'll hit the middle, right where the Spirit element would be."

"No probs, bestie." Peyton winked at me and hopped to her designated rune.

I didn't fail to notice the emphasis she placed on the word and the smile that widened on her face as she passed me. It was super uncomfortable to hear a shadower refer to me as her best friend, but I couldn't keep lying to myself. I cared for Peyton, shadower or not, and it was throwing my entire perspective on life off orbit. The soul suckers I've vanquished in Stamwick were vicious and cruel and they wanted nothing more than to hurt humans. But Peyton was different. She was sweet and I did not get any evil energy off her at all, even after I found out she was a shadower. Plus, her eagerness to help me save this town was endearing. She was willing to risk her life to help me, a witch, and I simply couldn't believe it was true. Maybe not every shadower was bad. It was possible that what we've been taught by the High Coven wasn't entirely true. I mean, they lied about so many other things, why not this too?

Peyton's shoulder brushed against mine and I reached for her elbow to stop her in her tracks. "Thanks for helping," I whispered. "I mean it."

"I know." She smiled. "Like I told you before, girl, I got your back."

I knew she meant that, and my shoulders slumped in relief.

As the others settled into their spots on the freezing cold ground, River walked over to me. I was so distracted going over the correct placement of amethyst dust and peach wood that I didn't see him approach. By the time I noticed, he was already crouching on the ground next to me and his hand was on my shoulder. Warmth rushed through me, and I buckled back as the sudden urge to hold him overtook me. He was so close that I could jump his bones before the others even noticed what happened. *Focus!* I growled at myself and shook the thought away though the racing of my heartbeat refused to simmer down. His fingers grabbed mine and I looked up at him, tears welling behind my eyes. How could someone this beautiful be interested in someone like me? I couldn't believe it.

"Are you sure you're ready for this?" he asked and pulled me in closer. "We don't have to do this you know."

Behind him, Savannah said something nasty, and I laughed when Peyton flipped her off. My friend looked my way, signaling that she could finish off Savannah if I wanted her too and it only made me laugh harder. Having a soul sucker on my side might prove useful after all. I wiped the tears that fell as I laughed from my face and turned to look at a very confused River. His eyebrows arched and he looked between me and Peyton like he was trying to size us up.

Good luck figuring this out, hunter! I giggled and squeezed his hand to get his attention. "I'm fine. And we most def need to do this."

"But we're going in blind."

"What he said!" Jayden yelled out in agreement. "You sure we can take this witch?"

I looked around the circle and forced a smile. "I'm not."

Jayden and Savannah groaned in unison, but to my surprise, it was Peyton who spoke up next. The red streaks in her hair looked almost pink in the moonlight and the thick eyeliner around her eyes made her appear even more dangerous than I already knew she was. Her voice was loud and boomed over the circle in a commanding manner I haven't heard her use before.

"Correct me if I'm wrong," she said, "but aren't you lot supposed to be hunters? Maybe I got something wrong here, but I expected, oh, I don't know, some courage?"

The hunters didn't respond, but I could see her words struck a chord. Savannah arched a manicured eyebrow and her teeth clenched together, making her high AF cheekbones even more defined. I touched my own face and frowned.

"Okay, cool," Peyton continued. "So, if you three wussies are ready, I'd like to get this over with so I can get back to binging Survivor."

She turned and gave me a thumbs up.

"What she said," I choked out, mimicking Jayden's words. "You guys ready?"

"As long as you're sure," River said and stood up. He looked back at the group. "Whatever happens, we protect Billie at all costs."

Everyone except Peyton nodded. Instead, my best friend hissed like a cat and buried her feet into the earth next to her rune. *She is so freaking weird.*

I walked around them, shifting their weight to align them into the best position. As I reached River, I took my sweet time as I rearranged his body. A cocky grin formed on his lips, deepening his unbearably cute dimple, and I pinched his side and rolled my eyes, roping my hand over his waist to move him forward a few inches. His own hands wrapped around mine and I found myself frozen, holding him in a tight hug from behind. My thighs shook as I took in his scent, and I leaned in to give him a quick kiss on the cheek when I was sure no one else was watching.

River's cheeks blushed and I had to force myself to step away.

"So, what now?" Savannah asked, drawing me back to the circle.

I stepped around River and took my place in the center. "Now, we draw blood."

"Oh, hell no!" Jayden yelled. "Uh-uh!"

"Relax, it's just a drop."

I pulled out the dagger from my boot and ignored the gasps of surprise from the circle. I tossed it, hilt first, to River. "Nick your index finger and trace the rune by your feet with the blood."

He nodded and did as I asked, passing the dagger to Peyton beside him. They went around the circle until it was Savannah's turn, and though she took her sweet ass time to follow suit, she finally finished the job. Her eyes narrowed on mine as she tossed the dagger back to me and I had to refrain from squirming, worried she was aiming for my throat. I caught the blade and brought it my palm, slicing across the center, and slamming my hand into the earth.

Around me, magic whirled in circles as it rushed into my body. The air thickened and I found it hard to keep my eyes on the rune in front of me. Power surged inside me, and it was unlike anything I've ever felt before. I could sense the energy of the circle members and it called for me, begging for me to drink it in. My eyes closed and my head rolled back as I opened myself up, letting the life forces of my friends to enter me. My lids fluttered and the ground under my feet grew dark, dying as I sucked its energy in with the rest. Gasps sounded all around, but I couldn't pinpoint who they belonged to. On my finger, the moonstone ring throbbed and ebbed, and I fought the urge to rip it off. My blood felt like it was boiling and sweat dripped down my face and back.

Suddenly, the energy shifted, and a cold breeze whipped by me, throwing my loose hair into my eyes. My body froze and I snapped my eyes open to follow the source.

My head whipped around just as a shadowy figure stepped out of the trees close to us. As it approached us, my jaw tightened and my hands fisted at my side, gripping the dagger with more strength than I thought I had.

She came.

My eyes narrowed in the witch's direction, and I squared my shoulders, rising to my feet. It wasn't until she was just outside our circle, I realized who I was looking at and my entire world exploded.

Chapter Thirty-six

"Mom?"

"Ms. Hunting?"

"Evanora?"

We all yelled out in unison. My jaw dragged on the ground and my knees were so weak, I couldn't stand straight. To my left, River's face was the same shade of grey as the concrete walls in the magical prison and my heart broke for him.

Evanora threw her head back and laughed, then walked around the circle so she could face me. Her hair was braided off her face and she wore a dark, wool coat over one of her signature suits. In her right hand, she clasped a handful of crystals, and I could see a tightly knit bushel of herbs tied around her neckline.

SHE'S THE KILLER? No, this can't be right. River's mom is the witch I'm after?

My pulse skyrocketed and a heavy pressure formed behind my temples until I could barely see a foot ahead. My gaze jerked to River, but he couldn't see me staring, his eyes were only on Evanora. I could see him try to form words, but his mouth only opened and closed like he didn't know where to start. He was a fish out of water, and I was watching him struggle to breathe right in front of me.

"It's you?" I asked, though I already knew the answer. "Why?"

The rest of the circle was quiet while we waited for her to respond. Peyton kept looking from me to Evanora to River and the confusion on her face mimicked my own. Next to her, Jayden's expression looked like he was trying to solve a math equation while Savannah was a mystery as always. Her tight curls bounced as she shook her head 'no', but her face was angered and determined. Her hand reached to the waist-line of her leather leggings where I knew she stashed a knife, or two, in case things went off the rails. Both she and Jayden looked like they didn't know whether to listen or kill Evanora on the spot. I waved my hand at my side, hoping to get their attention before they did something stupid and got themselves killed. To my relief, Savannah saw me and let her arms drop to the sides. The glare I got from her told me I'd regret it later, but it relieved me she knew well enough to listen.

"*Why not* is what you should ask," Evanora said, ice in her voice.

Time had seemed to stop, and I didn't even remember asking her a question at all but as soon as she spoke, I was back in the circle, my eyes fiercely trained on hers.

"Mom, what the hell are you doing here?"

"Language!" Evanora snapped and walked to her son. "I taught you better than to forget your manners."

"Manners are the least of my worries right now! You're a WITCH?"

Evanora sneered and ruffled River's hair with her

slender fingers. "I'm sorry you had to find out this way, darling, but it was bound to come out sooner or later. I had hoped for later."

"Why, Mom? Why are you doing this?" River shook his head, his eyes red. "You killed those students..."

"I did what had to be done."

"Bullshit!" I yelled out and took a step toward her.

Evanora tightened her grip on River's hair to send me a warning. If I didn't watch myself, he would pay the price. My heart broke into a million pieces as I thought about what River must have been feeling. His own mother is a killer. One that was threatening his life right now just to get what she wanted. *Goddess*. And I thought Beatrix was bad.

"You know, I'm starting to see where you're getting those unpleasant habits," Evanora purred and let go of his hair. My shoulders sank and I breathed out a sigh of relief but didn't move an inch. "It would appall your father to see you with the likes of her."

"You called Dad an inbred imbecile, remember?"

Evanora's lips curled into a sinister smile, and she let out a howling laugh. It echoed through the field and though I couldn't be certain, I was willing to bet I heard a flock of birds take off from the sound. "Not that idiot. Your *real* father."

Everyone in the circle turned to look at River, myself including.

"My..." he stammered. "What?"

"Your actual father, River. Or did you think you were the fruit of the wasted space that left us without so much as a good bye?"

"I... I..."

River's gaze met mine and the hurt that flashed across his

features broke me. I wanted to run to him, to wrap my arms around him, and tell him it would be all right, but that would have been an even dumber move that this entire ritual. I shouldn't have brought him here. Any of them. I should have done this on my own and then maybe River's heart wouldn't be breaking in front of me. Tears fell down my cheeks and I sniffled my nose, wiping it with the sleeve of my jacket.

"I should have told you," Evanora said, "but I didn't think you'd understand."

"So, you what? Pushed me into witch hunting? But you're a witch! WHY WOULD YOU DO THAT?"

His shout rose over us, reaching as far as the cornfield and I was suddenly very aware of the hunters hiding in the stalks. How much have they heard? And why were they still hiding?

Evanora turned to face her son. She reached for his face, but River shrunk away from her, his lips smashed into a tight line. "Just tell me why."

"Because witches ruin everything."

"*You're* a witch!"

"Yes, yes I am." She smiled, and it almost looked genuine. "But I am not like the rest of them. They ruined my life, River. They ruined *our* life! They forced me to kill your father just because he wasn't like them. Could you imagine what that felt like?"

The night somehow got darker to match Evanora's gaze. Her eyes were vacant, and she stared somewhere past my shoulder, her face paling with each moment that passed. A few tears glistened at the edge of her eyes, but she blinked them away in an instant. My thoughts were a mile a minute as I tried to connect the logic of her words. Witches forced her to kill River's father. But why? There was only one reason the High Coven would order a killing and—

Oh, my Goddess.

"Oh, I see someone is catching on," Evanora said my way. Her eyes burned into me, and I looked away, worried she might see more than what she came here for. "Your father was a shadower. A shifter, and the strongest, kindest man I've ever met. But they couldn't see that. All they saw was that he was different and as soon as the coven found out I was pregnant, I had to choose. Him or you. I was still a kid but even then, I knew I could never not pick you. Your father knew it too, so when I showed up to vanquish him, he didn't even fight back. That's how much he loved us."

"A shadower? High Coven?" Savannah asked.

River's mom snapped her head in Savannah's direction and the girl jumped back. "Yes. You know, for witch hunters, you children are ill-equipped in the way of knowledge. I really should have done a better job of pointing you in the right direction. Perhaps after all this is done, I can help train you better."

My blood bubbled and anger rose in my throat. *She's a freaking lunatic!* Whatever beef Evanora had with the High Coven didn't excuse her actions. She was a murderer. She killed innocent kids. And for what? To avenge a choice she made herself long ago? It was pathetic.

"You chose for yourself," I said. "You killed him just like you killed all those kids. You're a monster."

"Excuse me?"

"You heard me."

Evanora stepped over the salt threshold of the circle and walked up to me. She was my height to the tee, and I could feel her breath on my face as she leaned into me. "I'm not surprised to see you defend them. I was just like you once, you know." She sighed and turned her back to me. "I was young and impressionable. When the High Coven found me, I had already run away from home and had nowhere to go. So, it was easy to fall for their lies because they were my kind, my people. They were witches and witches stick together. At least they do until someone steps out of line. Then they toss you away like you're nothing, but not before they break you until you wish you were dead."

A scowl formed on her lips, and she crossed her arms, tightening her overcoat closed. Her shoulders dropped and she shifted her weight from foot to foot like she was unsure if she should stay or go. Darkness passed over her features and tears fell down her cheeks, her shoulders bobbing as she tried to stop herself from crying. She was so heartbroken that I almost felt sorry for her. Or at least I did until I remembered why we were in the field. My eyes instinctively drifted to River. The slouch of his shoulders and the redness in his eyes told me he was in more shock than the rest of us. I couldn't blame him. If I found out my mother was a lying murderer and that my dad was some rando shifter, I'd lose it. It all started to make sense now. My immediate draw to him, the darkness I felt rolling off him when we touched. It spelled shadower blood through and through, and I never let myself see it. What would that mean for him now? For us? I wanted to reach for him, to tell him everything will be fine and that I'll help him through it, but my feet were planted too firmly to move. And he hasn't said a word since Evanora showed up, so I doubted he needed me to make matters worse. All things considering, he was doing a pretty good job of not ripping her head off. Unlike me, who wanted nothing more than to pounce on her and get it over with.

"YOU KILLED KIDS!" I yelled, forcing her to face me again. "You're a murderer!"

Evanora laughed again except this time, it was a piercing shrill that chilled my bones. "No more so than you, WITCH! Or do you want me to believe that you have never vanquished an underage shadower before?"

Behind me, Savannah and Jayden gasped, and I spun to see their mouths wide open as they stared at me. At their side, Peyton's eyes filled with worry, and she moved toward me but I held my hand up to motion her to stop. My face flushed with anger, and I turned to face Evanora, ready to lash out, when I noticed River staring at me over her shoulder. I didn't think it was possible for him to get paler but there he was, frozen in his spot with a ghostly complexion over his otherwise bronze skin.

"What?" he asked in almost a whisper.

Evanora winked at me and the hairs on my arms stood rigid. She walked back to her son, resting her hand around his shoulder. "I told you she was bad news, darling."

A coldness ran through me, and I felt the earth give way under my feet. I tried to move toward him but my body was unwilling to cooperate. My arms fell flaccid at my sides, and I met his gaze, tears streaming down my face. "River, please, I can explain," I tried to say but he shook his head.

"Stop lying." His voice was so cold that it hit me in the face like a mallet. "Both of you. I hate you both."

"Darling," Evanora purred.

"Shut," River hissed, "UP!"

"Honey, you didn't think I would have a problem with you seeing her for no good reason, did you?"

"You've been known to do things for no good reason

before. Is this why you pushed so hard for me to be a hunter? For your own personal gain?"

Evanora's features darkened and she faced her son. "For *our* gain, sweetheart. Witches can't be trusted."

"No, YOU can't be trusted, Mom! How could you do this?" River yelled. Sweat beaded on his forehead, plastering his wet hair to his face. His eyes were wild and restless, and my own anger mirrored his as I remembered my outrage when I found out about Beatrix's betrayal.

"River..." I whispered.

His eyes snapped to me and the hatred in them was palpable. "Don't! I don't want to hear anything you have to say. Ever."

Deflated, I took a step back and set my gaze on my boots. My heart twisted and my ribs constricted as I tried to breathe. He didn't deserve this, any of it, and I should never have kept this from him. Instead of worrying about my own damn self, I should have thought of him. I should have trusted him enough to tell him the truth before it came to this. He hated me and I couldn't even blame him. I hated myself.

Thunder roared in the distance and somehow, the night grew even darker around us. The chill in the air was unbearable and my teeth chattered as I tried to keep my balance. In my peripheral, I saw Evanora move to River, her hands trembling as she reached for him. He pushed her off and turned away, stepping out of the circle to head for the trees beyond. As his back retreated, my insides thrashed until I was ready to throw up on my boots. Just before he was out of sight, River turned back, his eyes narrowed on me. He took a deep breath then turned to his mother. "Do whatever you want

with her," he said, "and when you're done, I never want to
see you again."

He was gone before I could say anything at all.

Chapter Thirty-seven

"Guys, listen..."

I struggled to say, but I was too late. Savannah already had a knife in each hand, though from this angle, they looked more like sharpened machetes. Beside her, Jayden cocked the safety of his rifle and pointed it at my head. *Why does he have a rifle? Did I know he had a rifle? That would have been excellent information to have.* I scowled and raised my hands defensively. "I just want to talk."

"Should have thought of that before," Savannah hissed. "You lying witch!"

The knives in her hand caught the light of the moon and my stomach turned. Even if I was quick enough to knock her out, she could still do some damage with those things before I could get close enough. Not to mention Jayden's damn rifle. I was fast but I was not faster than a bullet. Jayden shifted his weight and I saw his finger move a half an inch away from the trigger. My lungs contracted and I released a slight breath. Small victories were all I had left it seemed.

"Dudes, are you serious?" Peyton chimed in from her spot on the Air rune. "She's not the bad guy here!"

Savannah and Jayden looked to each other, disregarding her entirely. Their faces faltered and I took a step toward them, hopeful the gesture wouldn't appear confrontational. I really didn't want to fight them, not when the actual killer was still standing next to me with a wicked smile plastered on her face.

"She's right, guys. *I'm* not the one that killed those students. I'm not the one that killed your friend."

Close to me, Evanora groaned in disgust. "You're hunters, children. Finish the job."

Another flash of the knives jerked my gaze away from River's mom and back to Savannah. I tightened my hold on my dagger, expecting her to charge for me, but to my surprise, she stood still. Her gaze drifted over me like she was trying to decide if she should kill me or not. Next to her, Jayden moved the rifle's tip from my head to Evanora's then back again.

They're faltering.

I grabbed my chance while I still had it and took two more steps toward the hunters. My eyes widened and I held the dagger to the side to show them I would not use it, though I didn't let go of my grip. I had to be ready, just in case. "We came here to find the person responsible for the murders. We found her." I gestured to Evanora with a tilt of the head. "You can deal with me later, but right now, I need your help."

Evanora laughed like she couldn't believe I was bold enough to convince them to work against her, but I knew how wrong she was. I could see it in their eyes. Sure, they were witch hunters, but there was only one witch in this circle that posed a threat right now and that sure as shit wasn't me. My eyes met Savannah's and I smiled before raising a questioning eyebrow her way. My lips parted and I whispered *please* just loud enough for her to hear.

Then I closed my eyes and waited for her to decide.

It happened so fast, I barely had time to snap my eyes open. One moment, I was standing defenseless a foot away from two giant knives and a loaded rifle and the next, I was being pushed out of the way. My shoulder throbbed from the hit, and I spun around, tripping over loose rock and plummeting to the ground below. My tailbone hit the earth and I squirmed from the pain. Swallowing hard, I locked my eyes on Savannah, who was running toward Evanora with the knives slashing across the air. She was fast and fearless, and I fell silent, in awe of how fast she could switch sides. Her legs pumped and the slender muscle of her thighs pulsed against her leather leggings. She looked like a freaking superhero.

Savannah sliced the air again and skidded to a stop a few feet from Evanora. Her eyes narrowed on the witch, and she growled like a jungle cat. In one quick motion, Savannah swung back and catapulted the knives forward, aiming straight for Evanora's heart.

Before the knives could reach her, Evanora tightened her fist around the crystals in her hand and shot her hands up. Her face hardly moved as she thrust her magic at Savannah. A gasp escaped me, and I clutched my hands into the earth to hold on as a heavy gust of wind shot out of Evanora's hands and rushed for the knives. The blades flung in the opposite direction as soon as the wind hit them, but Evanora didn't stop there. She buried her weight into the earth and pushed more magic out, intensifying the wind until it was a hurricane barreling straight for Savannah.

"NOOOOO!" I shouted and jumped up.

I ran for the hunter, throwing my body her way, but I was too slow. I was nowhere near Savannah by the time the wind hit her head on and shot her out of the circle and across the field. Her body fell with a thud and the breath that knocked out of her rose in a puffy white smoke over her lips.

"Savannah!" Jayden yelled and started for his friend.

He was still running when Evanora threw her magic at his back and sent him flying ten feet past where Savannah's body lay still. I cringed at the sound of him hitting the earth and had to turn away when I noticed that his left arm was lying at an unnatural angle at his side. From where I stood, I couldn't see either of them move but I couldn't just let them die. I also couldn't leave Evanora in the circle with Peyton.

Time slowed down as I tried to take in my options, but I knew I had none left.

"Peyton!" I yelled. "Check if they're okay!"

In seconds, my best friend was sprinting down the field toward the fallen hunters, her red streaks flashing in the moonlight behind her. My eyes watered while I watched for her to check Savannah's pulse and throw two thumbs up my way. By the time she reached Jayden, I could hear him scream in pain. His arm was for sure broken, but at least he was alive.

I breathed out and turned to Evanora.

"Why? They're River's friends. What the hell is wrong with you?" I screamed. "Witches don't do this!"

"Witches do much worse," she snapped back.

Her fingers twitched at her side, and I could see her fumble for the next crystal. I couldn't tell which one she picked and without knowing what element she was about to unleash, I had no way to protect myself. All I had was the amber in my pocket, the amethyst on my neck, and a silver dagger. I was ill-equipped for this fight, and I knew it. Goddess, how I wished Evanora was a shadower so I could just vanquish her ass and get it over with, but that was not the case. She was a witch and as much I hated to admit it, she was more powerful than me even before she had fae blood running through her veins.

I had to keep her talking until I could figure out my next move.

The hair on the back of my neck stood rigid and I lowered the dagger to my side. "You know you're surrounded. Even without Savannah and Jayden, we still have people."

"You mean the other children?" Evanora laughed and pointed to the cornfield. "I took care of them already."

"Took care of them?" My heart leaped into my throat as I thought about what those words could mean. "You killed them?"

Evanora cackled and pressed two fingers to her temple. "Goddess, no. You're quite morbid, are you not? I could never hurt those kids. As you said, they're River's friends, and besides, once this ritual is complete, I'll need them to help me take down the High Coven."

"Didn't stop you from killing Grady," I mumbled.

"Yes, well, a means to an end that one. I'm not sure you realize how difficult it is to find fae blood in this town. I mean, it took me years just to track them all down. And you," she pointed a French-manicured nail my way, "were the most difficult to find."

"You know that you're not better than them, right? The High Coven?"

Evanora's smile faltered. "Maybe so, but I will make them pay, regardless. I will make the world right again."

I started to object but her hand snapped up and she curled her fingers into a fist. The air in my lungs expelled as Evanora reached for it, pulling it out of my throat and into her hand. My lungs screamed for air, and I desperately tried to suck in a breath. The world blurred around me, and I toppled to the ground, hands ripping at my throat. Not far from me, Peyton shouted my name, but her voice was garbled and unclear. My vision blurred and I blinked with little success of regaining it.

"No more chit chat," Evanora said, her shadowy figure looming over me. "Time to begin."

Her hand flipped again, and I could breathe. I sucked in the icy air, tears streaming down my cheeks in relief. Before I could stand again, something hard hit me on the head and the night closed in around me.

Chapter Thirty-eight

My lids fluttered open, and the blurry field inched into focus. Cold earth spread around me, and I struggled to lift my pounding head to see. I was on my back, my arms splayed wide to either side, my head pointing straight for the middle.

Oh, Goddess, no. The ritual.

Above me, Evanora's voice boomed over the circle. She whispered something over and over and the sound whooshed around me like she was running in circles over my body. Which was exactly what she was doing. Maybe not so much running, but my vision was still not perfect, and I was sure I got a concussion from when she knocked me out, so really, she could've been standing still just as well. I tried to make out the words, but they made no sense to me. Either I was in worse shape than I thought or Evanora was not speaking English anymore.

My body shook and nausea filled me to the brim as the force of her magic pushed itself into me. It was like my limbs were being stretched to the sides with ropes and the pain was too agonizing to bear. My jaw clenched and I ground my teeth into each other to keep from screaming. Straining, I felt my fingers over the earth as I tried to locate my dagger, but it was nowhere to be found. The witch stripped me of all my weapons, even the amethyst pendant was gone from my neck.

Evanora whispered something else, and I got sucker-punched with her magic. I choked on my spit and coughed, my throat burning like wildfire.

"Billie!" Peyton's panicked voice rose somewhere beyond the circle, and I snapped to attention.

My eyes widened and my pulse skyrocketed. Peyton was about to do something stupid and if I didn't act fast, Evanora would kill her. But I couldn't act fast. I couldn't act at all.

With a low growl, Evanora stopped her chanting and reached for something on the ground next to my feet. My breath caught in my throat when I realized that she had my blade in her hand. I kicked my feet from under me, trying to stand up, but my body was glued to the earth, Evanora's magic was too strong. Eyes full of tears, I watched as she swung the dagger toward Peyton's voice. There was a yelp and a crunch, followed by a thud. *No, no, no!* "Peyton!"

There was nothing but silence.

The next few seconds were the most excruciating moments of my life. Time slowed around me, and my limbs grew heavy under their own weight. Peyton tried to save me and got herself killed. She was no doubt lying in the field bleeding out somewhere with my dagger in her chest. This was all my fault. All of this was my—

A groan sounded about ten feet away and I breathed out.

My shoulders dropped and I threw my head back, hitting the cold earth with my messy hair. *She's alive. SHE'S OKAY.*

"I am tired of these interruptions!" Evanora screeched.

Her feet shuffled next to me until I could see her face come into view above me. Her braid fell heavy over her shoulder and she sneered before kneeling beside me and placing both her palms on my forehead. Something rough scratched at my skin as she ran her hands over my face then down my neck. Amethyst dust. *Shit!* My body jerked but it did nothing to deter her. Evanora moved like a snake over me, whispering those foreign words over and over. Her gaze met mine and she cocked her head to the side before tracing something in the earth by my head with a peach wood branch.

"Thank you for your element," she whispered and slammed her hands into the earth.

My entire body screamed in agony. I riled on the ground, squirming to be free of my skin. Around me, the air grew so cold that I couldn't feel my toes inside my boots and my tears formed icicles on my lashes. I felt like she was ripping my magic straight out of me, like she was ripping out my heart. I opened my mouth to scream, but only silence poured out. Silence and death.

Inch by inch, my skin contracted and dried as my life force drained out of me and into Evanora. She laughed and I shuddered. Or at least I thought I did, I couldn't feel anything anymore to be sure. My eyes grew heavy and started to close and I let them. Fighting was no use. She was stronger and she had me trapped. I failed.

It's funny, but when they tell you that your life flashes before your eyes when you're about to die, they always forget to mention one thing. It's never the parts you actually want to see. All I saw was Beatrix taking my small hand right before Sebyl led her away. I watched her as clear as day, like it was happening in that very instant. I watched her smile and remembered how confused I felt when she said good bye to me. Why did my mom have to leave? I didn't understand. Her hands clasped mine and I felt something heavy in my palm. When I opened them, a pretty moonstone ring sat in the center, more beautiful than anything I've ever owned in my young life. Beatrix whispered something but I couldn't understand her through her tears. My gaze shifted from her to the ring and back again and I remembered it like it wasn't a memory at all. I remembered it like it was my life. And it was. The life I wanted to forget but never could.

My eyes fluttered open I was back in the field again, back under the hold of Evanora's magic and back on my deathbed. My fingers curled as my breathing slowed and I sensed something cool on my ring finger. *The ring!* I still had my ring. It wasn't much, but I was happy to die with it on. I reached my thumb for the stone in the center as I often did and pictured my mother's face.

As soon as my skin touched the stone, a sharp pain shot through my arm. It was so quick, I almost didn't notice it, but when it was gone, I could move my hands again. The skin that was dried out and deadened before was regaining color and I could feel my blood pump faster through my veins. Next to me, Evanora's eyes were still shut as she continued to speak the words I didn't understand over and over. My eyes jerked to my ring, and I turned it around on my finger to press the stone into the soft part of my palm. I fisted my hand and focused on my mother's face that continued to flash in my vision.

Suddenly, Beatrix was gone, and I hated to admit that I missed seeing her. Her face evaporated from my thoughts and was replaced by something very different. A shadow of a man.

He was tall, with wide shoulders and a long neck, but that was all I could see. It was like I was looking through the darkness that was his body. The man moved and the shadow dispersed, spreading over my vision until all I saw was night. My eyes shot open, but when they did, I found myself in pitch black. The field disappeared, as did the circle and Evanora, and I was lying amid shadows so thick, I couldn't see an inch ahead.

My hand shook and I raised myself on my forearms to look around but no matter where I turned my head, the shadows followed. They had swallowed me whole.

Somewhere near me, Evanora gasped, and I snapped my head in her direction. Granted, I couldn't see her, but I assumed that's where she was based on the sound. Trembling, I brought my palms to my face to inspect them, and the shadows reflected the movement. They covered my hands in darkness but through it, I could see the moonstone of my ring glow brighter than the sun.

"What are you?" Evanora whispered.

I pointed my ring hand to where her voice was and pushed my magic out. A guttural scream escaped me as I let it go free and slam into her. The shadows followed the scream, bursting from my body, and wrapping around her neck as I twisted my fingers like I was squeezing Evanora's skin. She choked and gasped as the shadows tightened their hold on her windpipe and my jaw dropped to the ground.

This wasn't possible! A moonstone crystal was only useful to create balance. It had no power on its own, at least not one that manifested physically. *How am I doing this?* Bile rose in my throat as I replayed Evanora's words in my mind.

What in the hell was I?

Chapter
Thirty-nine

The shadows spread across Evanora's body like vines until only her head could be seen. Her eyes bulged and spit collected at the side of her lips as she grit her teeth together. Watching her struggle to breathe brought me more joy than I cared to admit, and I raised my hands, directing the shadows to bring her off the ground.

Evanora's horror-stricken eyes jumped in every direction as she tried to find a way out of this, but I knew she couldn't escape me now. Her crystals and my dagger lay on the floor below her feet and the bushel of herbs around her neck did not offer enough energy to free her. She was mine.

My lips curved into a vicious sneer, and I squeezed my fingers tighter, watching the blood rush to her face from the pressure. I could almost laugh at the situation. Just seconds ago, Evanora had me on my deathbed and now, she was under my control. I was stronger than a witch with four fae lines inside her and it made me giddy.

Bet you'll never talk down to me now, Sebyl. Ooooh! I

wonder if I could be a high priestess now that I'm kick-ass strong? Man, I LOVE this!

The thought of telling Sebyl and the other high priestesses what to do for once felt amazing but Evanora's agonizing screams brought me back to reality. As I watched her crumble under the hold of my shadows—I still couldn't bring myself to refer to whatever it was I was doing as magic—a sickness spread through me. What I was doing wasn't right and what was worse, if I killed Evanora, I would be just like her.

I couldn't do that. Not even to her.

For sure not to River.

My gaze met hers one more time and then I pulled the shadows back into myself. To my shock, they obliged without question and Evanora fell to the ground from five feet high, dropping to her knees like a sack of potatoes.

I can't kill her. I had to bring her to the High Coven, just as I planned.

Slouching, I turned to pick up my dagger from the ground when something hit my back and knocked me forward. My palms scraped the earth and the skin on them burnt from the friction. I slid on my knees, turning to see Evanora back on her feet, clear quartz in one hand and sapphire in the other. Her fingers tightened around the quartz, and she slammed her magic in my face.

The wind that rushed from her knocked me further back until I was on my ass in the dirt. I reached for my magic, but Evanora was one step ahead, working the sapphire in an epic display of power. A stream of water shot out from her palm and into my open mouth, sending me reeling back from the impact. The water rushed down my throat and I coughed and choked, trying to get it out of my system. My body jerked and I fell forward and retched onto the earth. My throat still burnt when I looked back to Evanora, just as she was about to fire again. Her braid was loose, and her hair whipped around her face making her look like an evil villain from a movie. She was petrifying and I couldn't believe a witch this evil could create someone as kind as River.

My head hurt thinking about him, but I shook the thought away. I would never see that hot specimen of a man again.

Evanora threw her arm out and I readied for her attack when suddenly, something knocked her off balance. The sapphire flew from her hand, landing somewhere too far to see. Next to her feet, a knife stood on end, the tip impaled in the earth. Evanora's eyes snapped back, and I followed her lead.

NO!

Close to us stood River. His hand was still outstretched from throwing the knife and he was breathing so hard, I could see his pecs move up and down under this shirt. My eyes traveled down his body to the waistband of his jeans. *YUM...*

For the love of the Goddess, can you get a grip?!?

Reluctantly, I forced my gaze back up his body, pausing only a little to admire his chest again. A girl had to get what she could, right? Our eyes locked and confusion spread over my face. He came back and he stopped his mother from killing me. But why? *He can't be here to save my sorry ass, could he? No. Uh-uh. That's not what's happening here.* River was a witch hunter and I was a witch. There had to be another explanation for this.

"You're back?" I asked.

"Why, son?" Evanora said at the same time.

River peeled his gaze from mine and glared at her. "I can't let you kill her, Mom. I just can't."

"River Hunting," Evanora scolded. "You are a witch hunter, and you will step aside and let me do the job for you if you cannot. You kill witches, son."

"I won't kill this one," River said. "And you won't either."

Despite Evanora's screams otherwise, River walked to stand by my side. His hand reached for mine and when I felt his fingers, my soul relaxed. He was my personal Valium, and I couldn't get enough of his touch. And he was here. With me. He came back for me.

I was still in shock mode when River squeezed my hand and urged my attention toward him. "I'm sorry I left. And I'm sorry for what I said," he whispered. "You're not like her, Billie. I know that. You can't be. You just can't be. I don't know what I was thinking."

"You were thinking that you just found I'm a witch and I don't blame you. Thanks for coming back."

"I know, but—"

Before he could finish the sentence, his body shot back and away from me. He landed on the ground with a loud bang and groaned as he rolled over to the side. Rubbing his chest, River jumped back to his feet and glared at Evanora. "What the hell, Mom? Did you for real just do that?"

Evanora chuckled and blew him a kiss then threw another gust of wind our way. It aimed at me, and it didn't miss its target. My feet skidded across the ground as it pushed me back with a force so strong, I thought I got hit by a truck. My back collided with River's chest, and we tumbled back, limbs knocking against each other as we rolled.

With a grunt, I pushed myself off River and crouched, slamming my shadows into Evanora's chest to knock her back. She catapulted through the air, landing on her back inside the circle.

"Doesn't feel great, does it?" I yelled and brushed the dirt off my knees.

I walked toward her, steps quickening the closer I came. Both my arms stretched in her direction, and I saw the shadows grow around them as I built my magic, ready to charge. Evanora crab walked away from me and the fear on her face told me everything I needed to know. I was going to win this. The shadows burst out of me and pinned her body to the ground as I came to stand over her. Cringing, I pulled my arms apart, forcing my shadows to spread Evanora's arms to match mine. She was inside the circle and laid out in a cross, just like her victims had been. A laugh bubbled to the surface as I thought about how good it would feel to end her right there and then, in exactly this position.

"Billie, NO!" River shouted and ran to my side. "You can't kill her!"

"She killed those students! Your friend was one of them!"

My voice shook as I yelled, but my hold on Evanora stayed strong. I couldn't let her get away this time.

"Please," River begged. "She's still my mom. Please, Billie."

A shiver ran up my spine and I turned to look at him. "Then what? We can't just let her go. She will not stop. She's a freaking lunatic."

"I know."

"You might as well kill me because I don't think I can

live knowing my son is dating some filthy little High Coven supporter," Evanora sniped.

My eyes snapped to her, and I flicked my finger. At my command, a shadow crept from her shoulder and wrapped around her mouth like a muzzle. "Stay quiet or you'll get what you're wishing for," I hissed then turned back to River. "So, what do we do?"

"I don't know, can't you just trap her somehow? With magic?"

"That's what I'm doing now!" I yelled and rolled my eyes. "I can't hold her like this forever. I can feel myself draining already and I don't know how long I can last this way."

"Okay, fine. So, we tie her up."

"She'll just escape," I murmured. "Unless..."

The field around us grew quiet as my thoughts ran a million miles a minute. River was onto something here. I could trap her but not in the way he was thinking. I could use magic to hold her down, at least until the High Coven gets here. Something that didn't drain my energy and though the shadows didn't seem to do much to steal from my power, I worried at some, I would run dry. My eyes scanned the ground for the rest of Evanora's crystals. She came here to finish the ritual, which meant she must have brought something for all the elements in the circle. Slowly, I rotated my head in each direction until I found what I was looking for.

"Over there!" I yelled, gesturing with my head. "Get that emerald."

River ran to where I was pointing and snatched the crystal from the ground while Evanora squirmed under the shadows beneath me. I was still worried this new magic would suck me dry, so I was hopeful my plan would work, or we'd be royally screwed.

"Now what?" he asked when he jogged back to me.

"Put it in my hand."

He did as I said and as soon as the emerald was on my skin, I could feel its energy course through me. Careful not to let go of the shadows, I lowered to my knees. With one hand holding Evanora in place, I slammed the other to the earth and reached deep into it with my magic. The emerald burnt against my skin and my body shook as I took in its power. The little lights twinkled in my peripheral but for once, I was grateful for their presence. They meant I had gotten what I needed. The earth rumbled under us, and I noticed River try to hold his balance. Both his feet were stretched out wide, like he was surfing a wave and his panicked eyes bore into me. I wanted to reassure him, but this always worked better with my eyes closed. Against myself, I shut my lids and poured my magic into the earth. The ground shook more again, and my knees slid beneath me as I pulled on the deep-seated tree roots under us. They were so far that I wasn't sure I could reach them, but after a few more tries and a lot of unattractive heaving, I had them in my grasp. I pulled my magic up, taking the roots with me until they spun out of the earth all around Evanora. My body was vibrating from the magic, and I had to drop the shadows I had around her to wield the roots with both my hands. As soon as she was free, Evanora bolted but I was faster this time. I crossed my arms, directing the massive roots that hovered above her. They intertwined around her body, locking her in and forcing her back to the earth.

Still shaking, I stood up and inspected my work. Evanora's limbs and mid-section were covered in a weave of tree roots. There was no way she getting away now. As a final 'screw you', I flicked my finger and sent a root to wrap around her mouth. Then I turned to River.

I was on him like a freaking spider monkey before I could stop myself. My lips crashed to his and I wrapped one leg around his as I pressed into him. My body was on fire from the feel of him, and I breathed out so heavily, it sounded like a moan. River shivered and parted his full lips, his tongue brushing against mine. My magic went into over-drive, but I didn't stop it. Instead, I let it pour out of me, covering us in shadows that swirled at tornado speed over our entwined bodies. My hair flew in every direction, and it didn't matter. A house could have crashed on me and all I would know was River. He pulled back from me, his panty dropping dimple making an appearance.

"Not that I don't want to do this forever," he whispered and pressed his forehead to mine, "but we should figure out what to do about my mom."

Right. Time to get back to Kansas, Dorothy. "Ew," I laughed. "Don't talk about your mom when your tongue's down my throat, please."

"You are seriously twisted, witch."

"You're welcome to leave any time, *hunter*."

His lips found mine again but this time, the kiss was so short that I scowled when it stopped. I dropped my hands, calling the shadows to return until we could see around us again. My knees buckled and I could feel my energy draining by the minute. I'd need sleep for days after this for sure!

"So, what should we do about her?" River asked.

I looked over at Evanora, whose eyes said she wanted to rip my head off. *Feeling's mutual, asshole.*

"You need to get out of here," I said. "Like yesterday. I'll call the High Coven and wait with her until they arrive. They'll know what to do."

River's eyes widened.

"Don't worry, they won't kill her. But she'll be put in a magical prison. Hey, maybe she and my mom can be jail besties." His eyes got even larger. "It'll take them a few hours to get here from Stamwick, but that should be enough time for you to get the other hunters and Peyton out of here."

"Oh, my God! The others! I completely forgot!"

"They're fine, don't worry. But I'm not sure how many of them are conscious and I think Jayden broke his arm. Peyton's hurt bad too, so get them both to a hospital right away. And be careful with Peyton, she's a shadower, so I have no clue what she'll do if she wakes up and you're dragging her around."

"She's a what?"

"A shadower. I'll explain later."

"Shit! Okay, yeah, I'm on it!"

He ran off then darted back to give me another kiss. When he left, I dropped to sit next to Evanora's caged body, refusing to look at her. Soon, the High Coven would arrive and take her away and until then, I had to come up with a story for how things went down tonight. Somehow, I knew that telling them about my shadow magic was out of the question. Even *I* didn't know what the shadows meant and why I had magic no other witch seemed to wield and it would just complicate things even more. For now, I needed a simple and believable explanation for the events of the evening. One that didn't include my shadows, or the hunters and my shadower best friend. I was not ready to deal with those repercussions yet and I knew I couldn't betray my friends. Not after everything they did for me tonight.

My eyes drifted past Evanora and into the darkness of the trees on the horizon. I did exactly what the High Coven wanted. I found the killer witch and she would pay for her crimes against the coven. Everything was as is it should.

Then why did it feel like this wasn't over yet?

Chapter Forty

The High Coven showed up two hours later like clockwork. They marched in unison down the field, their multicolored robes swaying in the wind behind them. It shocked me to see so many witches arrive, but Evanora's tricks likely got a lot of attention back in the city. She was dangerous and the coven knew it.

A few steps ahead, the four high priestesses stomped toward me, and my stomach turned. Rhiamon and Luna held hands, their crystal bangles ringing against each other and echoing across the field. Next to them, Theodora skipped like she was a nymph in a Broadway play. Her sapphire hair stood high above her head, and she flashed her teeth my way as she approached. I peeled my eyes from her to look at Sebyl, who was the picture of calm considering the events of the evening. Her dark bangs had grown out since I last saw her and covered most of her eyes, which was likely a good thing since I doubted there was anything pleasant to see in them.

Sebyl looked past me to Evanora's trapped body in the

tree roots and curled one side of her lips. Lavender rushed into my nostrils, and I had to breathe through my mouth before I got too dizzy and passed out. "Well done, Wilhemina," she said but there was no warmth in her tone. "Sisters, collect the prisoner!"

Behind her, fourteen head witches rushed to Evanora's side. Their bodies were so adorned in crystals, I wondered how they moved so speedily, but they were on her like hungry dogs on a bone. Four of the head witches dug their fingers into the earth and I saw the roots give way and slither back into the ground. Evanora screamed but a witch bent over her and forced a fistful of dirt into her mouth. She pressed her palm atop the dirt and Evanora's eyes widened, unable to speak. The witches raised Evanora to her feet, tearing the bushel of herbs off her neck and searching her pockets for hidden crystals or weapons. When they finished, they bound her hands with anointed ropes and tossed her to the ground.

Forming a circle around Evanora, the witches salted the earth and worked their magic to render her useless until they could transfer her to the prison. In any other situation, I'd have been terrified for her, but I had no emotions left. She deserved everything she got for the horrific things she did.

"You'll take her to jail now?" I asked.

"She will be handled accordingly," Sebyl answered.

"Wait, what does that mean?"

The four high priestesses exchanged looks but none of them spoke up. Luna shifted her weight next to Rhiamon and refused to meet my eyes. Her green eyes locked on Rhiamon, who twisted the large crystal choker on her neck over and over.

"WHAT DOES THAT MEAN?" I demanded,

surprised at the strength of my voice. "You can't kill her. Those aren't the rules."

Sebyl glanced at Theodora and plastered a fake smile on her face. "Don't be silly, girl. We are not killing anyone."

"Then what?"

"The witch will be transported to the prison where we will use all means necessary to divulge any information she may process that might be useful to the coven. I think we can all agree that her knowledge of dark magic is exceptional and while we do not abide by its use, we cannot let it fester and rot inside the body of someone so wicked."

"You're going to torture her to tell you what she knows, aren't you?"

"As I said," Sebyl sneered, "we will do what is necessary."

My skin paled and the ground under my feet got so soft that I thought I was standing in quicksand. I tried to focus on Sebyl's face, but I could see it distorting in front of my eyes. Her grin spread across her cheeks until she didn't look like a person at all. It was as though her skin was melting like those Dali paintings I saw in a gallery once. Time stood still around me as I thought over her words. They would torture Evanora until they got what they wanted from her. But why did they need to know? What use could the High Coven have from dark magic or fae energies? And what was I going to tell River later?

"Billie?" Luna asked and I shook my head to look at her. "Is everything all right?"

I cleared my throat. "Yeah. Yes. Sorry, I think I'm wiped out from tonight. I used up a lot of magic and my body is not cooperating."

"You poor dear," Theodora said, her words almost believable. "Not to worry. As soon as we get back to Stamwick, we'll have the healer witches look at you and make sure everything is as it should be."

"Stamwick?"

"Well, of course. You've done us proud and it's time to come home."

A breath lodged itself in my throat and I rubbed my hands over my eyes so hard that my entire face flushed. I'm going home. I'm actually going home. Why wasn't I happy about that? My head ached and sweat formed at the base of my back as I pictured myself going back to the coven. Ever since I arrived in Shadowhurst, I wanted nothing more than to return but somewhere along the line, everything changed. *I* changed. I didn't want to go back, and I didn't want to be around the high priestesses, not when I knew how little they cared for me. Much like the other witches that stood obediently behind them with a restrained Evanora in their grasp, I was just a tool for the High Coven to use as they pleased. That wasn't the life I wanted. Not anymore.

"I don't think I should go back," I said.

"Pardon?" Sebyl arched one eyebrow, or at least I thought she did since I couldn't see her forehead under all that black hair. "You don't wish to return?"

"It's not that," I lied. "Of course I want to come back. I miss you all so much!"

My voice was so sugary sweet, I almost barfed. I was laying it on thick.

"Then what?"

I looked from one high priestess to the next and widened my smile, trying to look as reassuring as possible. "It's just that with all this stuff with the witch, I didn't have time to figure out who the hunters are. They're still dangerous and I can't leave until I find them. It's my duty to the coven."

Lowering my head, I peeked over to Evanora, whose eyes widened at my words. *Don't worry, bitch, I'm just as shocked as you right now.* I grimaced then squared my shoulders to face the priestesses again.

"So what do you think?"

The four looked past me then to each other.

"Ladies?" Sebyl asked.

My body froze as I waited for the others to speak, praying they wouldn't send me back just yet. There was still so much I wanted to see in Shadowhurst and I needed time to do that. I wanted more time with River and Peyton and the Chandlers. More so, I had to find out what these damn shadows were and why I had them in me. They were unlike any magic I've seen and being able to call on them without an elemental connection was both intoxicating and scary as hell. What worried me most was the extra energy boost I got when using them, unlike other times I've used my magic, the shadows stole nothing from me, and I felt more powerful than ever now. Somehow, I had the feeling that if the High Coven found out, I'd be a magical lab rat before I knew it. No, thank you.

In front of me, Theodora leaned in and grinned. "That is a wonderful idea, dear. But only if you're sure this is what you want. We are already very impressed with you, so if you're doing this to prove something, it isn't required."

"I'm doing this because it's the right thing to do."

"Very well," Sebyl said. "Then you're approved to stay. But you must keep us informed at all times on what you discover. We will not be kept in the dark like last time and if we ever feel that you are no longer needed in Shadowhurst, you will return immediately."

I nodded. "Thank you. And yes, of course."

"Very well. We will speak with the Chandlers and come up with a reason for you to stay."

"I don't think you have to," I interrupted. "I'm pretty sure they enjoy having me around and wouldn't mind. I can talk to them when I get back tonight."

There was a struggle to my right, and I turned to see Evanora wrestle with one of the head witches. Her face was bright red, and she was mumbling something over the dirt in her mouth. Her bound hands shook behind her, but she trained her eyes only on me.

"Control your prisoner, sisters!" Sebyl snapped.

My gaze met Evanora's and I narrowed my eyes. "It's okay. Let her speak. What harm can it do now?"

Reluctantly, Sebyl agreed and the head witch shoved her hand into Evanora's mouth and dug out the dirt, throwing it to the side in disgust. As soon as she was free to speak, Evanora growled and leaped forward, but the head witches yanked her restraints back so hard, I was shocked they didn't dislocate a shoulder. Her fiery eyes burnt into me, and I took a step back for fear she might break free and I'd have to fight her all over again.

"Believe nothing they tell you, kid!" she shouted as her eyes dropped to the moonstone on my finger. "Seek the truth. Find what they're hiding!"

"ENOUGH!" Sebyl roared. "Shut her up before I lose my patience!"

The head witch that bound Evanora before forced her to her knees and muzzled her once more. Tears streamed down Evanora's face but this time, she didn't struggle. Her eyes pled with me to listen, to hear what she was trying to say even though her words were unclear. I wanted to ask her more, but my gut told me it was best to keep quiet. This wasn't the first time someone warned me to watch out for the High Coven's lies and though I didn't believe Beatrix when she said it, I sure as hell was starting to believe her now. Something wasn't right in the coven, and I would get to the bottom of it.

As I watched the witches drag Evanora down the field, a fire blazed in my stomach. These women lied to me, in more ways than one it seemed. They pushed me into the shadows and forced me to hide who I was. They taught me to hate, and I let them. Well, not anymore. I didn't know if what Beatrix and Evanora said was true, and a big part of me wished it wasn't, but I needed to know for myself. And if I was wrong and the High Coven wasn't up to something, I would say good bye to everyone I met here and return to them. I would come home to my people and force myself into the shadows of Stamwick alleys as I had done for many years before. Except this time, I'd have some shadows of my own.

Chapter Forty-one

"You're staying?" River asked.

We sat on the front steps of his porch and his fingers had been playing with my hair for hours. It was starting to hurt a little, but I didn't want to ask him to stop for fear he may never touch me again, and not being touched by River was not an option. Sure, he was a hunter and trained to kill my kind, but he was so much more than that. Just like I was much more than what I've been raised to be. We were both the same kind of lost and confused and I hoped that maybe, by some luck, we could unravel the pieces together. Shadowhurst was not what I thought it would be, but a lot has changed since I first drove in through those massive iron gates. I changed. For the better, I hoped, but it was much too early to tell at this point. The only thing I was sure of was that I made the right decision in staying and not telling the High Coven what I knew. Witch or not, I would not betray the people that had my back when it mattered and that was enough for now. As far as a plan went, I had none. Keeping secrets from the High

Coven would be the most difficult thing I've ever had to do, but my choices were limited and if I wanted to protect my friends, I saw no other way than to keep the lies twisting. At least this time around, I had some support to help keep the balls in the air. My legs rested on River's and I leaned back on my elbows, staring at the hanging planters above our heads.

With Evanora gone, I was surprised to see the house hasn't fallen apart in seconds.

"Yep. Looks like you're stuck with me," I teased.

"I like being stuck with you."

River leaned in and pressed his lips to mine. His breath was heavy and hungry, paralleling my own. My legs tensed on top of him and when he pulled my hair to deepen our kiss, I almost imploded. I was still getting used to the fact that I was dating a witch hunter and every time we touched, a pang of guilt rushed through me. But one look at River's V made all of that go away because come on, how could it not? The boy was perfect.

He growled against my lips, and I laughed before pulling back, instantly missing the warmth of his body. Frigid Shadowhurst air wrapped around me, and I inched closer to him to nuzzle my head on his shoulder. "What will happen now? With you, I mean?"

River shrugged. "I don't know. My dad's coming back, so that should be interesting."

"For real? That's good, right? It's what you wanted."

"I guess. Not how I wanted it to go down, but yeah, it's good." He rearranged himself but kept my legs just where they were. "I still can't wrap my head around it. My real dad was a shifter. It's messed up."

"Yeah, it's not great."

"Thanks."

I laughed. "I'm kidding. Look, you're almost seventeen and you're as human as they come, so if you're worried about shifting, I don't think that's going to happen. And hey, even if it does, we'll deal with it."

"Like 'you'll vanquish me' deal with it?" he asked, eyebrows arched.

"Yeah, I'll smoke your ass, buddy. Watch out!" I joked. "No, I mean we'll figure it out. Together."

River's jaw relaxed and he lazily swirled his thumb over my thigh. Bolts of energy ran through me with each passing circle, and I cursed him for having this effect on me. River made it impossible to keep my head straight. "Thanks for helping me through this. I'm pretty sure if you weren't here, I'd lose it."

"I'll always help you," I whispered. "Ever since we met, I couldn't get you out of my head. When your mom told us about your shifter bloodline, I thought that it was just my magic reacting to your blood, but I don't think that anymore."

"What do you think now?"

My lips spread into a stupid grin as they often did when he was nearby. "I think I kinda like you, hunter," I said. "Sorry, do you prefer shifter? I wasn't sure what we were going with here."

"River's fine, *witch*," he teased.

A gust of wind ruffled his soft hair and I reached up to brush the strands back into place. The waves fell over his forehead, and I stared at him as I worked to imagine what he must have felt at that moment. His father that left him when he was young was coming back and despite the joy that must have brought, it couldn't be enough to make up for what his mother did. I knew a little about having a criminal for a parent, so I could totally relate but unlike River, I didn't also just find out that my mom was a witch that killed one of my close friends. My heart broke for him, and I pressed my lips to his again.

"What was that for?" he asked.

"For being you. And for taking all of this so well. Me, I mean."

River sighed and I pulled back, wondering if this was when he would break up with me. Instead, he smiled and flashed his adorable dimple my way. "To be honest, I'm surprised you're sticking around. Or that you haven't put some hex on me or something."

"What? Why?"

"Hello? Hunter over here!" He gestured to his body, and I tried not to picture him topless. "I'm impressed you're able to look past that."

I ran a finger over his pecs and grinned like an idiot. "Yeah, well, you're hard to hex, I guess." I laughed then looked up at him from under my lashes. "But seriously, it will not be easy. At least not at first. The rest of your friends are not going to come around to this anytime soon, especially not Savannah. Then there's your dad to worry about. And Peyton. It's going to be a hot mess for a while."

"Don't worry about the hunters, I'll talk to them. They might not like it, but most of them know you're not the bad guy here and I'm sure they're all pissed our parents didn't give us the entire story when they pushed us into this whole witch-hunting thing." His hand found mine again and he smiled. "And as far as my dad goes, he might not like the hunter business, but he knows how important it is to me. Though I don't think I will tell him about you being a witch just yet."

"Probably a good idea." I nodded. "And Peyton?"

River's jaw slacked like he was hearing about Peyton being a soul sucker for the first time. In the two days that followed Evanora's arrest, I tried to fill him on as much as I could about the paranormal world around us. I told him about the shadowers and explained the history of my kind in so much detail that I sounded like an occult encyclopedia rambling off facts. But he had to know everything if he was going to stay safe and now that we knew how dark Shadowhurst was, I couldn't leave him unprotected. As it turned out, Evanora didn't do much in the way of preparing the hunters for what was truly out there though I understood why. Opening that gateway would only distract from hating my kind so completely. So, it was up to me to get them ready in case any of the shadowers I've encountered came knocking. I even promised to help train the hunters to get them up to speed, though we decided it was best to keep Peyton's true identity a secret until she was ready to talk about it herself. After all, it was *her* life, and I would not force my friend out of the mystical closet if she didn't agree with it.

"I still can't believe Peyton is a badass," River said.

"The baddest badass. Soul suckers are no joke." I tucked a strand of hair behind my ear and rolled my shoulders. "What I can't believe is that I'm with a witch hunter and my best friend is a freaking shadower. That's cray."

"HA! I mean, if anyone messed with this crew, they're in deep shit."

A laugh bubbled out of me as I imagined that situation when it hit me. Evanora might be gone, but something still didn't sit right with me. In the wake of her arrest, I have given little thought to the High Coven situation and my stomach turned just remembering that they were still there.

As much as I wanted to go back to school and have a normal life, there were still too many unanswered questions, and I was more in the dark now than when I first came to town. Couple that with the new magic I now had, and I was a walking wreck. At least now, I didn't have the guilt of lying to River and my friends eating away at me, but somehow, it wasn't enough. Deep inside, I knew I wouldn't feel right until I figured out what the High Coven was keeping from me and the rest of the witches. Evanora might have been a murderer and my mom was a downright asshole, but they both hated the High Coven and I was determined to find out why.

"You're doing that thing again," River said and tugged my chin forward.

"What thing?"

"That thing where you get all wrapped up in your head."

I smiled at the notion that even after such a short time, he had my weirdo faces down pat. "Don't be a creep. Quit staring, I'm fine."

"I'm just worried you're overanalyzing, as always. Not that I mind how cute you look when you're all serious like that." His fingers tightened around my chin and his eyes took on a stern expression. "Stop freaking out. We will be fine."

Doubt that. "Promise?"

"Whatever happens, we'll figure it out. Together."

I was about to lose myself in River's kisses again when a bike skidded to a stop in front of us. Peyton jumped off, heaving over her thighs as she tried to breathe. My best friend's hair was an unbrushed mess and her eyes looked like she'd been crying. In an instant, I was off River's lap and kneeling by her side.

"Peyton? What's wrong? What happened?"

She held up a finger and took a few more ragged breaths before straightening her back and looking from me to River. "Sorry to bust up this make out sesh, but..." She took another wheezing breath. "God, I'm out of shape."

"What's going on?" River asked, his eyes stern and dark.

"We got trouble. Serious, Voldemort trouble."

My chest tightened and my cashmere sweater pressed against my body until I wanted to rip it right off. "What the hell are you talking about?"

"Okay, you know those shadowers that have been creeping around the last little while?"

"...Uh-huh."

"Well, there might be a tiny little thing I maybe, sort of forgot to mention."

"Peyton," I hissed. "Spill it."

My friend crouched so we could be eye level and put her hand on my shoulder while I fought the urge to back away. It was still difficult to let her touch me without thinking she could kill me where I stood in a heartbeat. But she wouldn't. She was my best friend.

"So long story short, there's like this big shadower resistance against the High Coven and one of the bigger factions is right here in Shadowhurst. I wanted nothing to do with it so I told them to screw off, but they've been insistent on having me join 'cause it turns out, they don't have that many soul suckers in the ranks and whatever. Anyway, that's what they were doing in my house that time when you showed up. Trying to recruit me."

"Dude, that's dark," River breathed out.

"Yep," Peyton agreed. "To get to the point, I met with two of their leads this morning."

"You did WHAT?!?" I shouted.

"Calm your tits, girl. I went there to get some information, so we know what we're up against."

River cocked an eyebrow. "And did you?"

"Hell, yes. But you won't like it." She gulped and locked her eyes on mine. "They've been trying to get you to leave since they knew you were a witch and didn't want you in town. But since the whole thing with Evanora, sorry, River, they're dead set on moving forward with their plans against the High Coven."

"Which are what exactly?"

"They want them all dead. Starting with you."

Behind me, River ran his fingers through his hair and groaned. "Well, shit."

Just when I thought things couldn't get worse, I had somehow found myself in the middle of some damn shadower rebellion that was gunning for me. Shadowhurst just couldn't give me a break. My eyes peeled away from Peyton's panicked face, and I turned to look at River, bile coating my mouth as I thought about what the future might hold.

There was no other way to look at this situation and River nailed it straight on the head. 'Well, shit' indeed.

Ready to dive into the next mystery to hit Shadowhurst? Billie's adventure is just getting started and there's no telling what the High Coven will do next. Will her relationship with River survive their differences? Why does the shadower resistance want her dead? Can she find out what else the High Coven is hiding from the witches? Find out in Book Two of the Shadowhurst Mysteries: **Book of Darkness.** CLICK HERE to read **Book of Darkness** now!

You can also check out the cover and description for the Book of Darkness below.

All I wanted was the normal life of a teenager. What I got was a deathtrap.

My name is Billie Stonewall, and I'm smack dab in the middle of a potential disaster. Again.

You'd think playing a key role in putting the witch who terrorized Shadowhurst behind bars would earn me a few points, but no such luck.

When my best friend informs me that a secret shadower resistance wants me dead, the normal life I thought I'd earned flashes before my eyes.

Now I must stay a step ahead. Of course, that would be a lot easier if everyone in town didn't want me dead. Then, there's the little problem with my boyfriend. He's part shapeshifter and at any moment now, his animal side might come out to play. If that happens, no one will be safe. Not even me.

Watch out, world! Things are about to get really interesting.

CLICK HERE to start reading the **Book of Darkness** now!

Interested in finding out what happened to Beatrix Stonewall? Read the prequel novella Coven of Deception for FREE!

READ COVEN OF DECEPTION

Who said fairy tales aren't real?

I have it under good authority, they're not only real, they can be a veritable nightmare.

Not only do I possess magic; I also belong to a secret coven of witches who've been living in plain sight.

First came the fun part. My powers manifested.

Next came reality. Trouble found me.

One minute, I'm living my life without a care in the world. The next, I'm dodging a mystery stranger who can't get enough of me.

So much for easing into this new life. It's time to see where these new skills will take me. Want to come along for the ride?

Start reading Coven of Deception by CLICKING HERE.

ACKNOWLEDGMENTS

Thank you, Scott, for everything. You are the best partner in crime and I'm so glad I have your ear to talk off with my ideas and plot lines. This book wouldn't be the same without your love and support.

A huge shout-out to my parents who have done their best with their overly enthusiastic child. You have shaped who I am and I will forever be grateful for you.

To my wonderful beta readers - thank you a million times! Your suggestions and notes are invaluable and my heart roars each time I get your thoughts on a book.

And my lovely reader, it is for you that this was written and I am at a loss for words that you have given this book a chance. Thank you!

Onto the next adventure and stay magical!

ABOUT THE AUTHOR

A.N. Sage has spent most of her life waiting to meet a witch, vampire, or at least get haunted by a ghost. In between failed seances and many questionable outfit choices, she has developed a keen eye for the extra-ordinary.

Since chasing the supernatural does not pay the bills, she dabbled in creative entrepreneurship, marketing and retail management. A.N. spends her free time reading and binge-watching television shows in her pajamas.

Currently, she resides in Toronto, Canada with her husband who is not a creature of the night.

A.N. Sage is a Scorpio and a massive advocate of leggings for pants.

For more books and updates:

www.ansage.ca

Connect on social media:
Facebook Group:
facebook.com/groups/945090619339423/
Instagram:
instagram.com/a.n.sage/
Twitter:
twitter.com/ANsageWrites
Facebook:

facebook.com/ansagewrites
Pinterest:
pinterest.ca/ansagewrites
Goodreads:
goodreads.com/author/show/18901100.Alexis_N_Sage
Amazon:
amazon.com/author/a.n.sage